BABYMOUSE A *

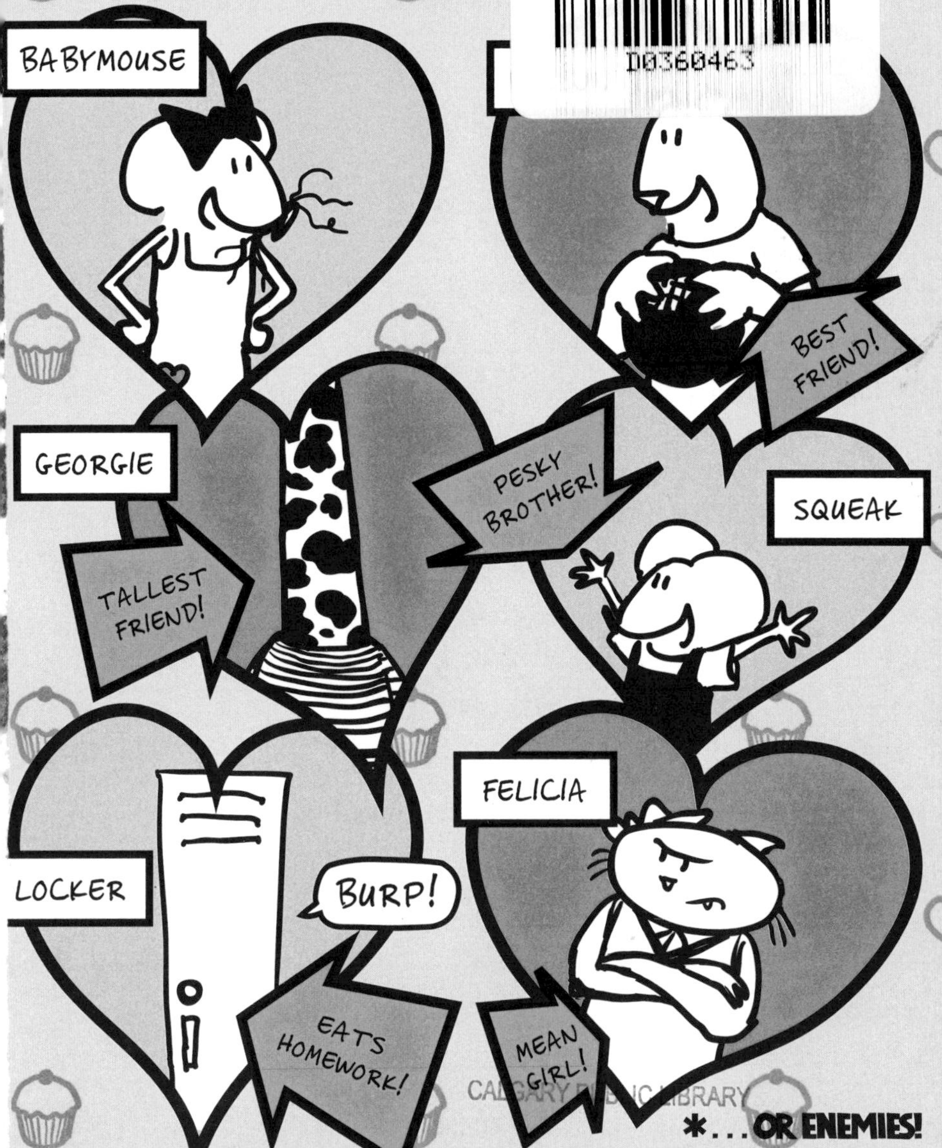
BABYMOUSE
BEST FRIEND!
GEORGIE
TALLEST FRIEND!
PESKY BROTHER!
SQUEAK
LOCKER
BURP!
EATS HOMEWORK!
FELICIA
MEAN GIRL!

*... OR ENEMIES!

Be sure to read **ALL** the **BABYMOUSE** books:

#1 BABYMOUSE: Queen of the World!
#2 BABYMOUSE: Our Hero
#3 BABYMOUSE: Beach Babe
#4 BABYMOUSE: Rock Star
#5 BABYMOUSE: Heartbreaker
#6 CAMP BABYMOUSE
#7 BABYMOUSE: Skater Girl
#8 BABYMOUSE: Puppy Love
#9 BABYMOUSE: Monster Mash
#10 BABYMOUSE: The Musical
#11 BABYMOUSE: Dragonslayer
#12 BABYMOUSE: Burns Rubber
#13 BABYMOUSE: Cupcake Tycoon
#14 BABYMOUSE: Mad Scientist
#15 A Very BABYMOUSE Christmas
#16 BABYMOUSE for President
#17 Extreme BABYMOUSE
#18 Happy Birthday, BABYMOUSE

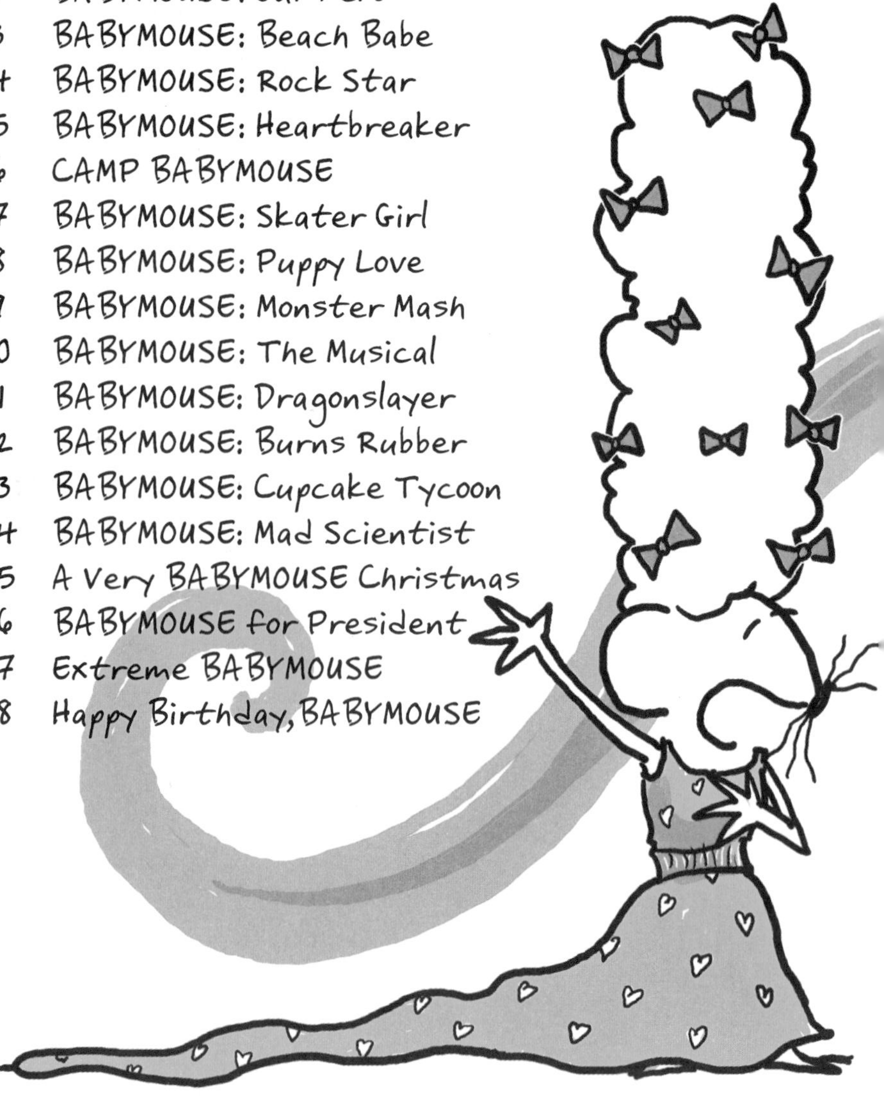

BABYMOUSE
THE MUSICAL

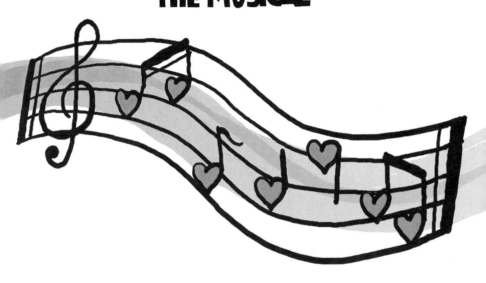

BY JENNIFER L. HOLM & MATTHEW HOLM

RANDOM HOUSE NEW YORK

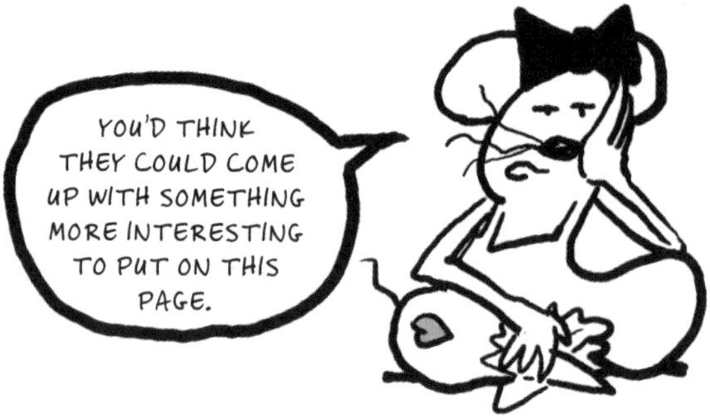
YOU'D THINK THEY COULD COME UP WITH SOMETHING MORE INTERESTING TO PUT ON THIS PAGE.

This is a work of fiction. Names, characters, places, and incidents either are the product of the authors' imagination or are used fictitiously. Any resemblance to actual persons, living or dead, events, or locales is entirely coincidental.

Published in the United States by Random House Children's Books,
a division of Random House LLC, a Penguin Random House Company, New York.

Random House and the colophon are registered trademarks of Random House LLC.

Visit us on the Web!
randomhouse.com/kids
Babymouse.com

Educators and librarians, for a variety of teaching tools, visit us at
RHTeachersLibrarians.com

Library of Congress Cataloging-in-Publication Data
Holm, Jennifer L.
Babymouse : the musical / by Jennifer & Matthew Holm.
p. cm.
Summary: As tryouts for the school musical begin, Babymouse takes the starring role in several imaginary Broadway productions, which also feature her debonair new classmate, Henry the Hedgehog.
ISBN 978-0-375-84388-4 (trade pbk.) — ISBN 978-0-375-93791-0 (lib. bdg.)
1. Graphic novels. [1. Graphic novels. 2. Musicals—Fiction. 3. Theater—Fiction. 4. Imagination—Fiction. 5. Mice—Fiction. 6. Animals—Fiction. 7. School—Fiction.] I. Holm, Matthew. II. Title.
PZ7.7.H65Bal 2009 [Fic]—dc22 2008010891

MANUFACTURED IN MALAYSIA 20 19 18 17 16 15 14 13 12 11 10 9 8

Random House Children's Books supports the First Amendment and celebrates the right to read.

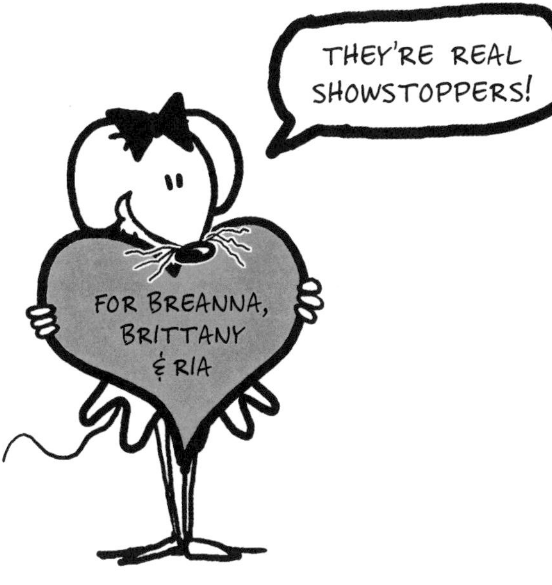
THEY'RE REAL SHOWSTOPPERS!
FOR BREANNA, BRITTANY & RIA

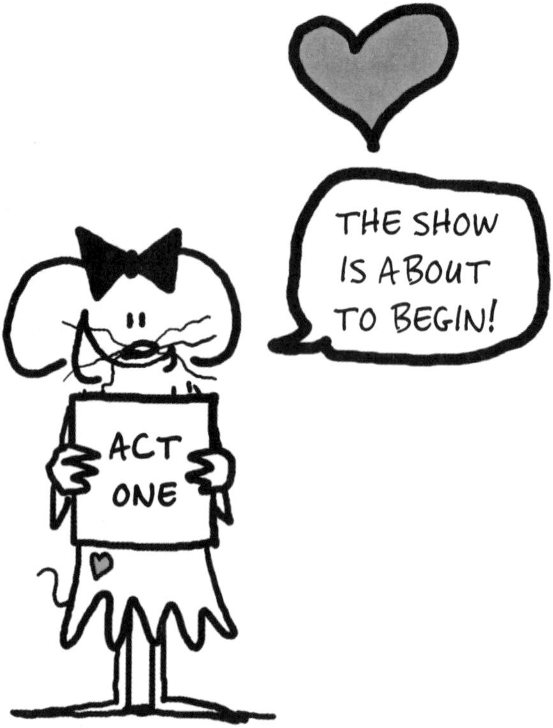
THE SHOW IS ABOUT TO BEGIN!
ACT ONE

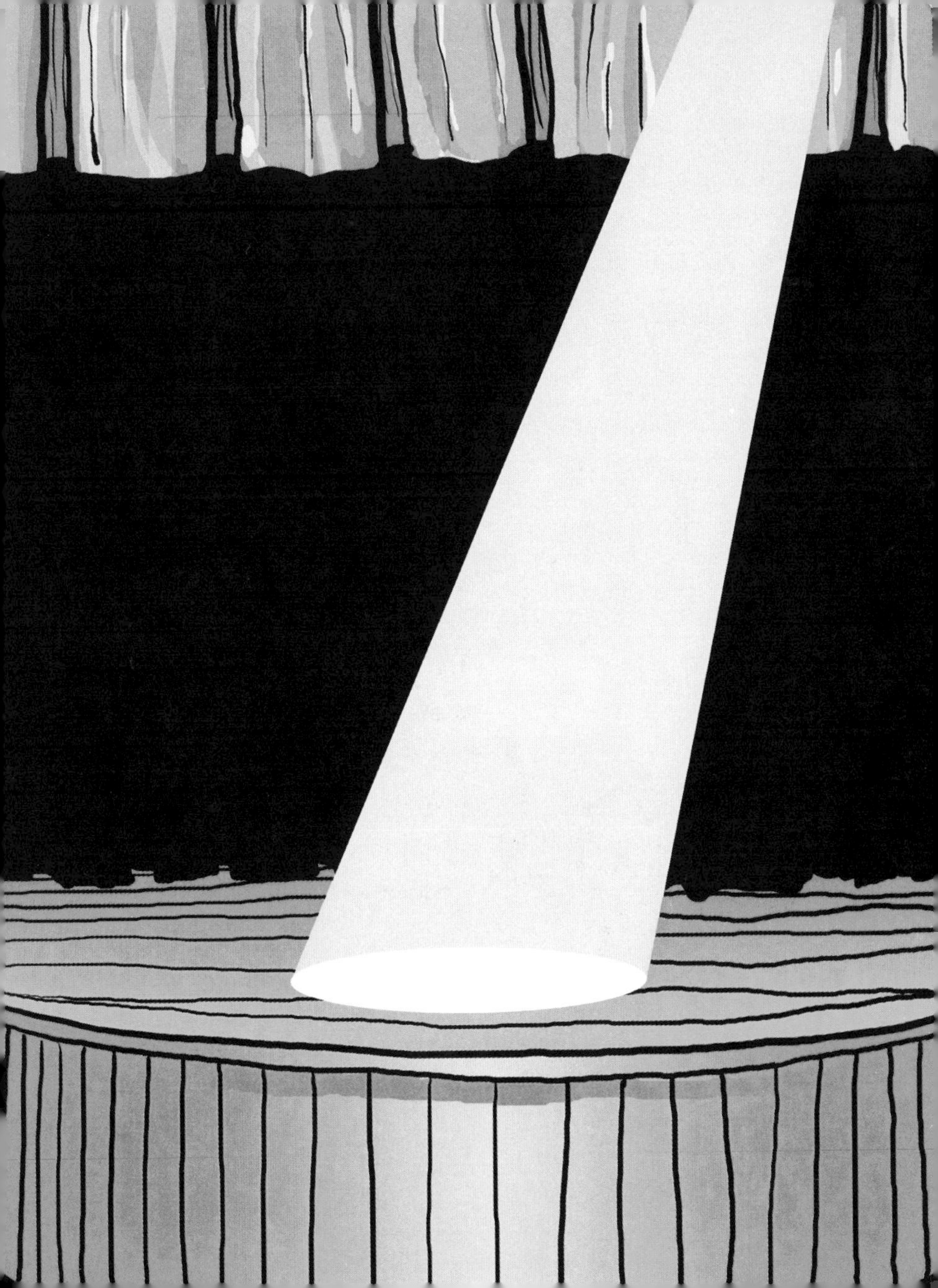

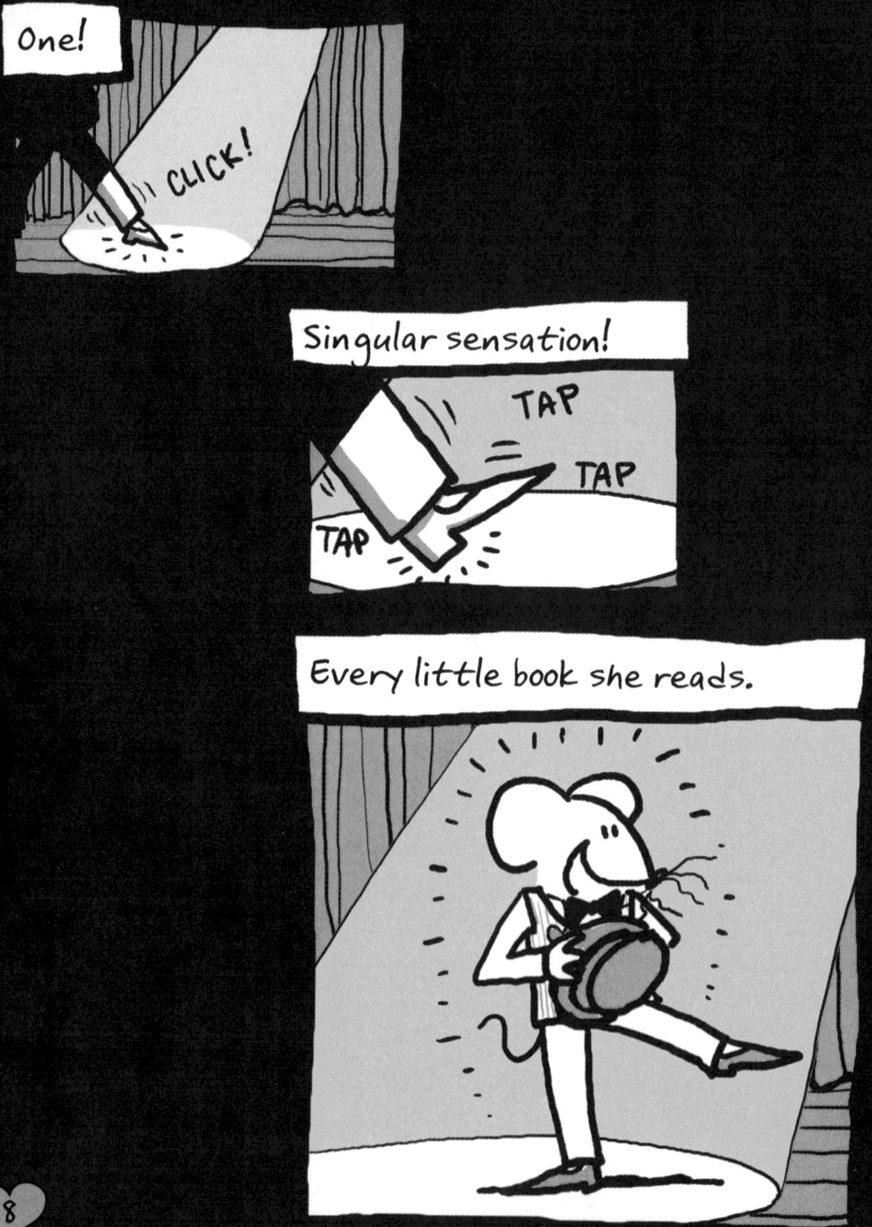
One!
CLICK!
Singular sensation!
TAP
TAP
TAP
Every little book she reads.

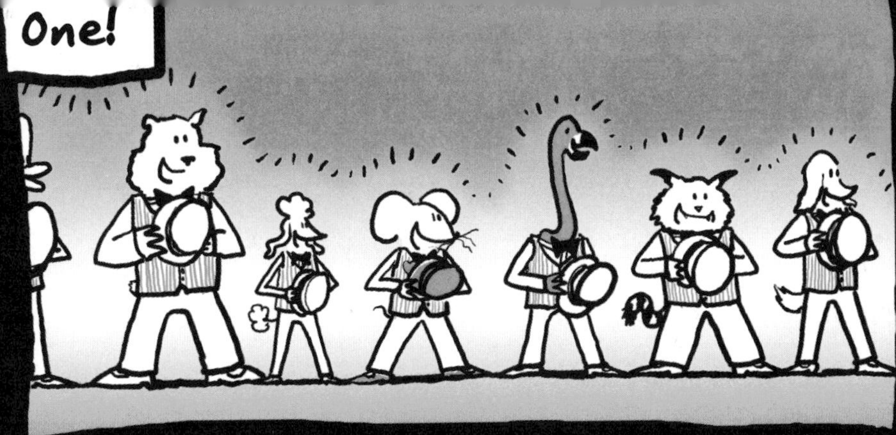
One!

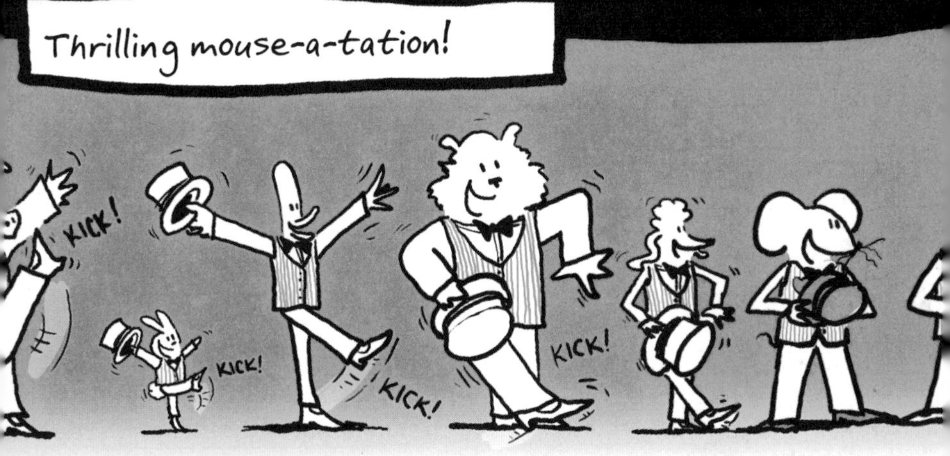
Thrilling mouse-a-tation!
KICK!
KICK!
KICK!
KICK!

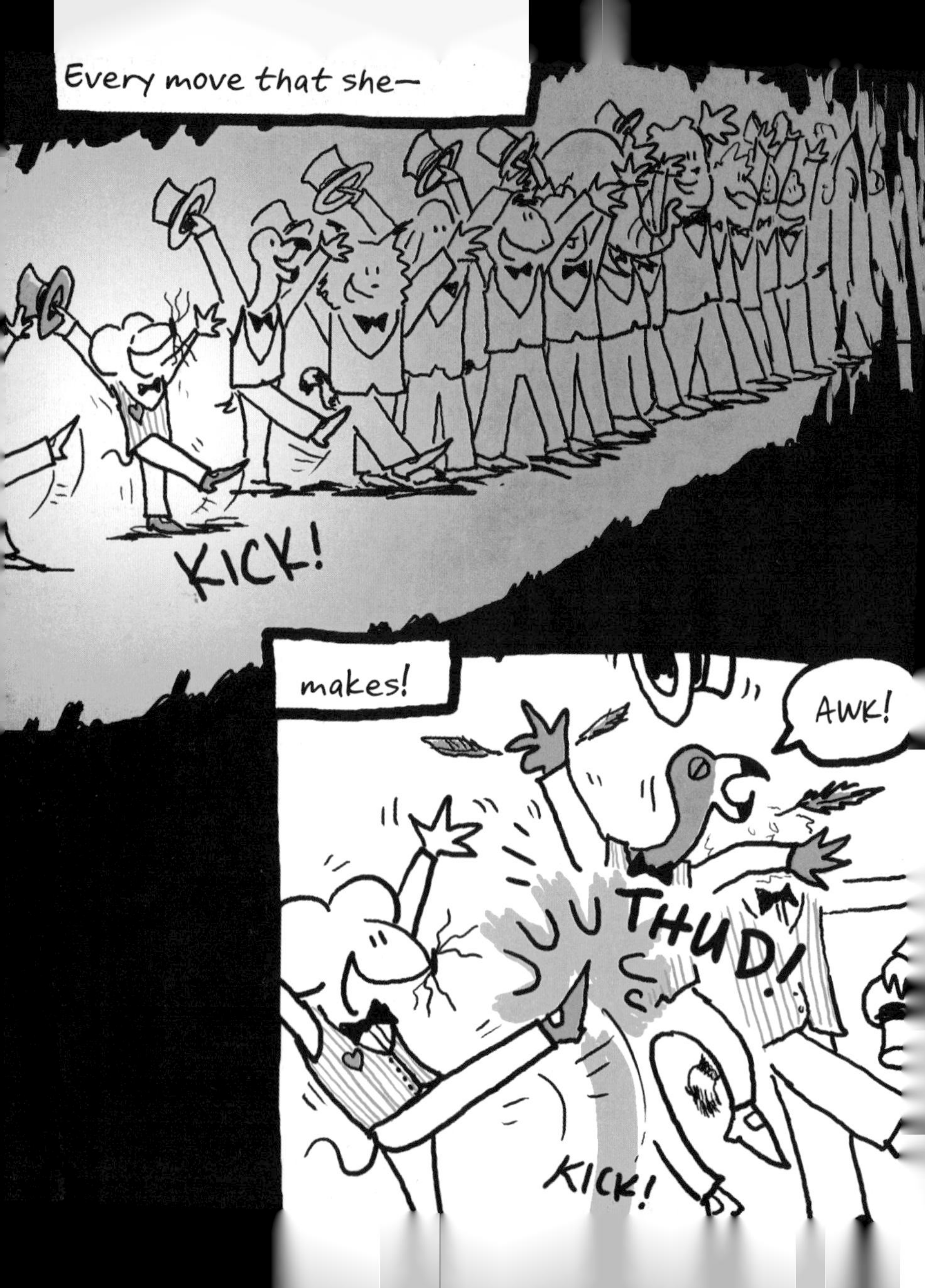
Every move that she—
KICK!
makes!
AWK!
THUD!
KICK!

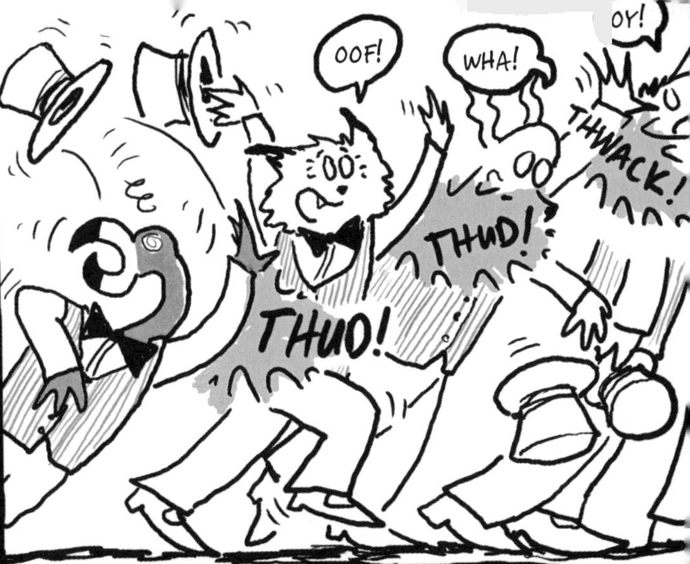
OOF!
WHA!
OY!
THWACK!
THUD!
THUD!

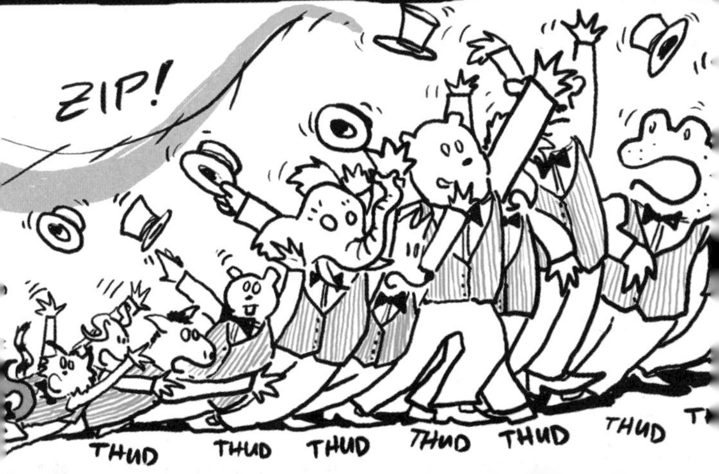
ZIP!
THUD
THUD
THUD
THUD
THUD
THUD

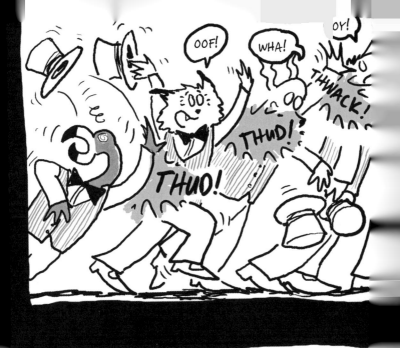

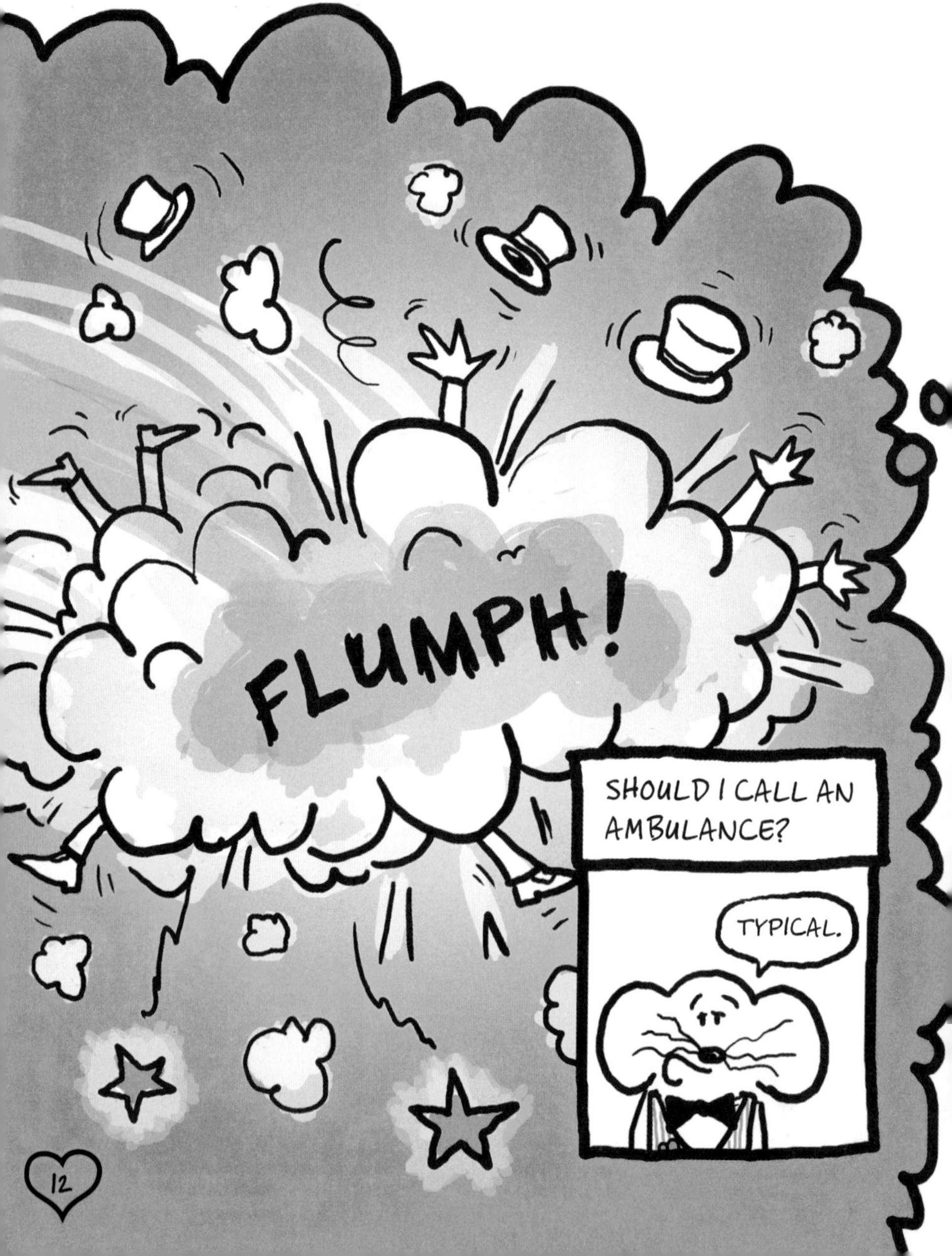
FLUMPH!
SHOULD I CALL AN AMBULANCE?
TYPICAL.

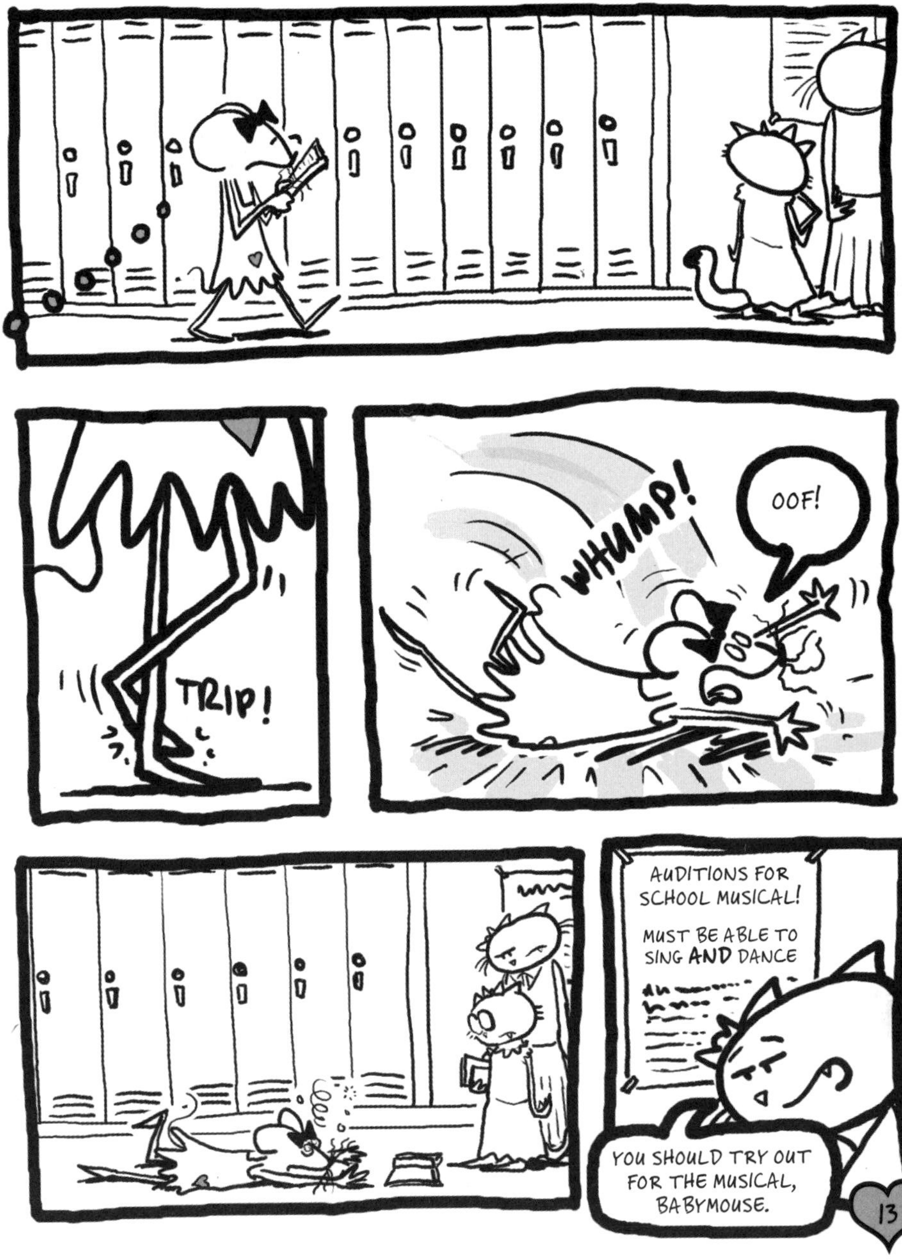
TRIP!
WHUMP!
OOF!
AUDITIONS FOR SCHOOL MUSICAL!
MUST BE ABLE TO SING AND DANCE
YOU SHOULD TRY OUT FOR THE MUSICAL, BABYMOUSE.

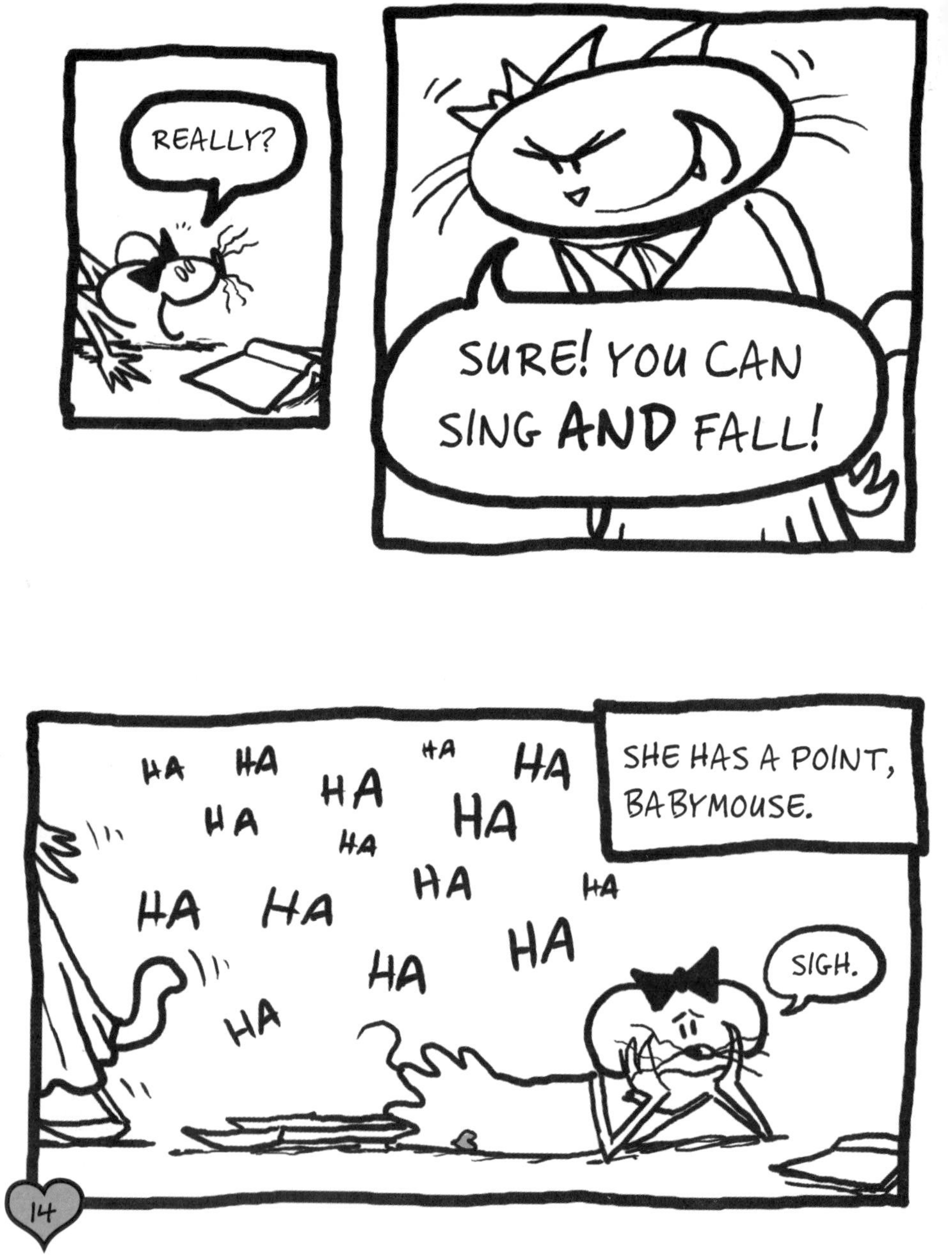
REALLY?
SURE! YOU CAN SING AND FALL!
HA HA HA HA HA HA HA HA HA HA HA HA HA HA HA HA
SHE HAS A POINT, BABYMOUSE.
SIGH.

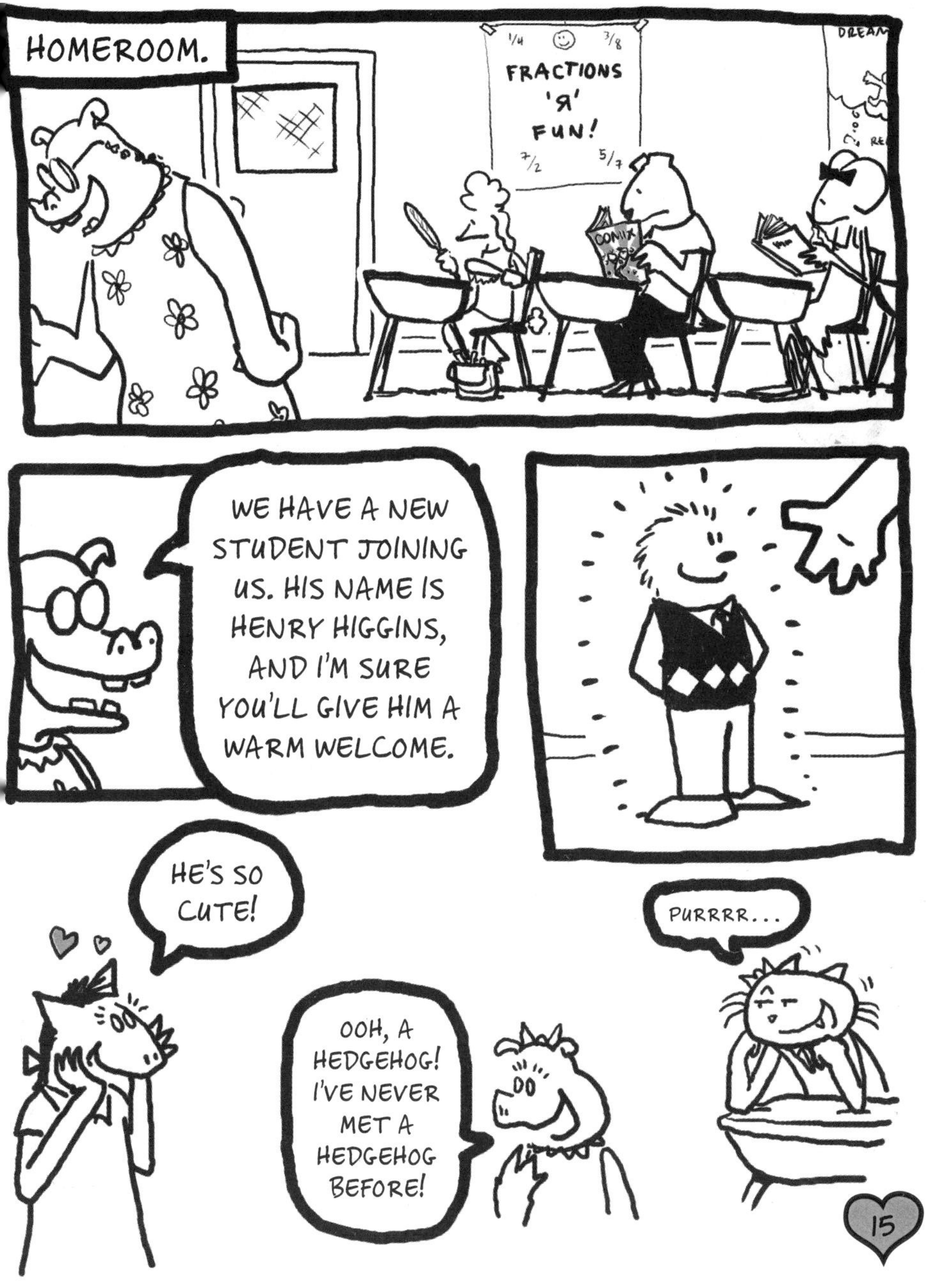
HOMEROOM.
1/4
3/8
FRACTIONS
'Я'
FUN!
7/2
5/7
COMIX
WE HAVE A NEW STUDENT JOINING US. HIS NAME IS HENRY HIGGINS, AND I'M SURE YOU'LL GIVE HIM A WARM WELCOME.
HE'S SO CUTE!
PURRRR...
OOH, A HEDGEHOG! I'VE NEVER MET A HEDGEHOG BEFORE!

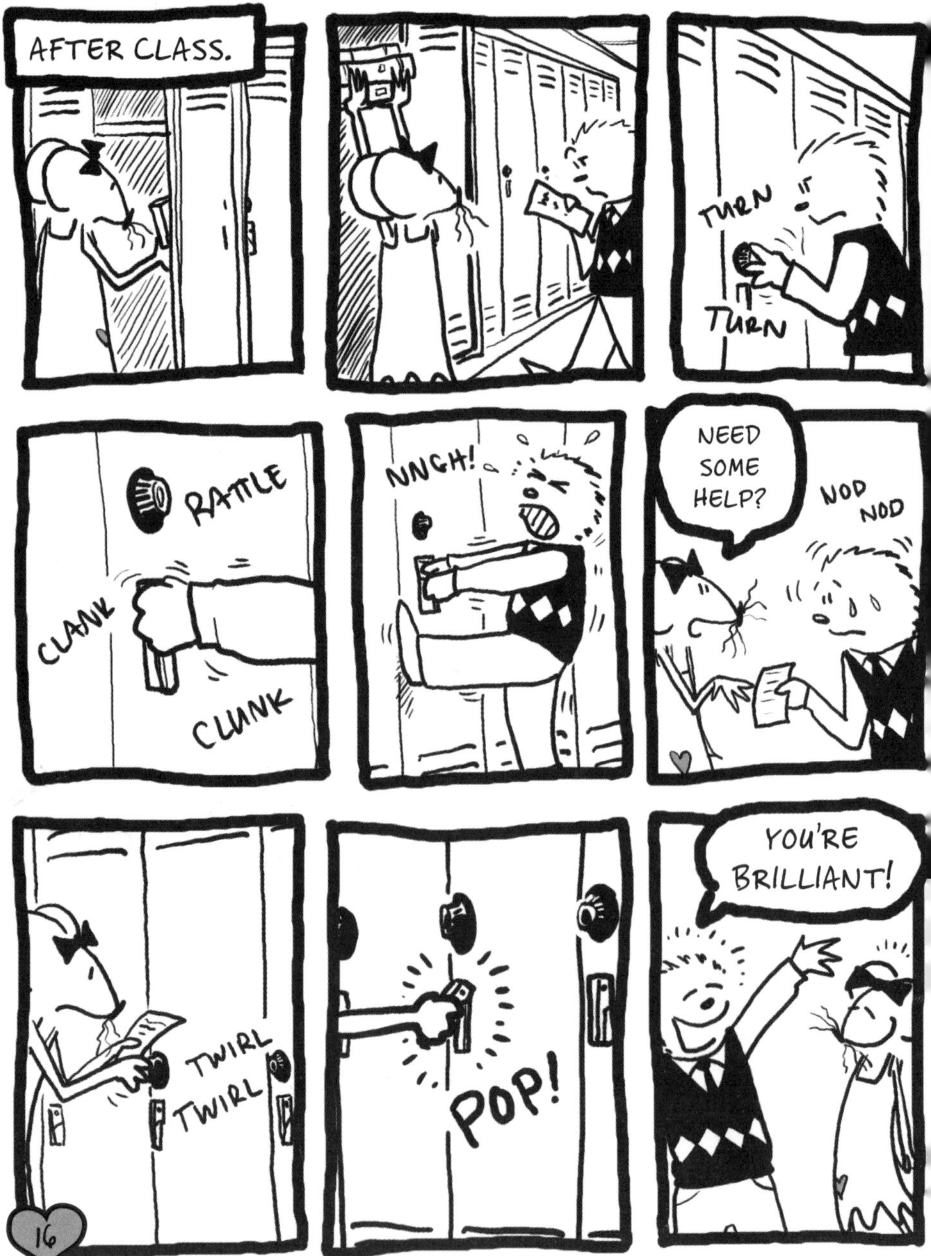
AFTER CLASS.
TURN
TURN
RATTLE
CLANK
CLUNK
NNGH!
NEED SOME HELP?
NOD
NOD
TWIRL
TWIRL
POP!
YOU'RE BRILLIANT!

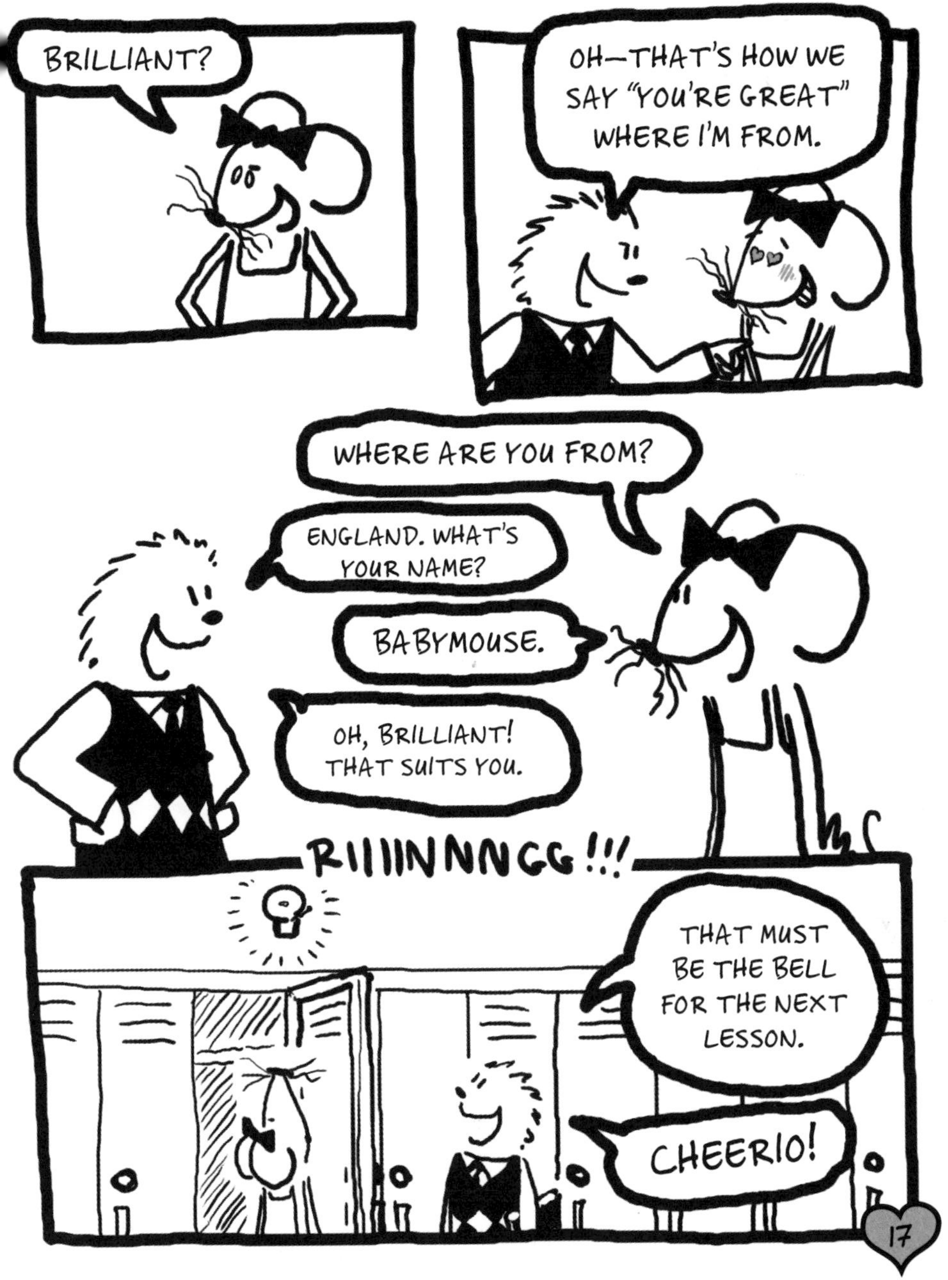
BRILLIANT?
OH—THAT'S HOW WE SAY "YOU'RE GREAT" WHERE I'M FROM.
WHERE ARE YOU FROM?
ENGLAND. WHAT'S YOUR NAME?
BABYMOUSE.
OH, BRILLIANT! THAT SUITS YOU.
RIIIINNNGG!!!
THAT MUST BE THE BELL FOR THE NEXT LESSON.
CHEERIO!

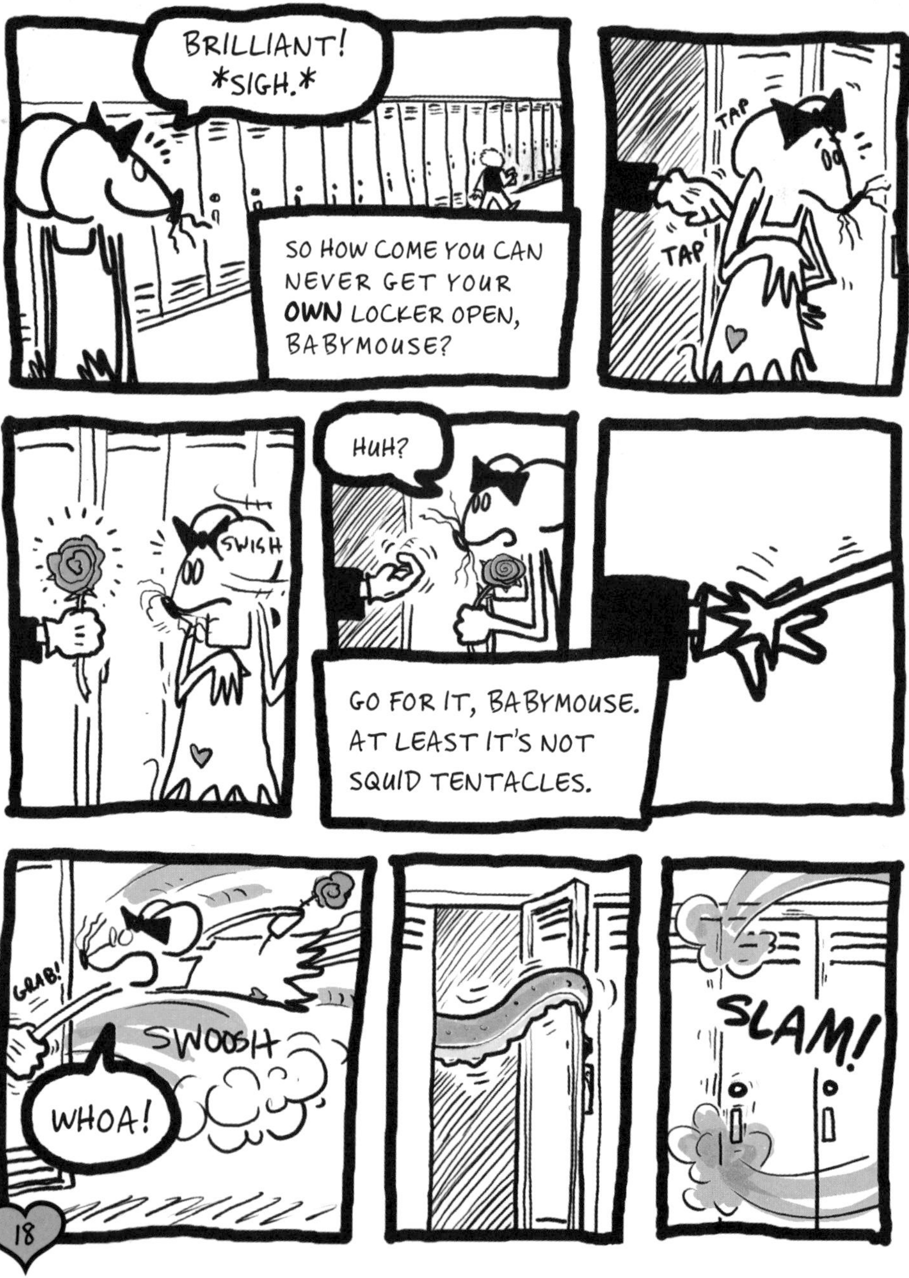
BRILLIANT! *SIGH.*
SO HOW COME YOU CAN NEVER GET YOUR **OWN** LOCKER OPEN, BABYMOUSE?
TAP
TAP
SWISH
HUH?
GO FOR IT, BABYMOUSE. AT LEAST IT'S NOT SQUID TENTACLES.
GRAB!
SWOOSH
WHOA!
SLAM!

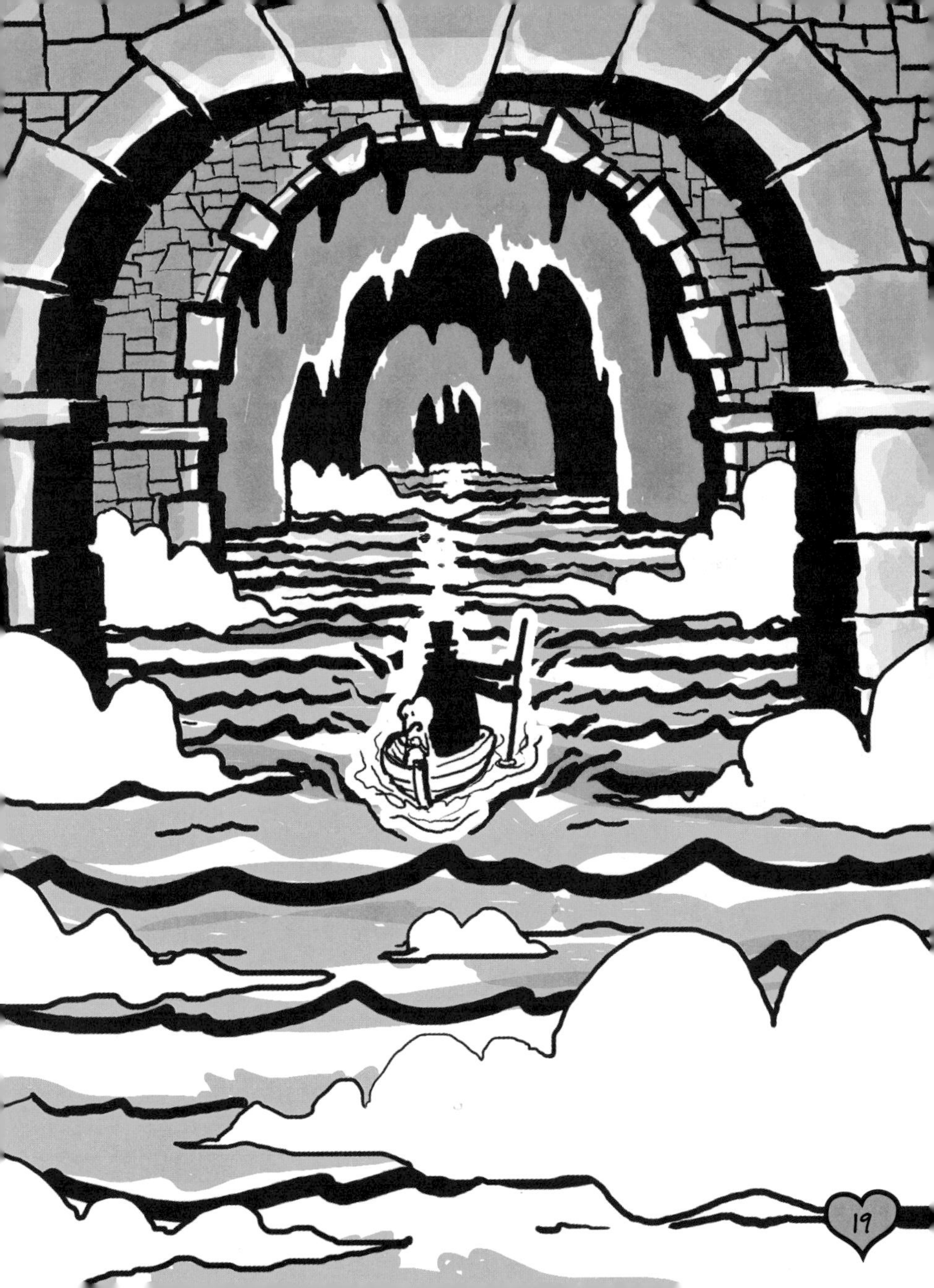

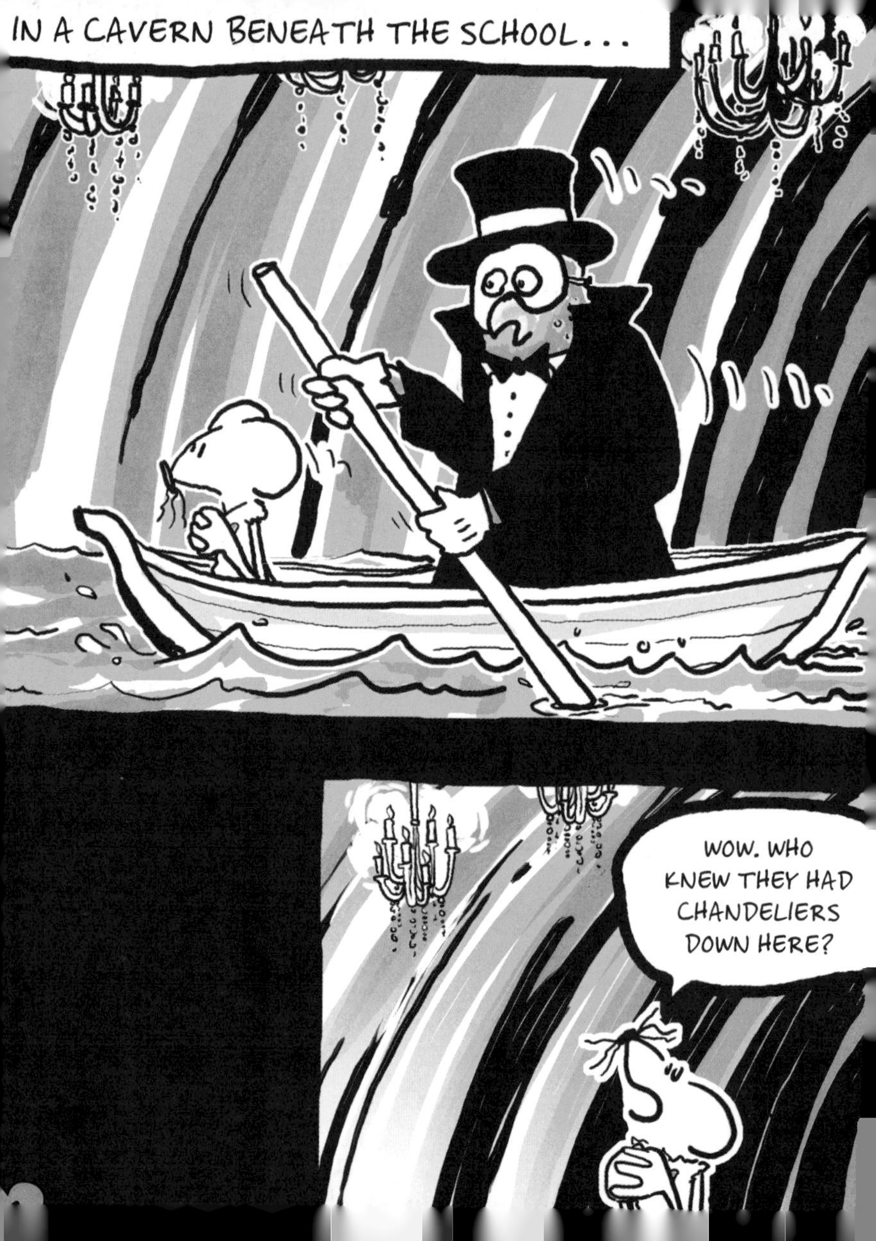
IN A CAVERN BENEATH THE SCHOOL...
WOW. WHO KNEW THEY HAD CHANDELIERS DOWN HERE?

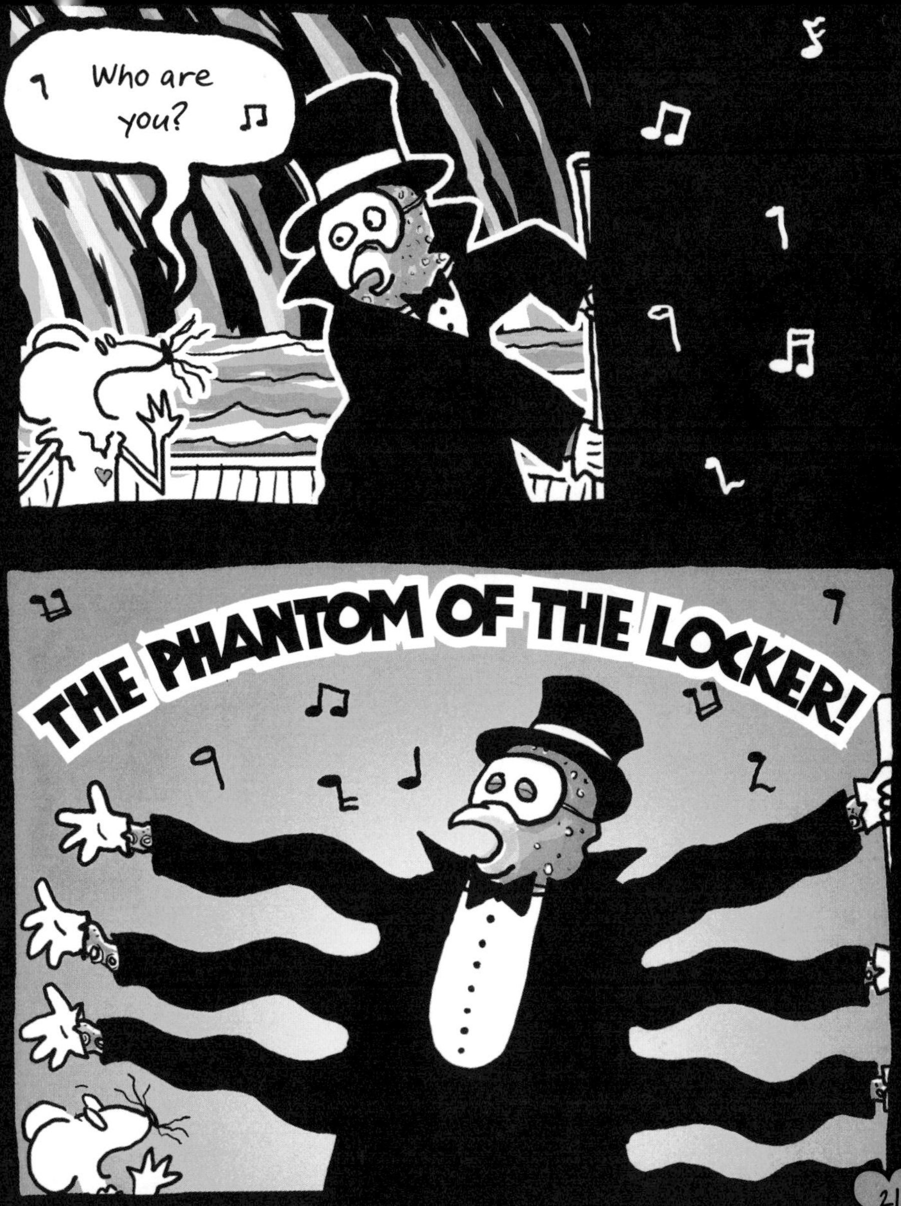
Who are you?
THE PHANTOM OF THE LOCKER!

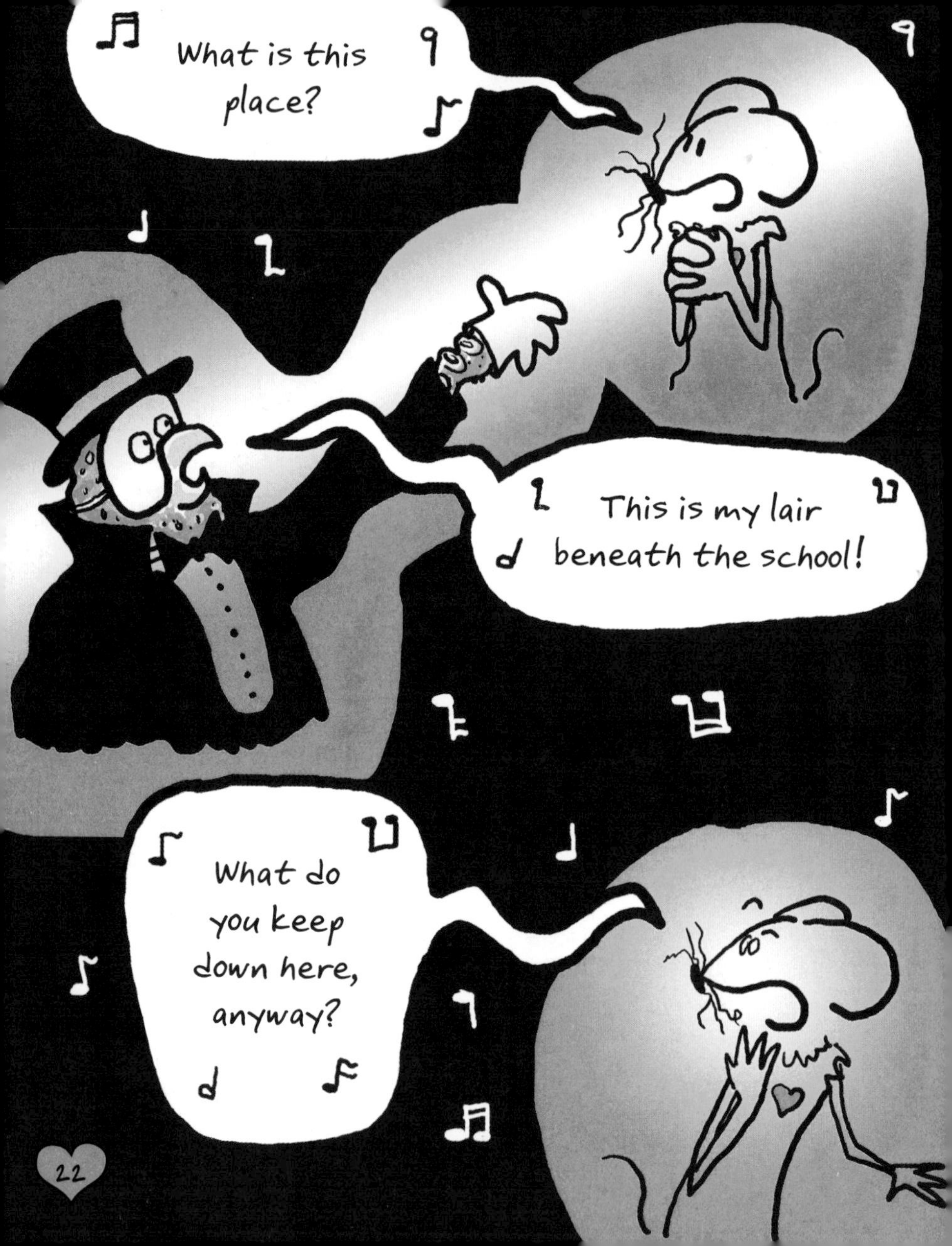
What is this place?
This is my lair beneath the school!
What do you keep down here, anyway?

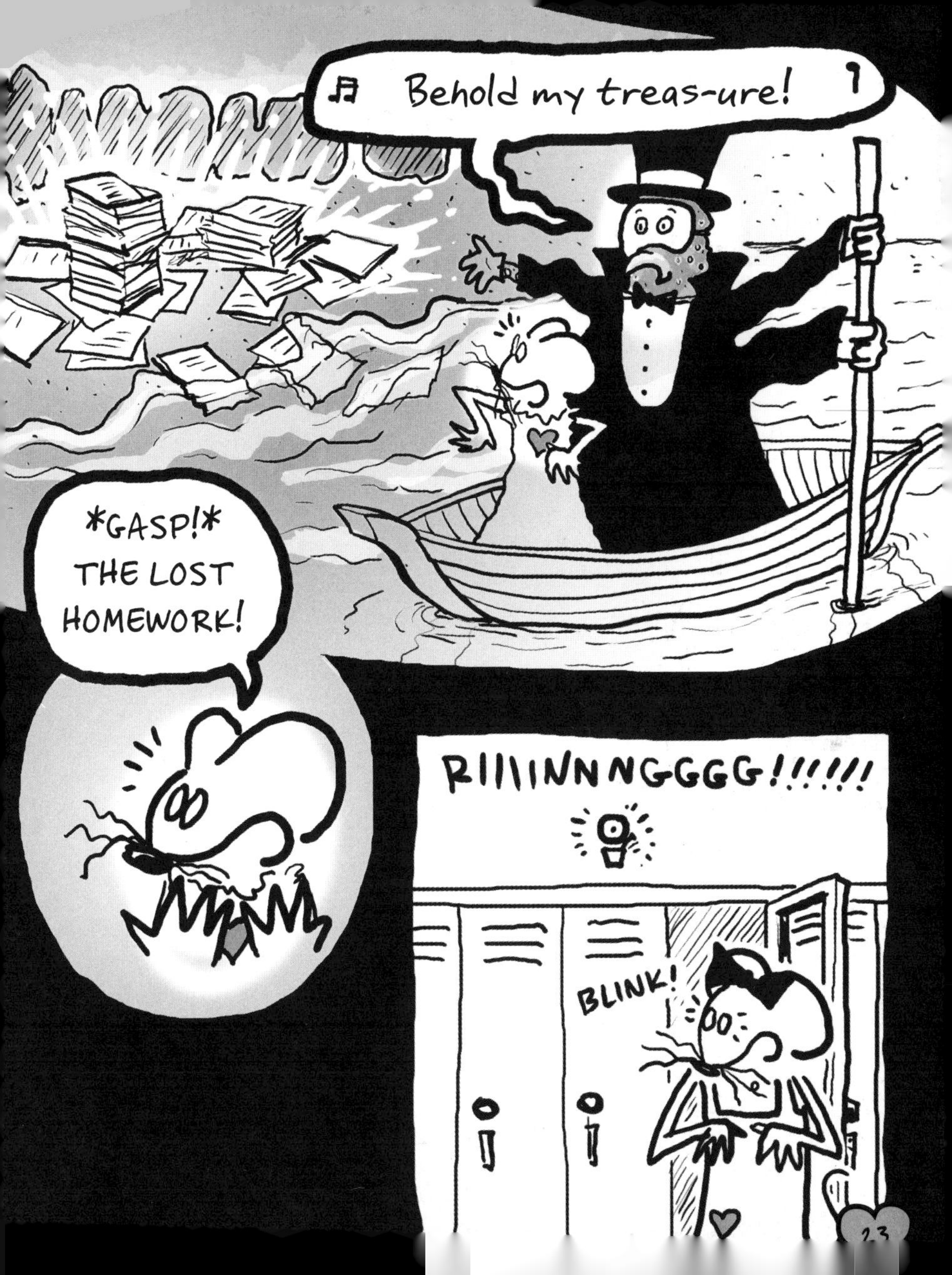
♫ Behold my treas-ure! ♪
GASP! THE LOST HOMEWORK!
RIIIINNNGGGG!!!!!!
BLINK!

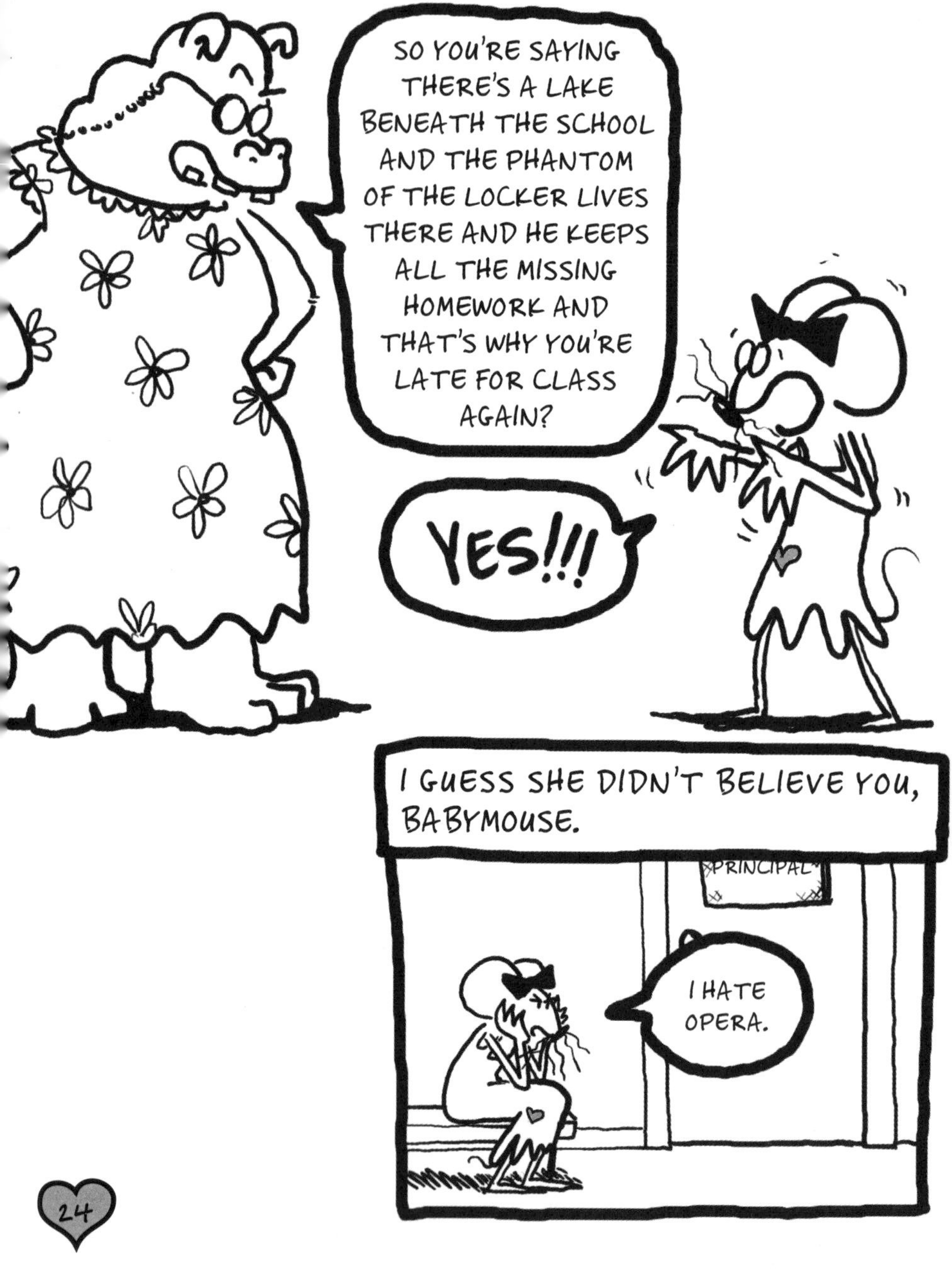
SO YOU'RE SAYING THERE'S A LAKE BENEATH THE SCHOOL AND THE PHANTOM OF THE LOCKER LIVES THERE AND HE KEEPS ALL THE MISSING HOMEWORK AND THAT'S WHY YOU'RE LATE FOR CLASS AGAIN?
YES!!!
I GUESS SHE DIDN'T BELIEVE YOU, BABYMOUSE.
PRINCIPAL
I HATE OPERA.

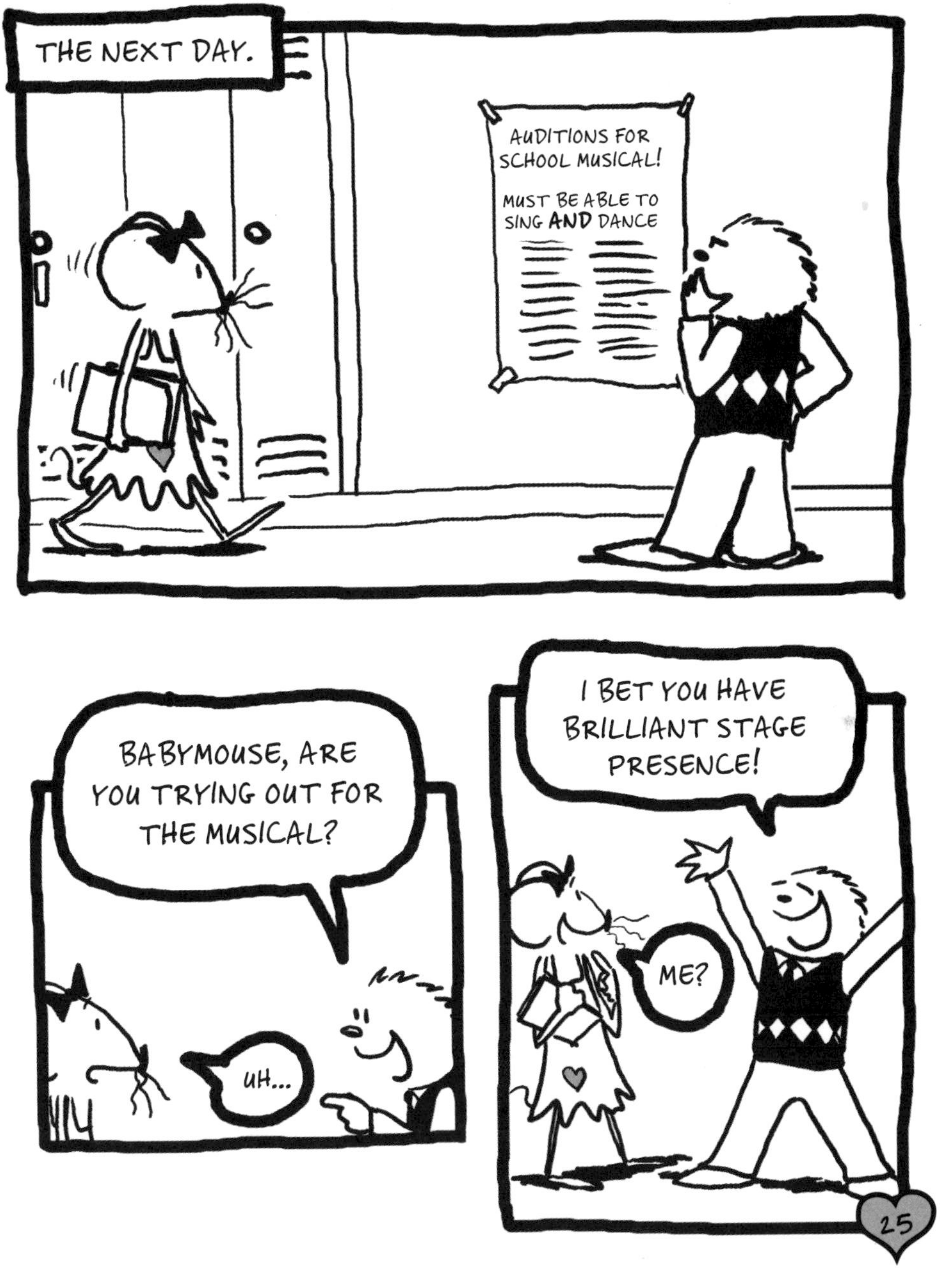
THE NEXT DAY.
AUDITIONS FOR SCHOOL MUSICAL!
MUST BE ABLE TO SING AND DANCE
BABYMOUSE, ARE YOU TRYING OUT FOR THE MUSICAL?
UH...
I BET YOU HAVE BRILLIANT STAGE PRESENCE!
ME?

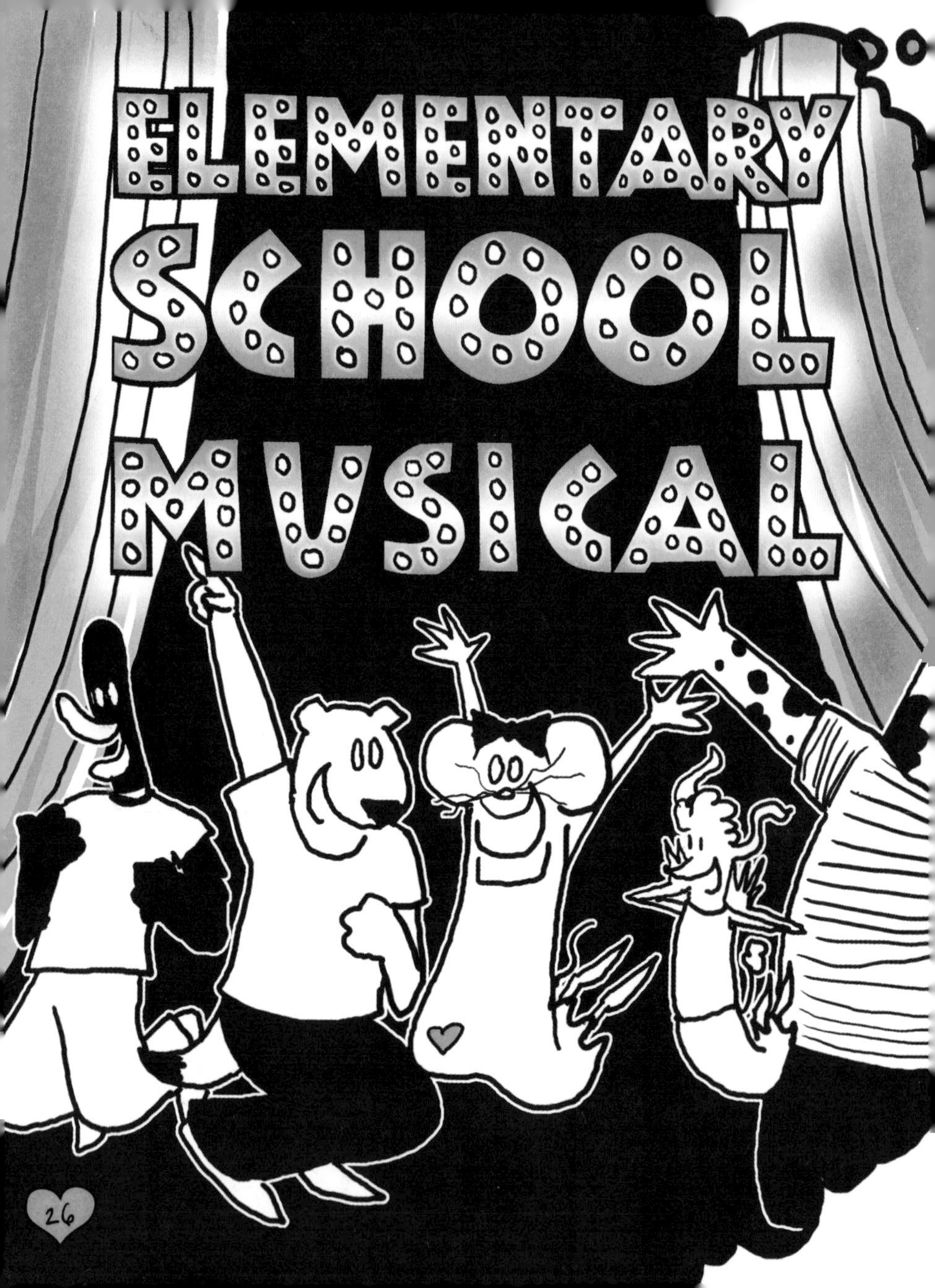
ELEMENTARY
SCHOOL
MUSICAL

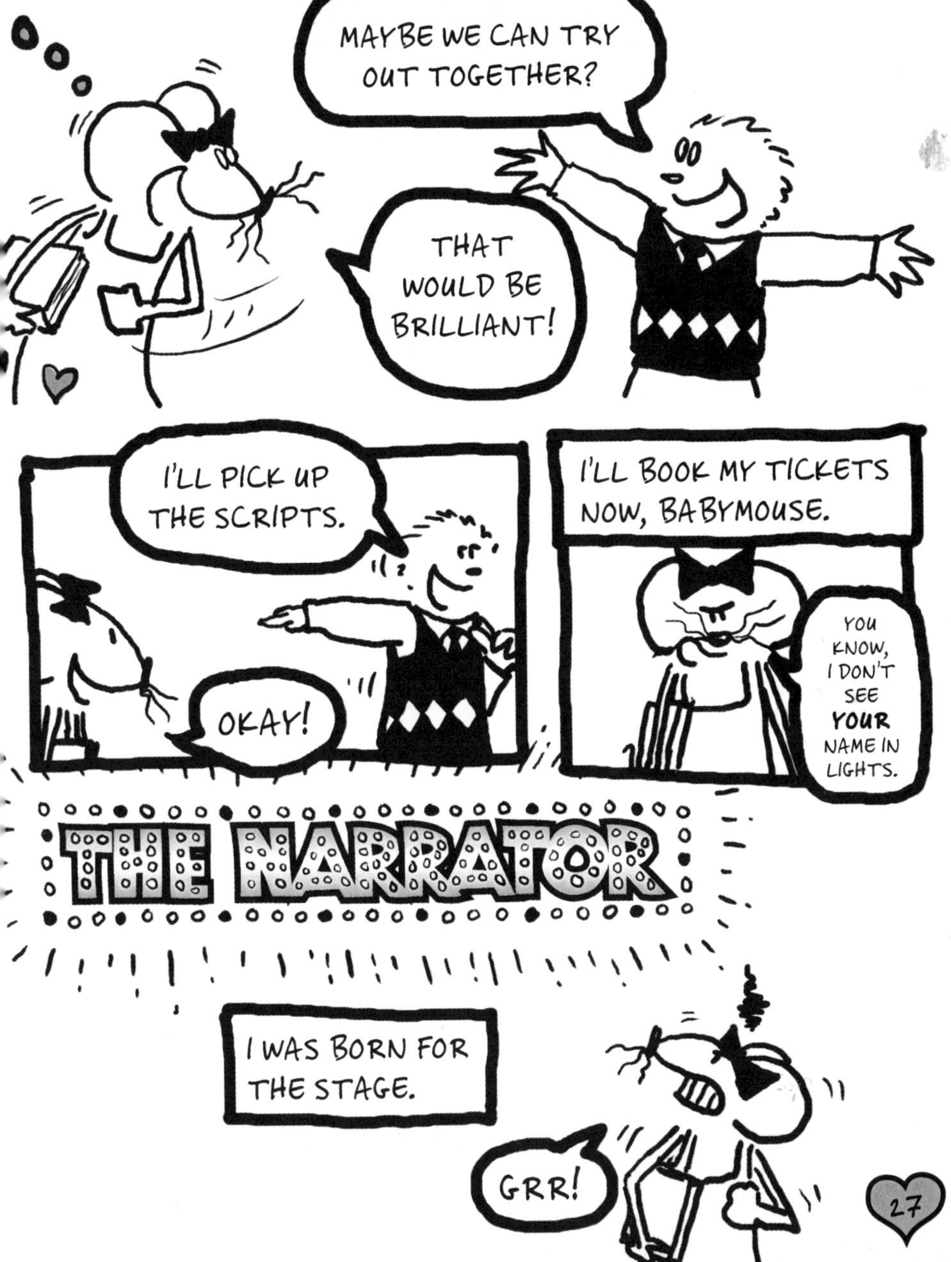
MAYBE WE CAN TRY OUT TOGETHER?
THAT WOULD BE BRILLIANT!
I'LL PICK UP THE SCRIPTS.
OKAY!
I'LL BOOK MY TICKETS NOW, BABYMOUSE.
YOU KNOW, I DON'T SEE **YOUR** NAME IN LIGHTS.
THE NARRATOR
I WAS BORN FOR THE STAGE.
GRR!

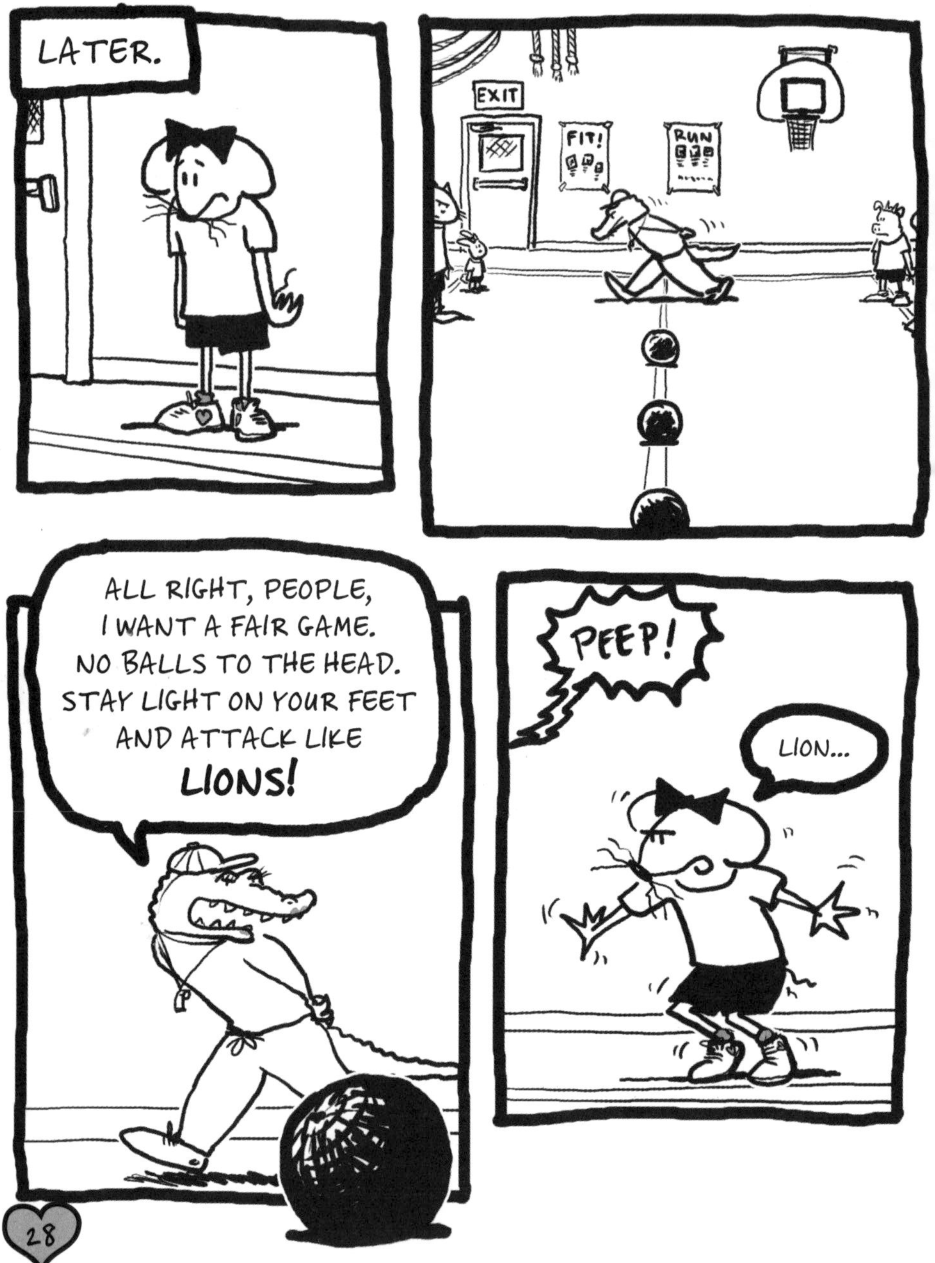
LATER.
EXIT
FIT!
RUN
ALL RIGHT, PEOPLE, I WANT A FAIR GAME. NO BALLS TO THE HEAD. STAY LIGHT ON YOUR FEET AND ATTACK LIKE **LIONS!**
PEEP!
LION...

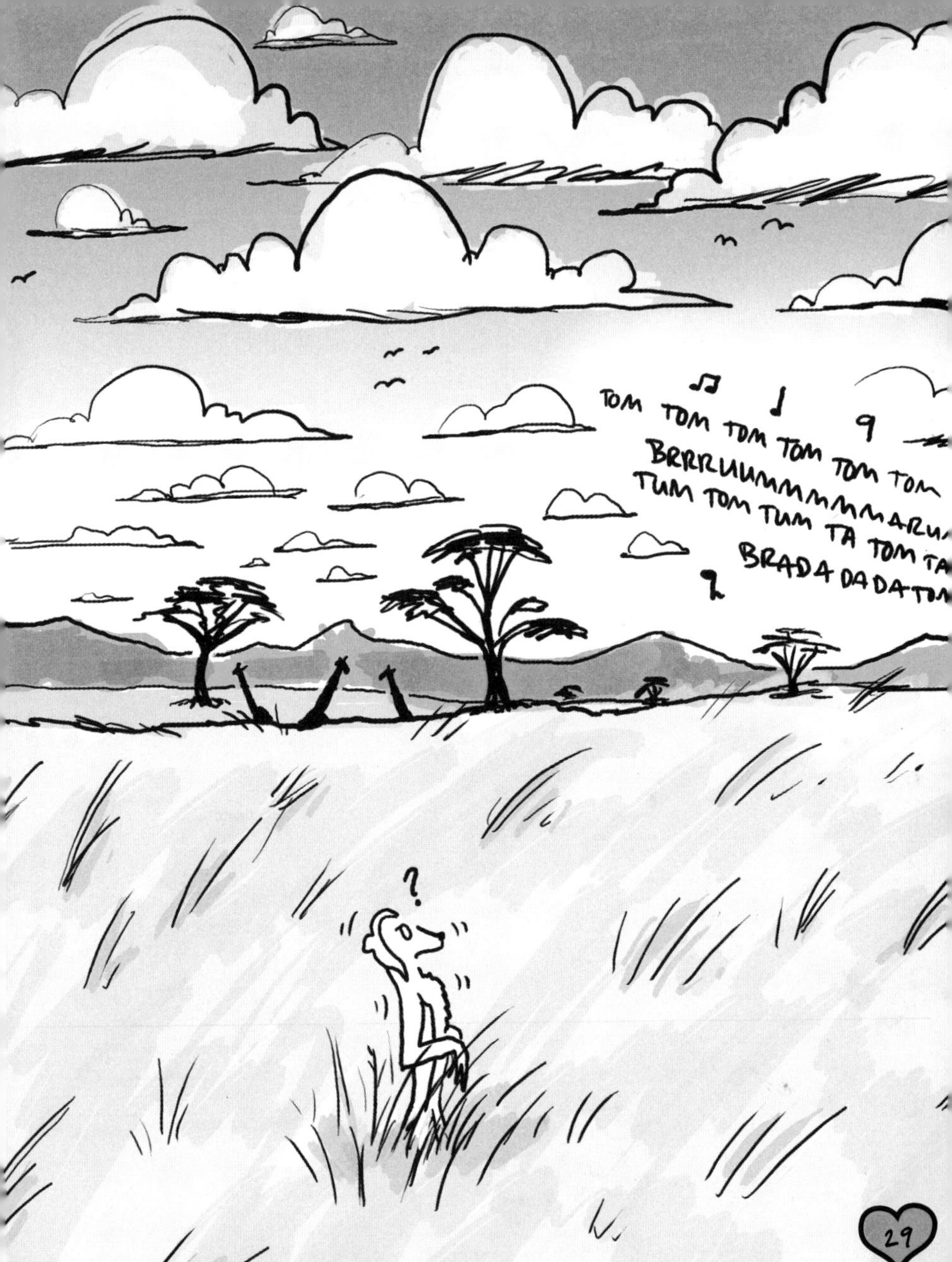
TOM TOM TOM TOM TOM TOM
BRRRUUMMMMMMARU
TUM TOM TUM TA TOM TA
BRADA DADATOM
?

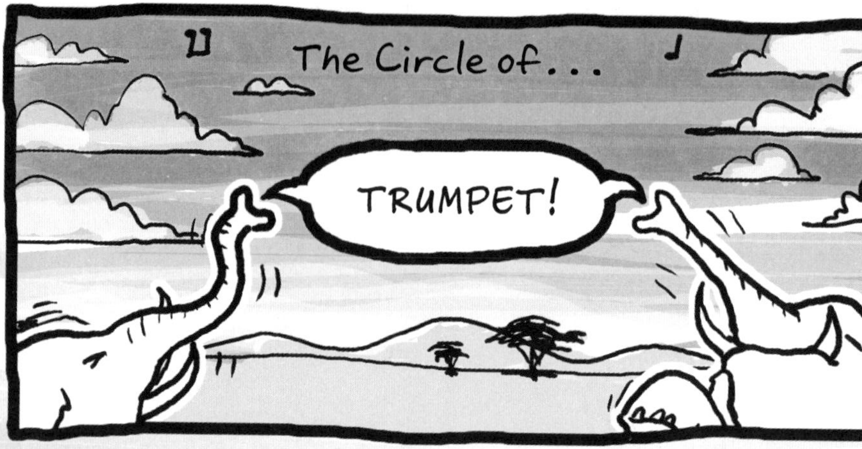
The Circle of...
TRUMPET!

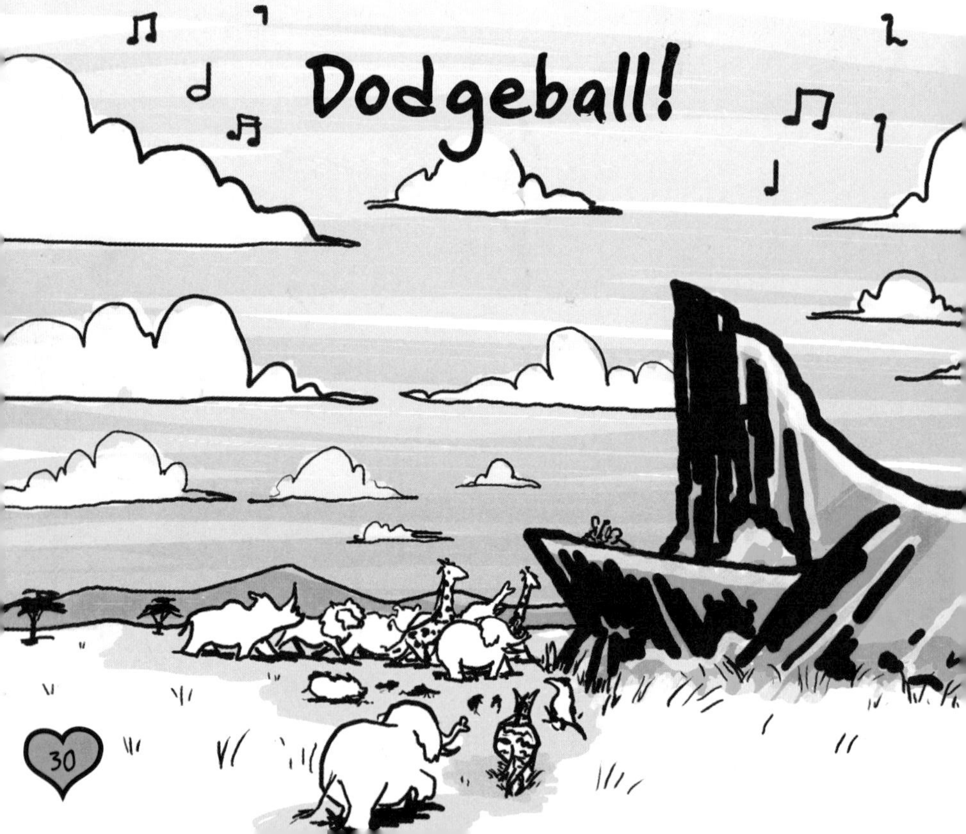
Dodgeball!

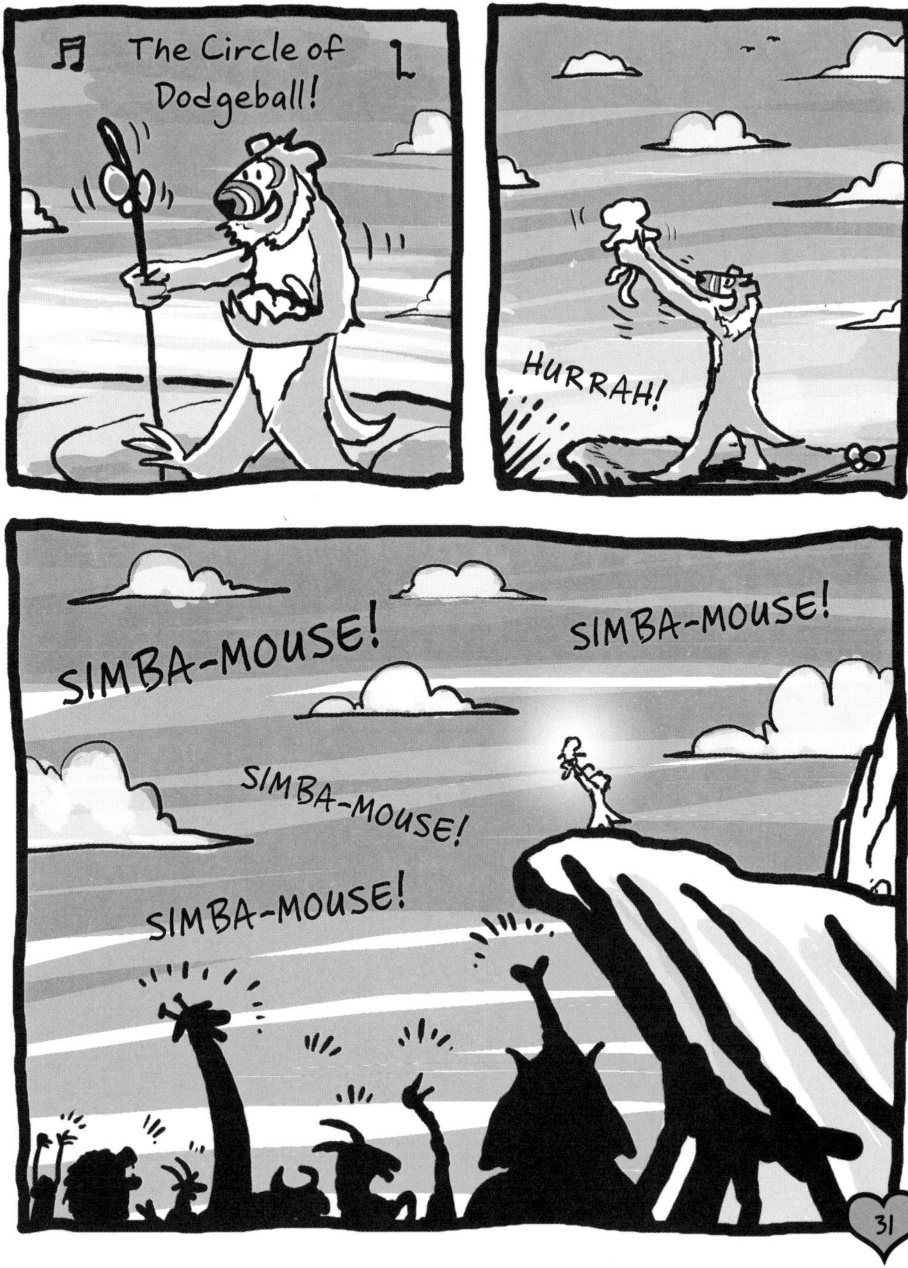

The Circle of Dodgeball!
HURRAH!
SIMBA-MOUSE!
SIMBA-MOUSE!
SIMBA-MOUSE!
SIMBA-MOUSE!

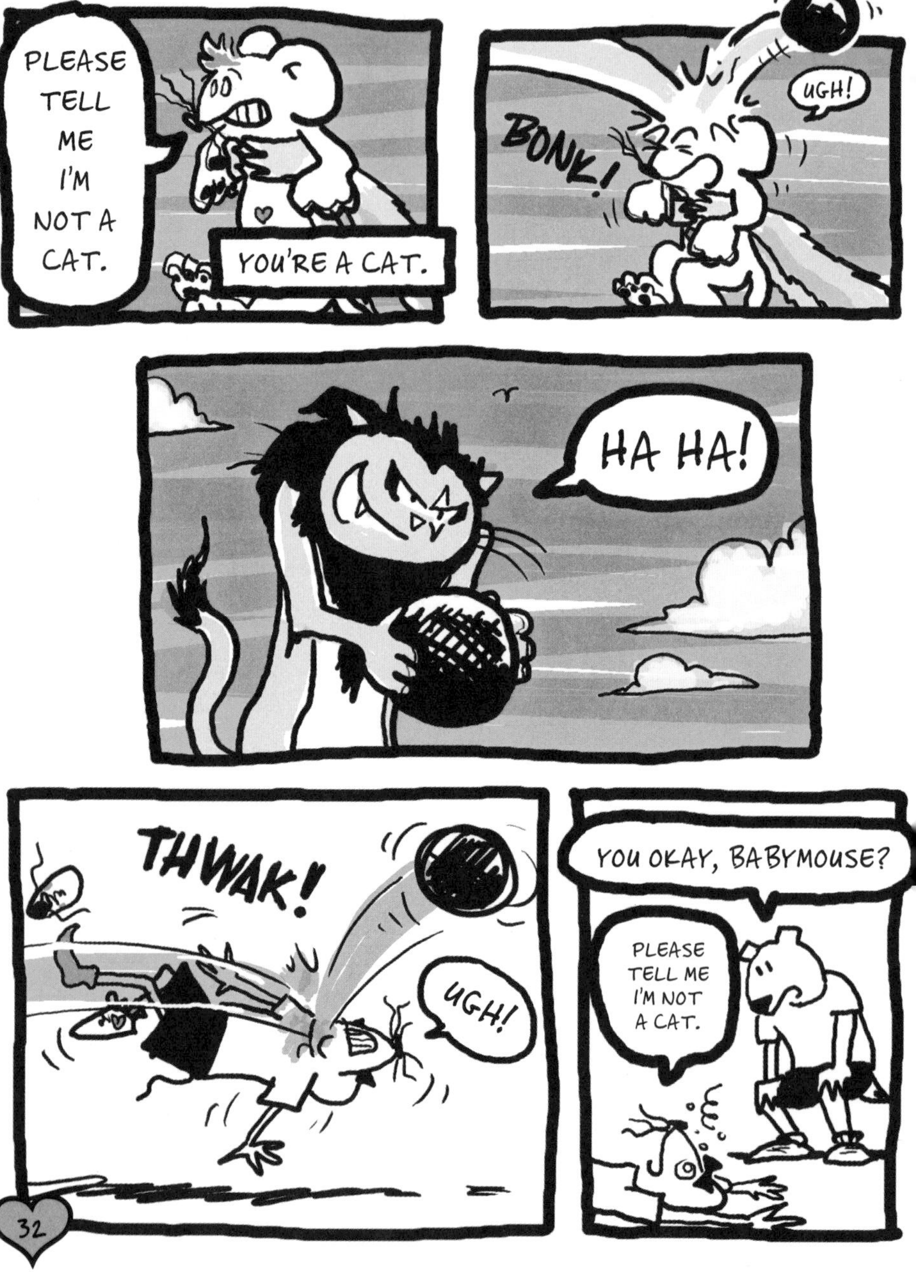
PLEASE TELL ME I'M NOT A CAT.
YOU'RE A CAT.
BONK!
UGH!
HA HA!
THWAK!
UGH!
YOU OKAY, BABYMOUSE?
PLEASE TELL ME I'M NOT A CAT.

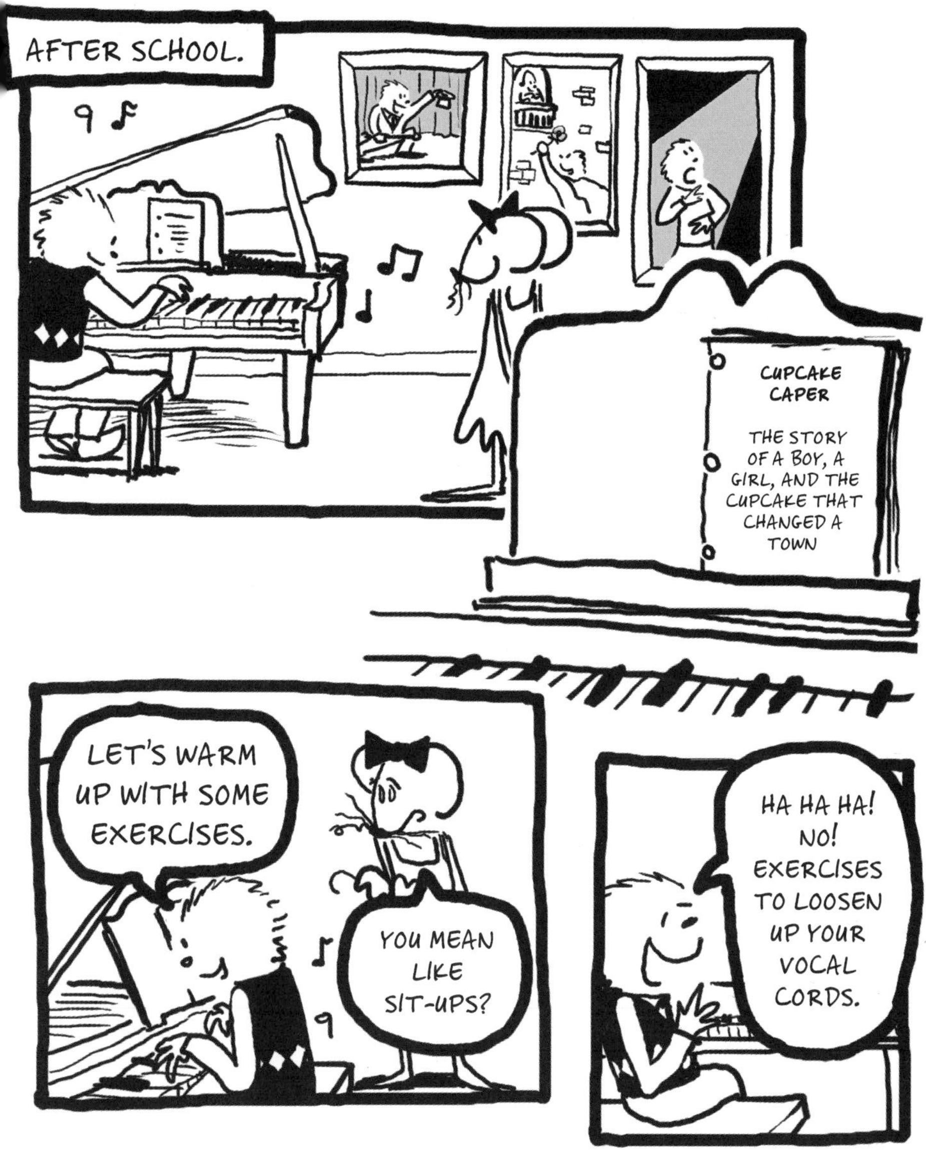

AFTER SCHOOL.
CUPCAKE CAPER
THE STORY OF A BOY, A GIRL, AND THE CUPCAKE THAT CHANGED A TOWN
LET'S WARM UP WITH SOME EXERCISES.
YOU MEAN LIKE SIT-UPS?
HA HA HA! NO! EXERCISES TO LOOSEN UP YOUR VOCAL CORDS.

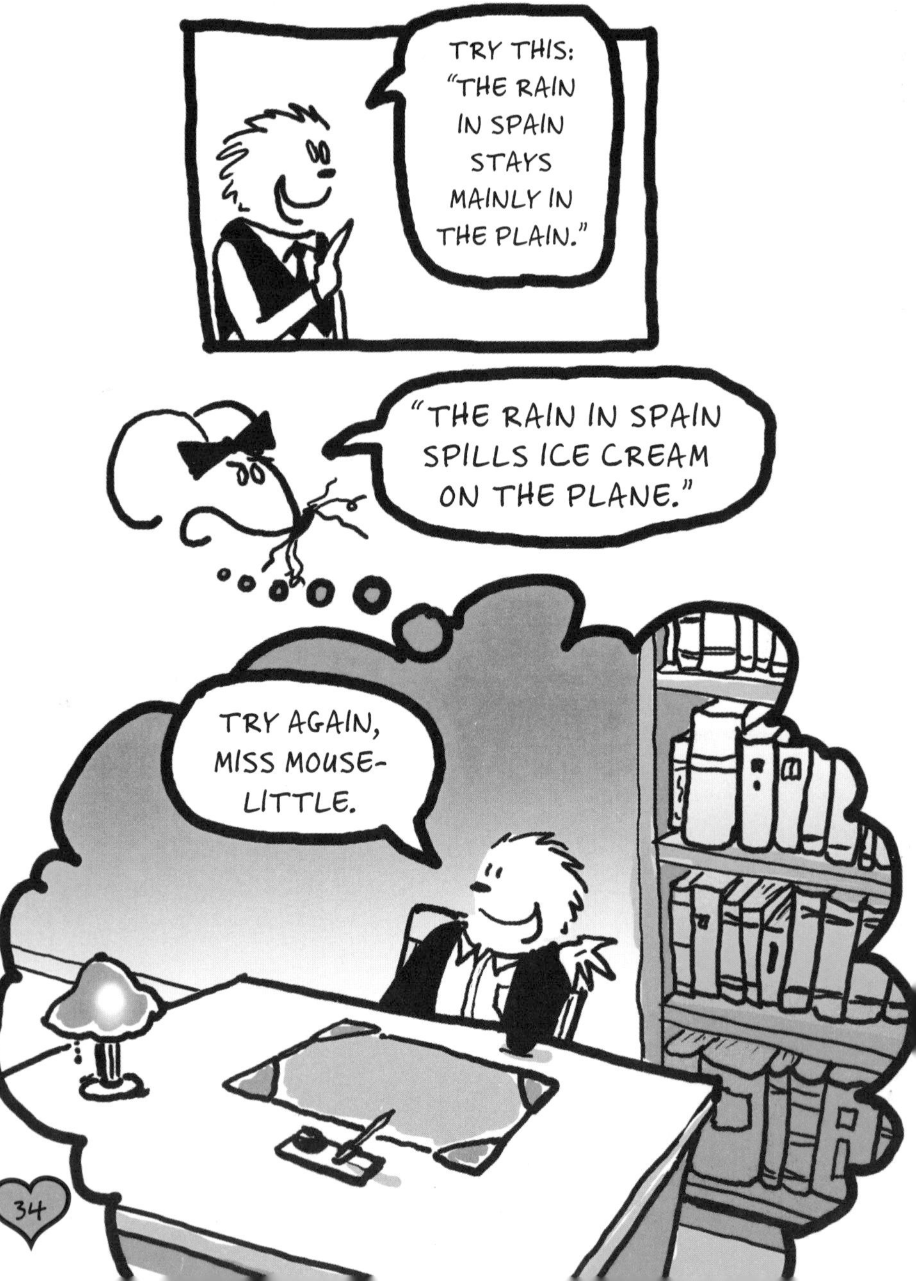
TRY THIS: "THE RAIN IN SPAIN STAYS MAINLY IN THE PLAIN."
"THE RAIN IN SPAIN SPILLS ICE CREAM ON THE PLANE."
TRY AGAIN, MISS MOUSE-LITTLE.

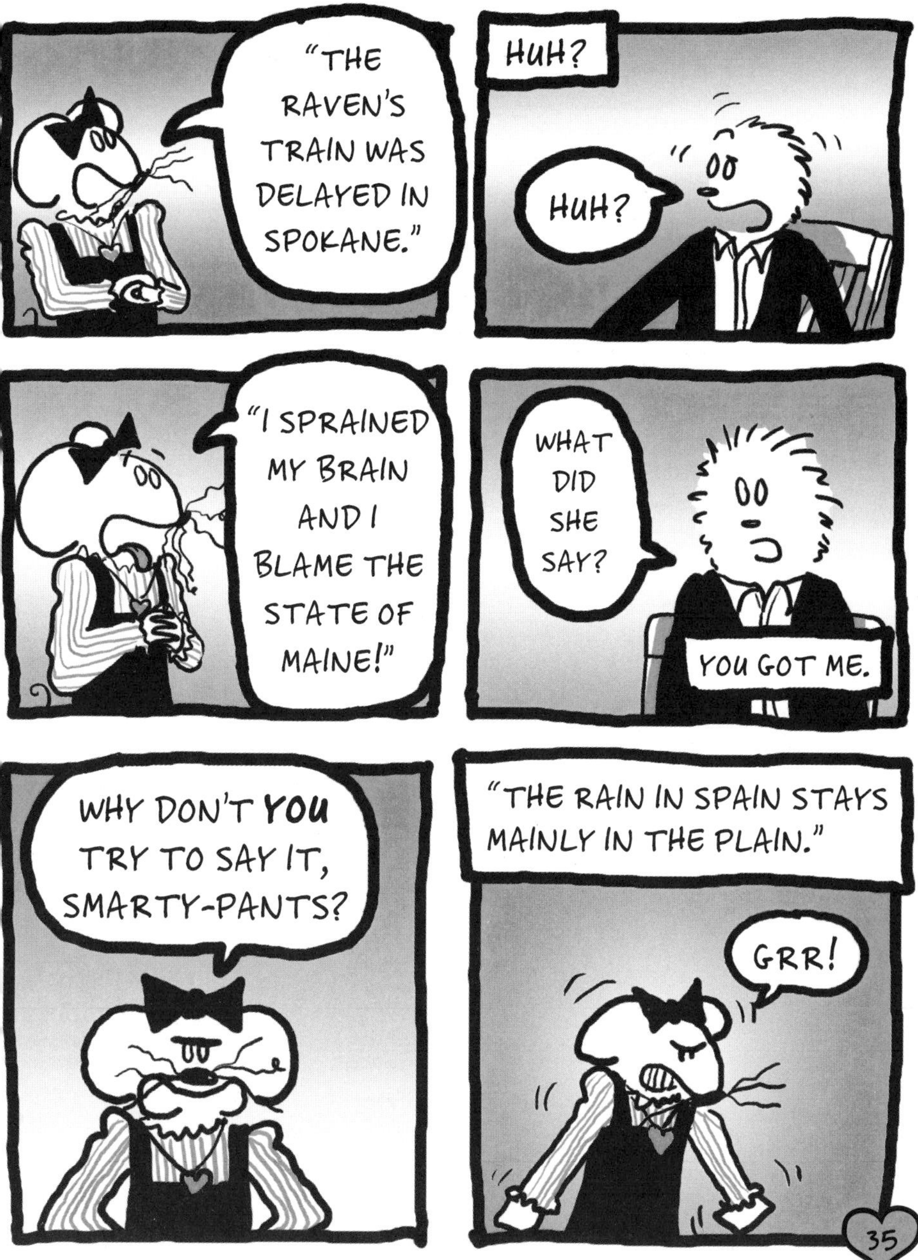
"THE RAVEN'S TRAIN WAS DELAYED IN SPOKANE."
HUH?
HUH?
"I SPRAINED MY BRAIN AND I BLAME THE STATE OF MAINE!"
WHAT DID SHE SAY?
YOU GOT ME.
WHY DON'T **YOU** TRY TO SAY IT, SMARTY-PANTS?
"THE RAIN IN SPAIN STAYS MAINLY IN THE PLAIN."
GRR!

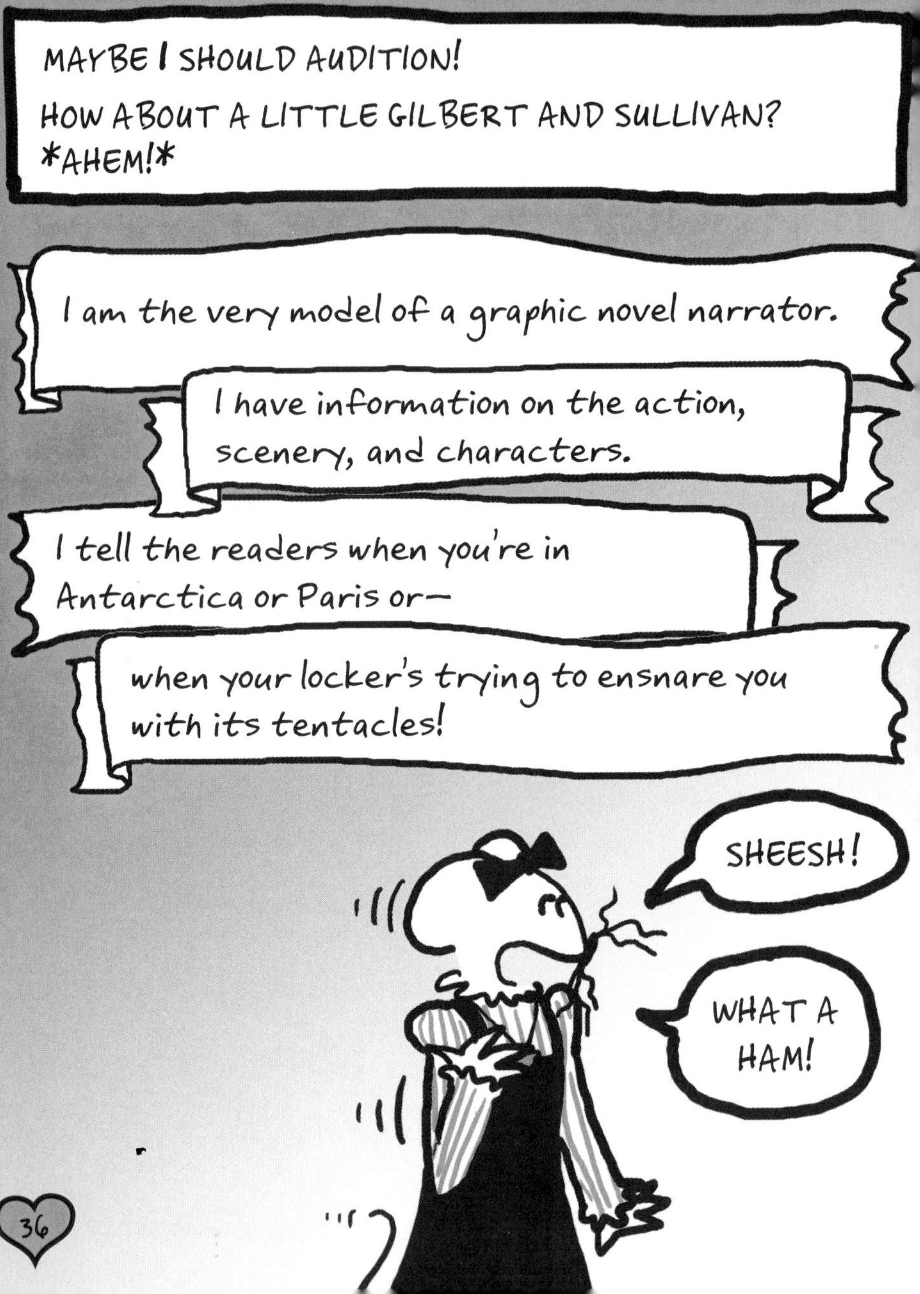
MAYBE I SHOULD AUDITION!
HOW ABOUT A LITTLE GILBERT AND SULLIVAN? *AHEM!*
I am the very model of a graphic novel narrator.
I have information on the action, scenery, and characters.
I tell the readers when you're in Antarctica or Paris or—
when your locker's trying to ensnare you with its tentacles!
SHEESH!
WHAT A HAM!

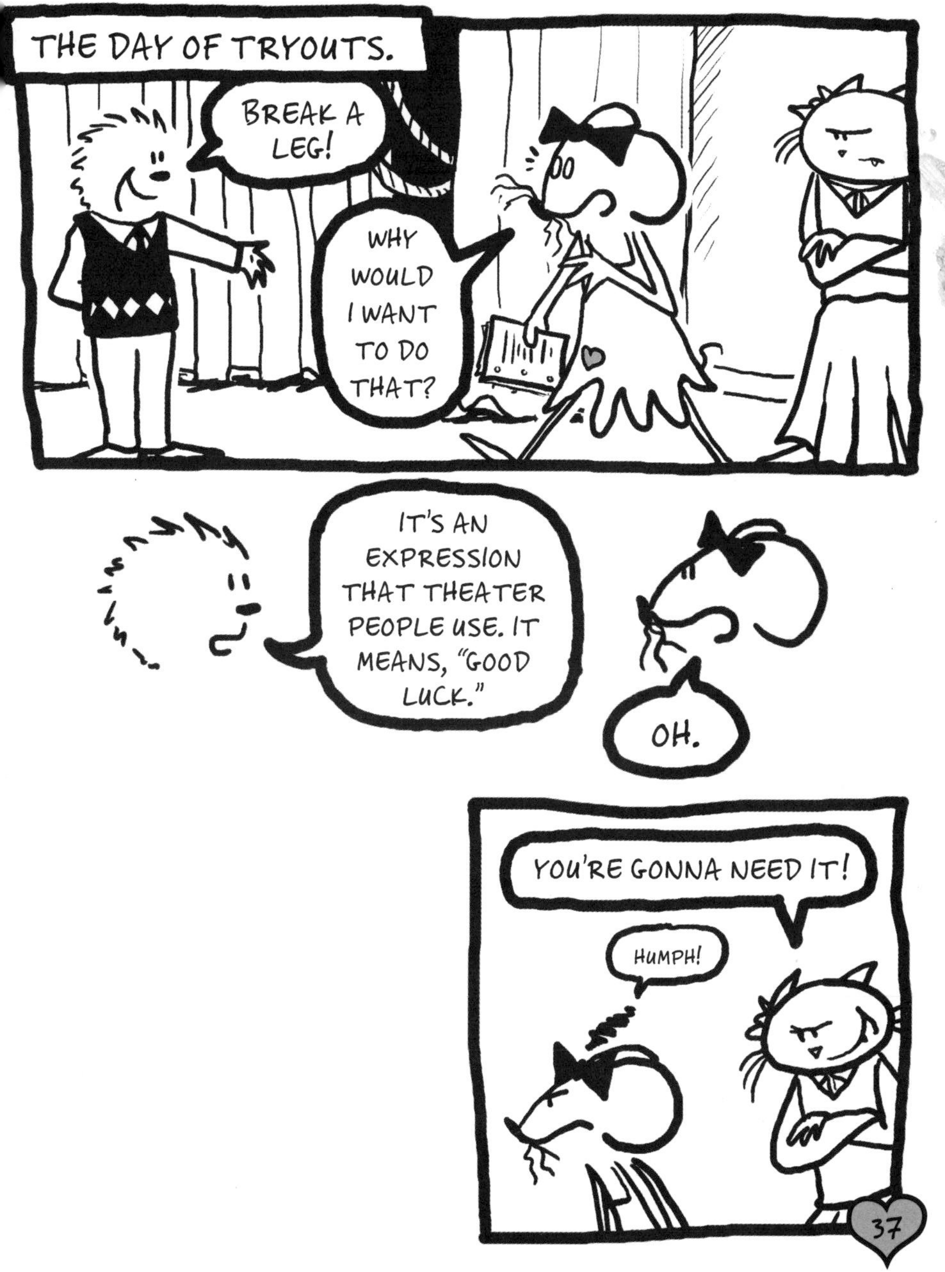
THE DAY OF TRYOUTS.
BREAK A LEG!
WHY WOULD I WANT TO DO THAT?
IT'S AN EXPRESSION THAT THEATER PEOPLE USE. IT MEANS, "GOOD LUCK."
OH.
YOU'RE GONNA NEED IT!
HUMPH!

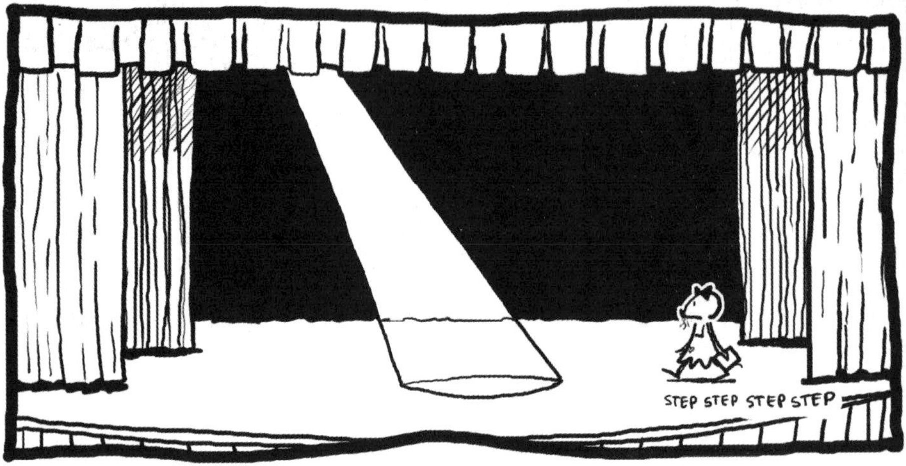
STEP STEP STEP STEP

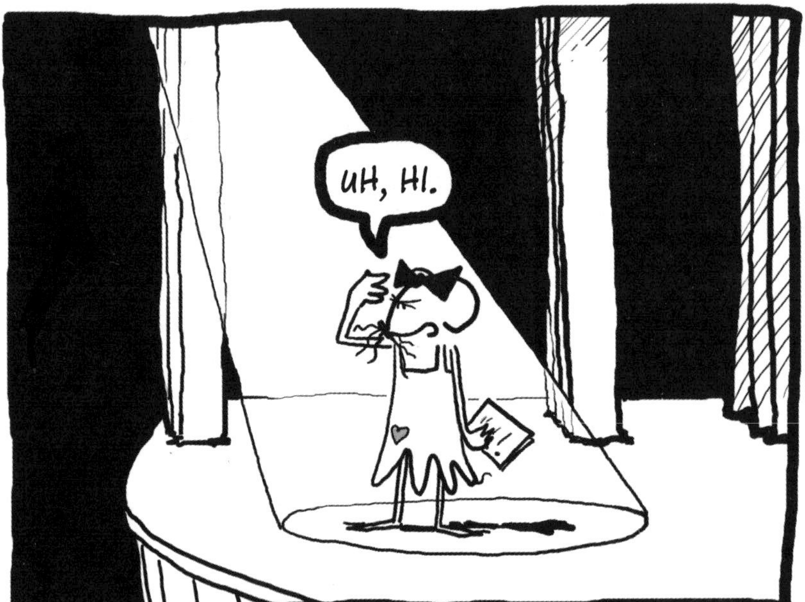
UH, HI.

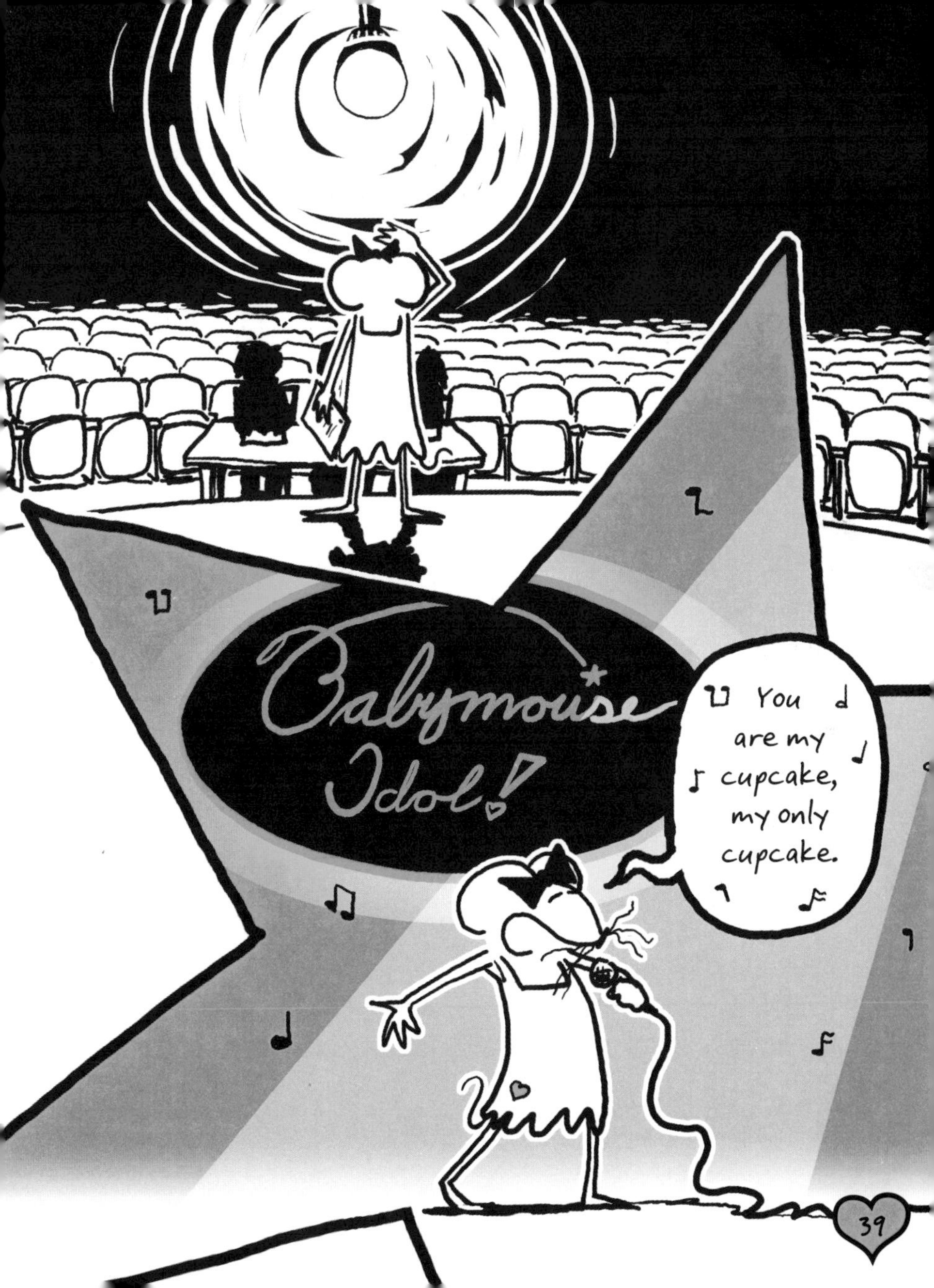
Babymouse Idol!
You are my cupcake, my only cupcake.

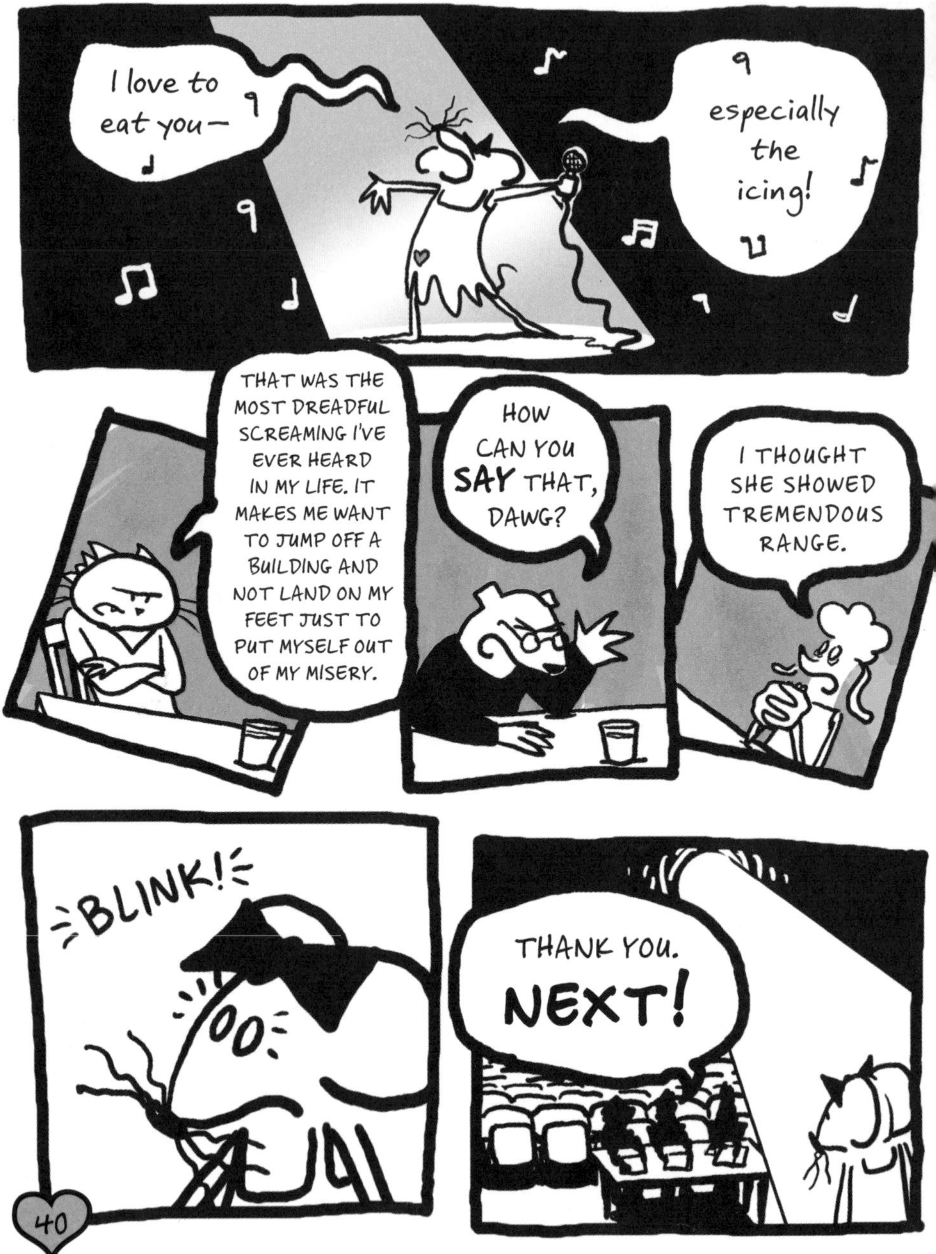
I love to eat you—
especially the icing!
THAT WAS THE MOST DREADFUL SCREAMING I'VE EVER HEARD IN MY LIFE. IT MAKES ME WANT TO JUMP OFF A BUILDING AND NOT LAND ON MY FEET JUST TO PUT MYSELF OUT OF MY MISERY.
HOW CAN YOU **SAY** THAT, DAWG?
I THOUGHT SHE SHOWED TREMENDOUS RANGE.
BLINK!
THANK YOU. **NEXT!**

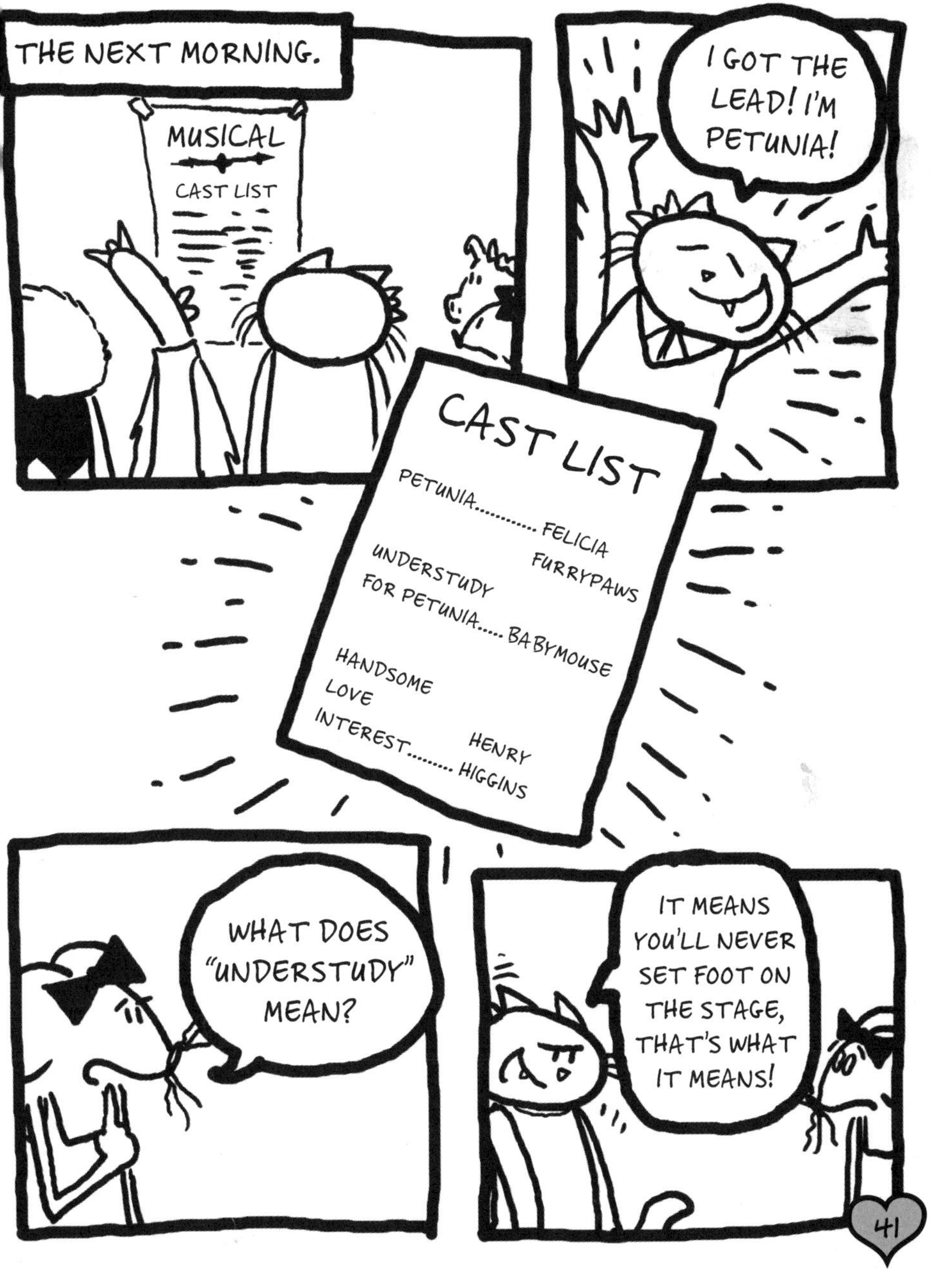
THE NEXT MORNING.
MUSICAL
CAST LIST
I GOT THE LEAD! I'M PETUNIA!
CAST LIST
PETUNIA........... FELICIA FURRYPAWS
UNDERSTUDY FOR PETUNIA..... BABYMOUSE
HANDSOME LOVE INTEREST......... HENRY HIGGINS
WHAT DOES "UNDERSTUDY" MEAN?
IT MEANS YOU'LL NEVER SET FOOT ON THE STAGE, THAT'S WHAT IT MEANS!

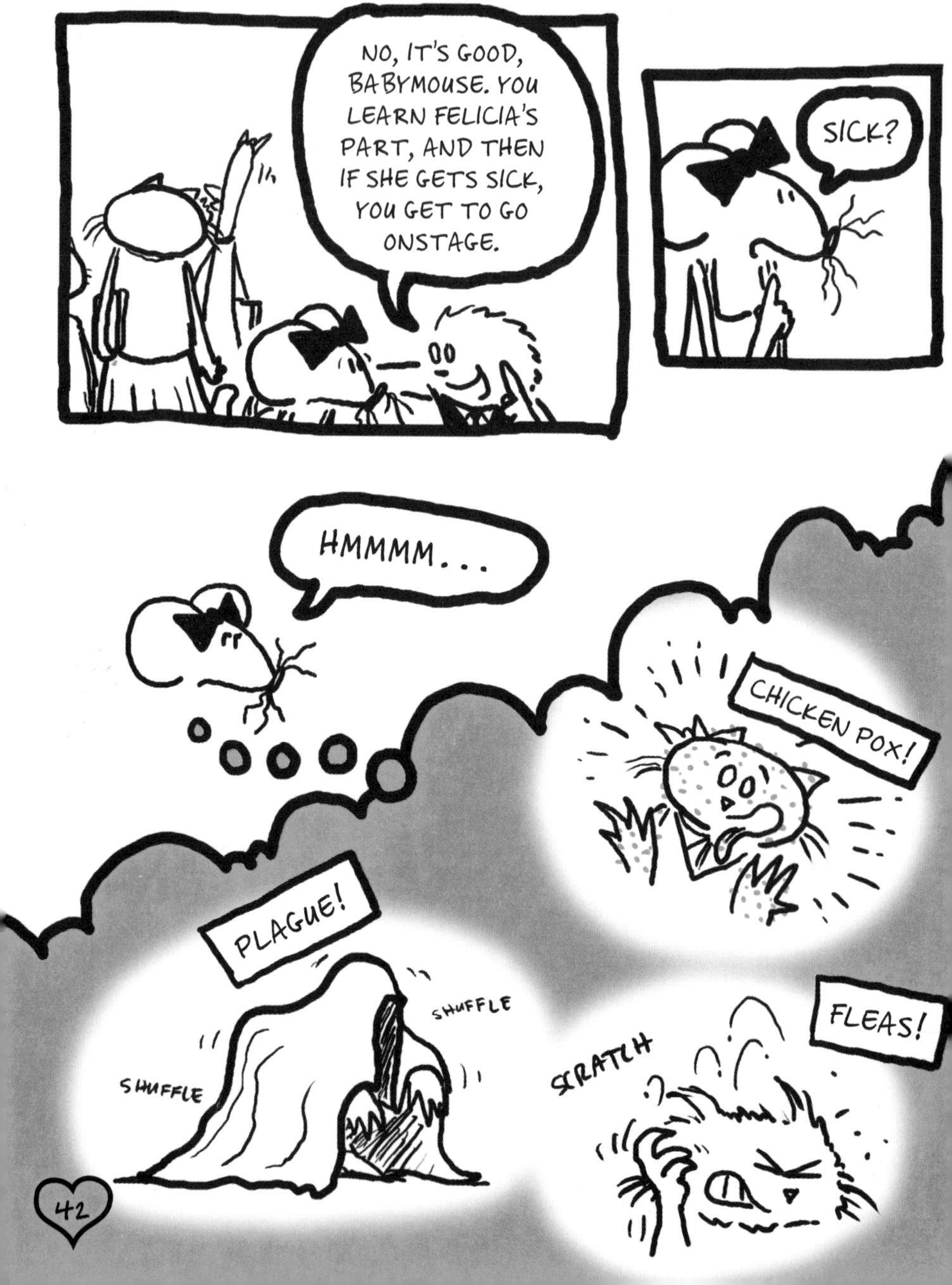
NO, IT'S GOOD, BABYMOUSE. YOU LEARN FELICIA'S PART, AND THEN IF SHE GETS SICK, YOU GET TO GO ONSTAGE.
SICK?
HMMMM...
CHICKEN POX!
PLAGUE!
SHUFFLE
SHUFFLE
FLEAS!
SCRATCH

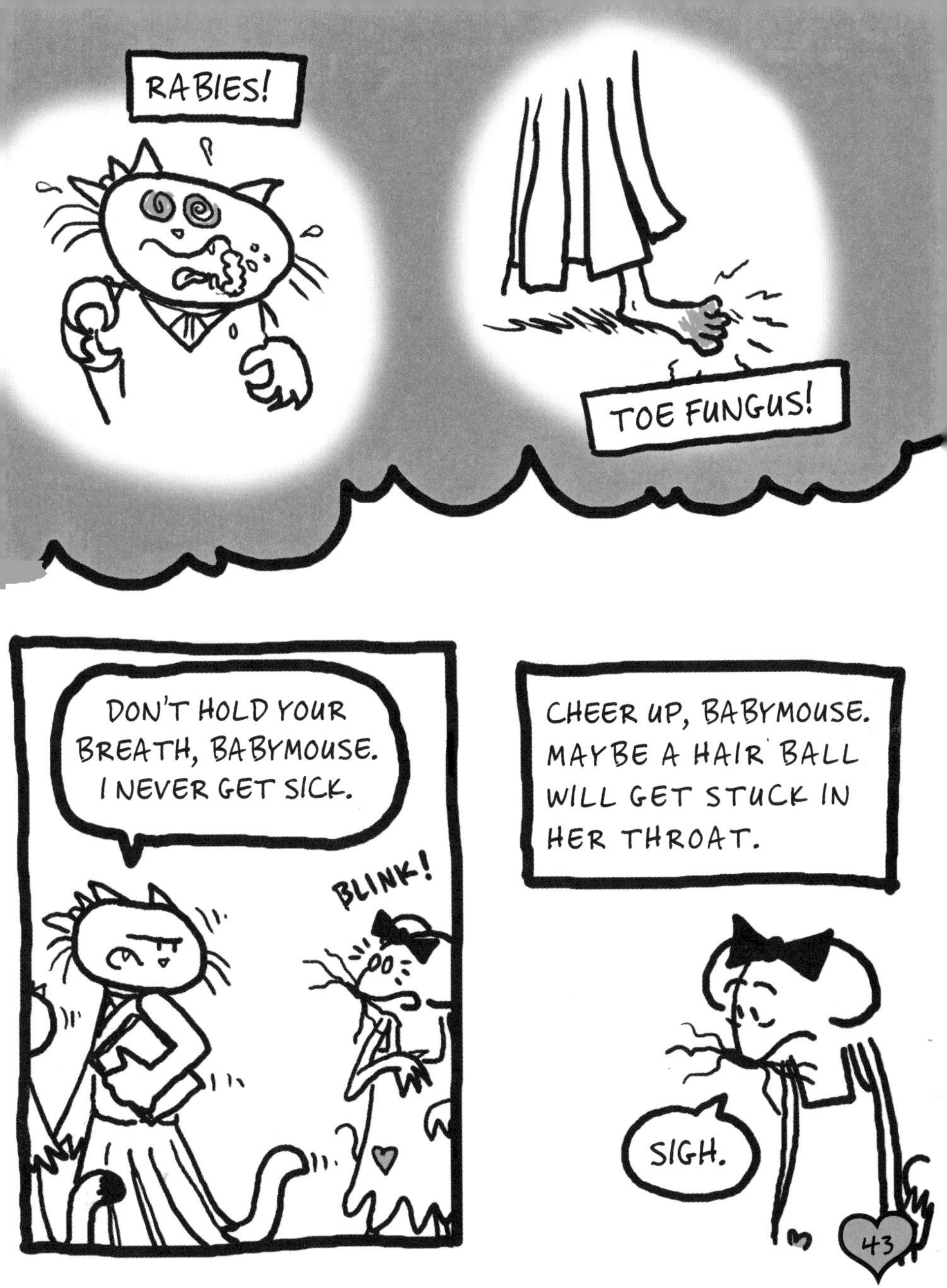
RABIES!
TOE FUNGUS!
DON'T HOLD YOUR BREATH, BABYMOUSE. I NEVER GET SICK.
BLINK!
CHEER UP, BABYMOUSE. MAYBE A HAIR BALL WILL GET STUCK IN HER THROAT.
SIGH.

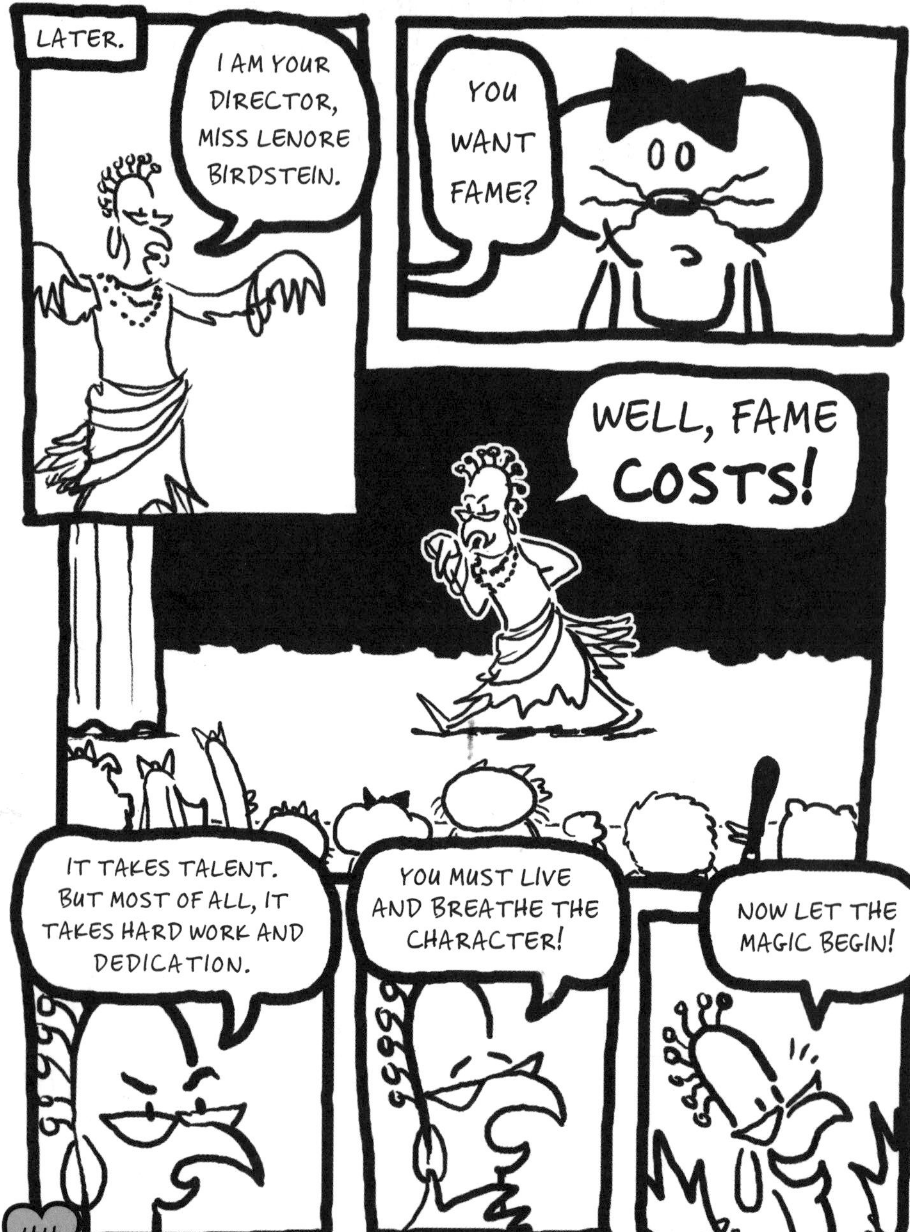
LATER.
I AM YOUR DIRECTOR, MISS LENORE BIRDSTEIN.
YOU WANT FAME?
WELL, FAME COSTS!
IT TAKES TALENT. BUT MOST OF ALL, IT TAKES HARD WORK AND DEDICATION.
YOU MUST LIVE AND BREATHE THE CHARACTER!
NOW LET THE MAGIC BEGIN!

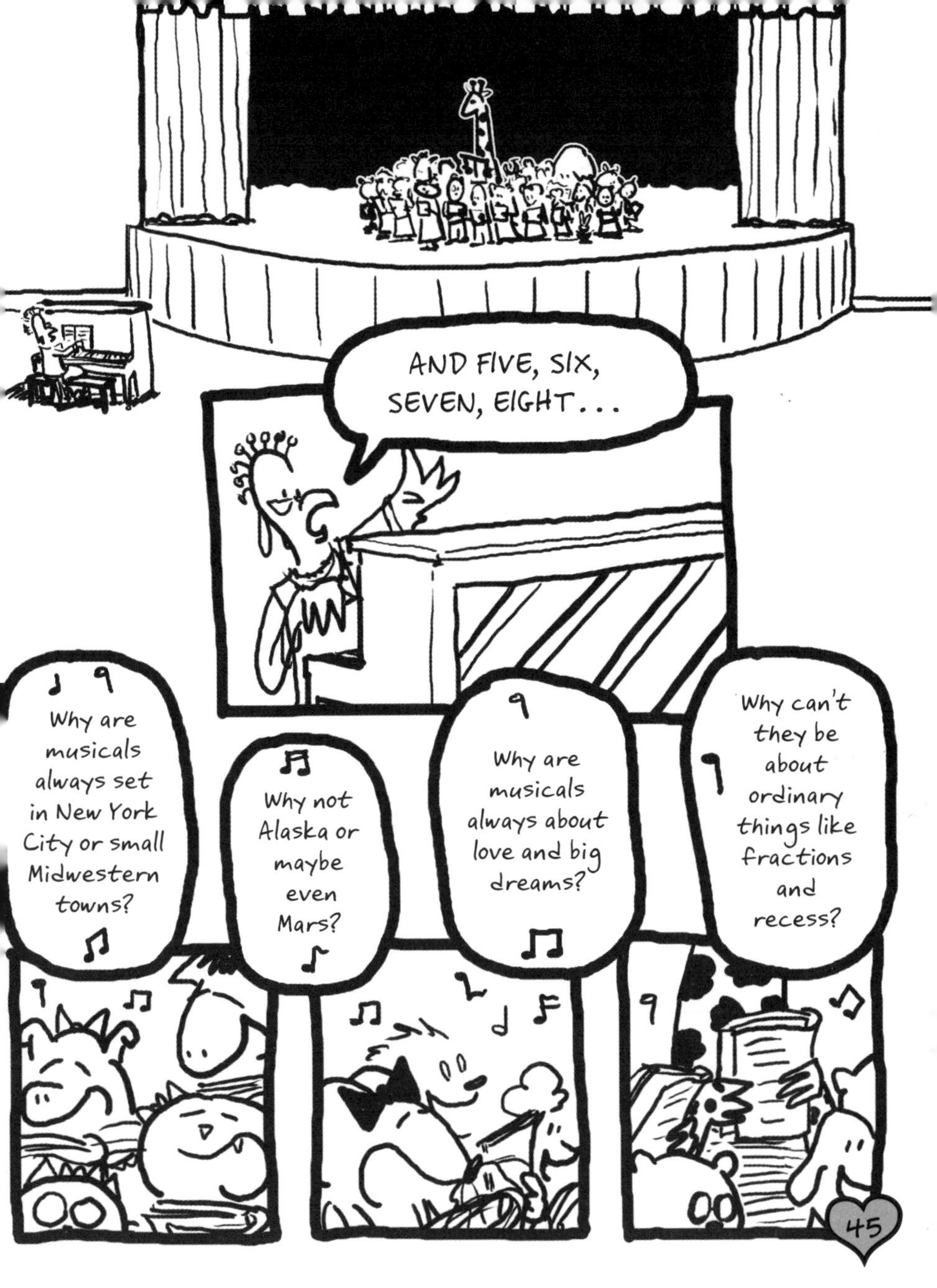
AND FIVE, SIX, SEVEN, EIGHT . . .
Why are musicals always set in New York City or small Midwestern towns?
Why not Alaska or maybe even Mars?
Why are musicals always about love and big dreams?
Why can't they be about ordinary things like fractions and recess?

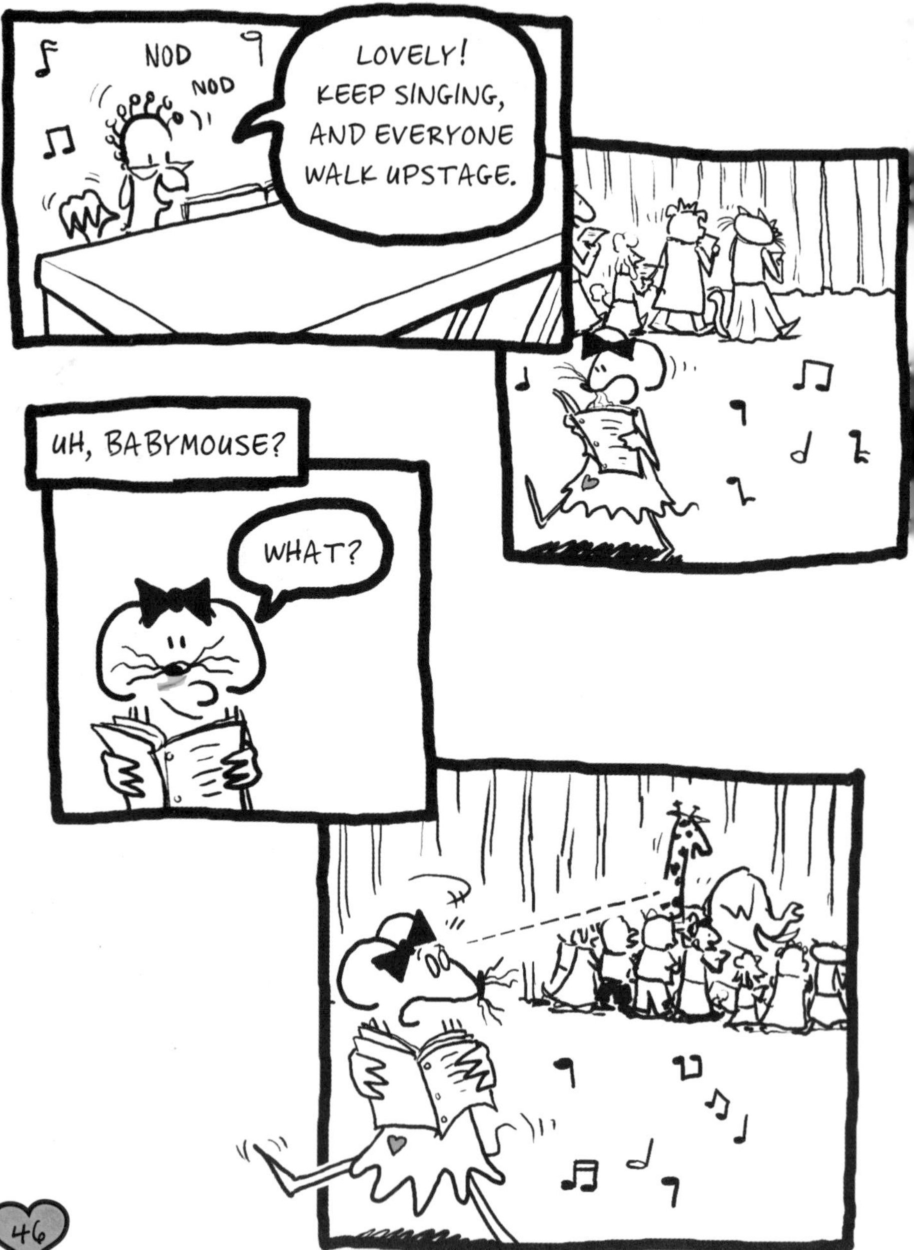
NOD
NOD
LOVELY! KEEP SINGING, AND EVERYONE WALK UPSTAGE.
UH, BABYMOUSE?
WHAT?

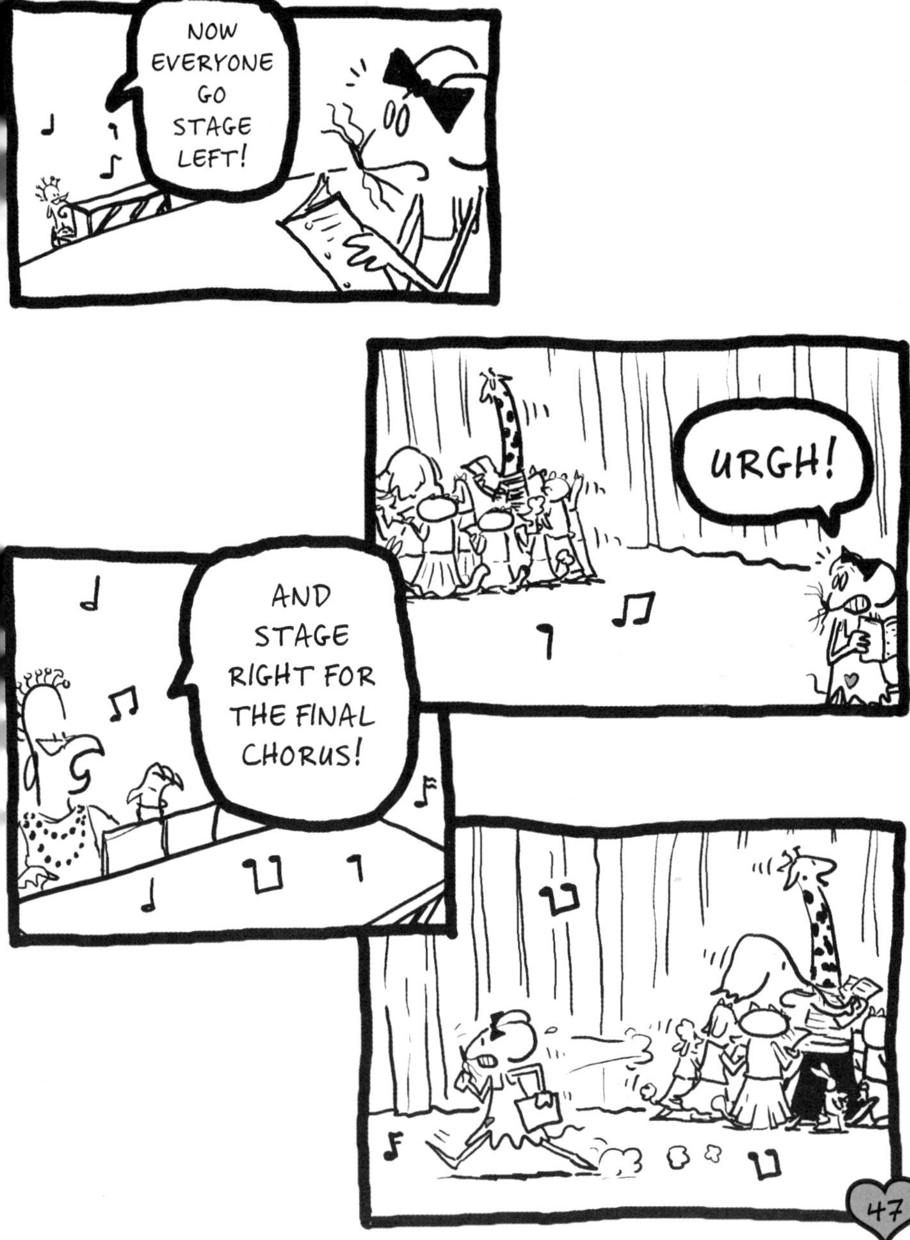
NOW EVERYONE GO STAGE LEFT!
URGH!
AND STAGE RIGHT FOR THE FINAL CHORUS!

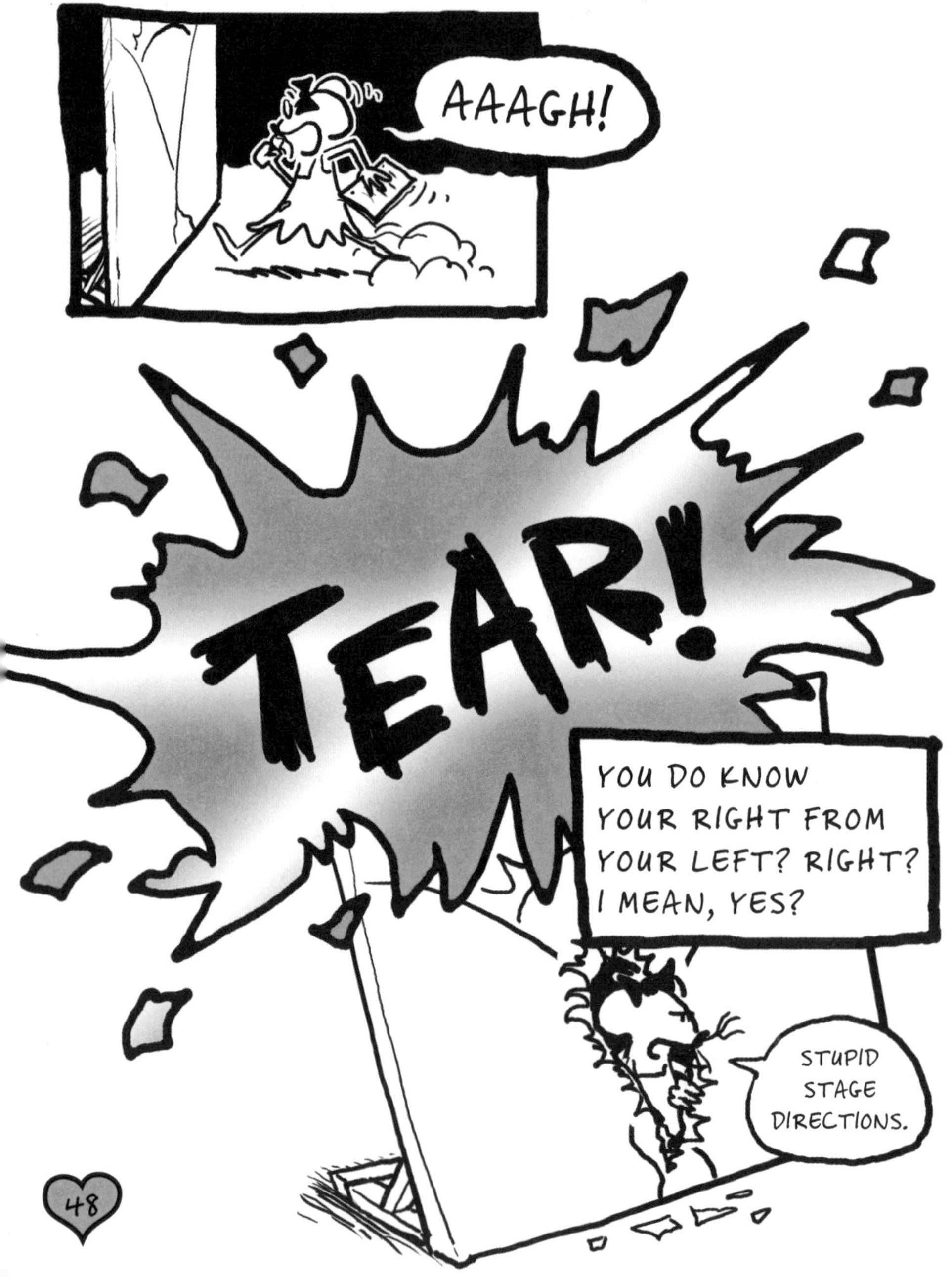
AAAGH!
TEAR!
YOU DO KNOW YOUR RIGHT FROM YOUR LEFT? RIGHT? I MEAN, YES?
STUPID STAGE DIRECTIONS.

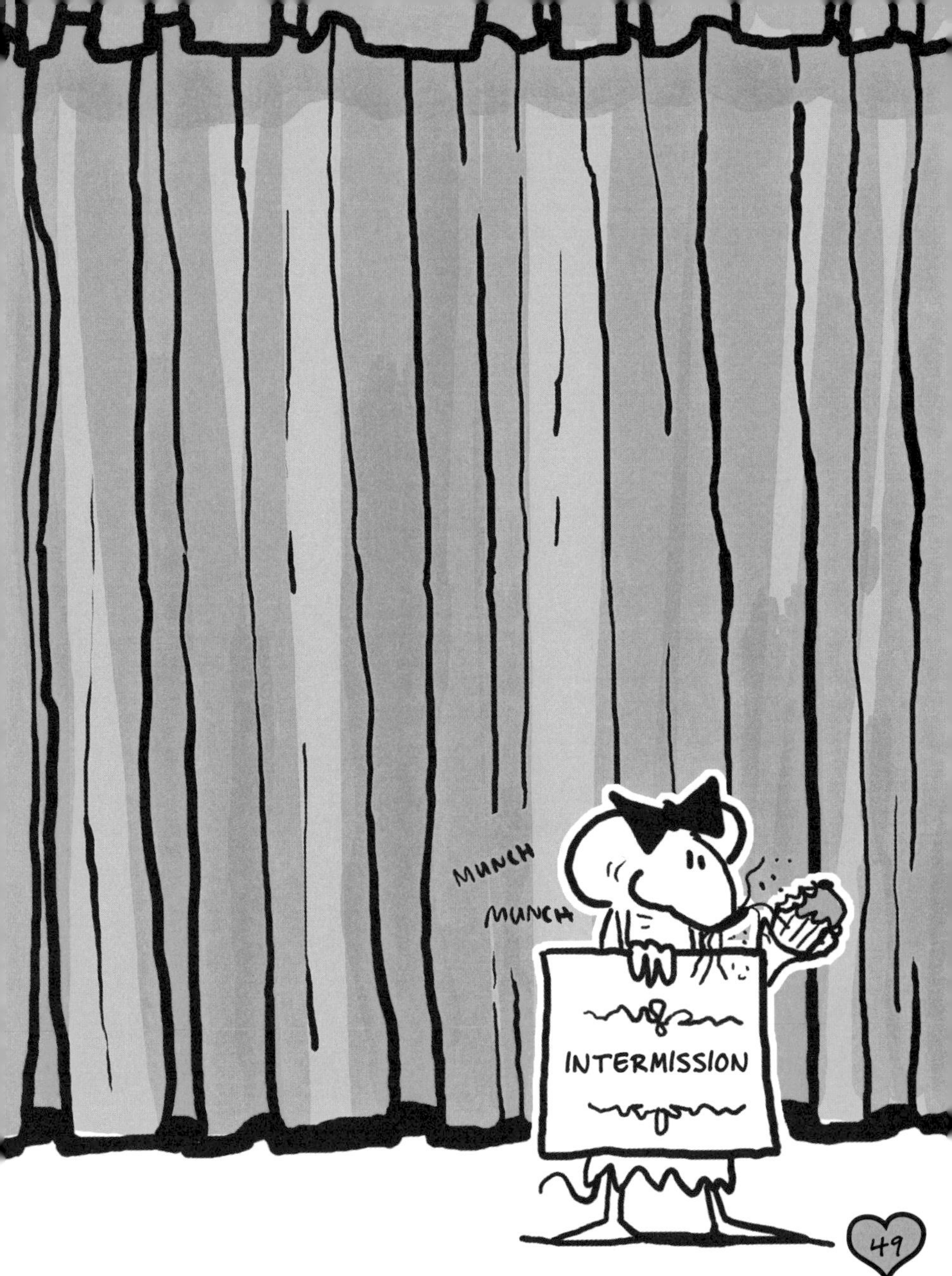
MUNCH
MUNCH
INTERMISSION

CAN WE GET BACK TO THE STORY, PLEASE?

THE LINE IS ALWAYS LONGER FOR THE GIRLS' BATHROOM!

ACT TWO

50

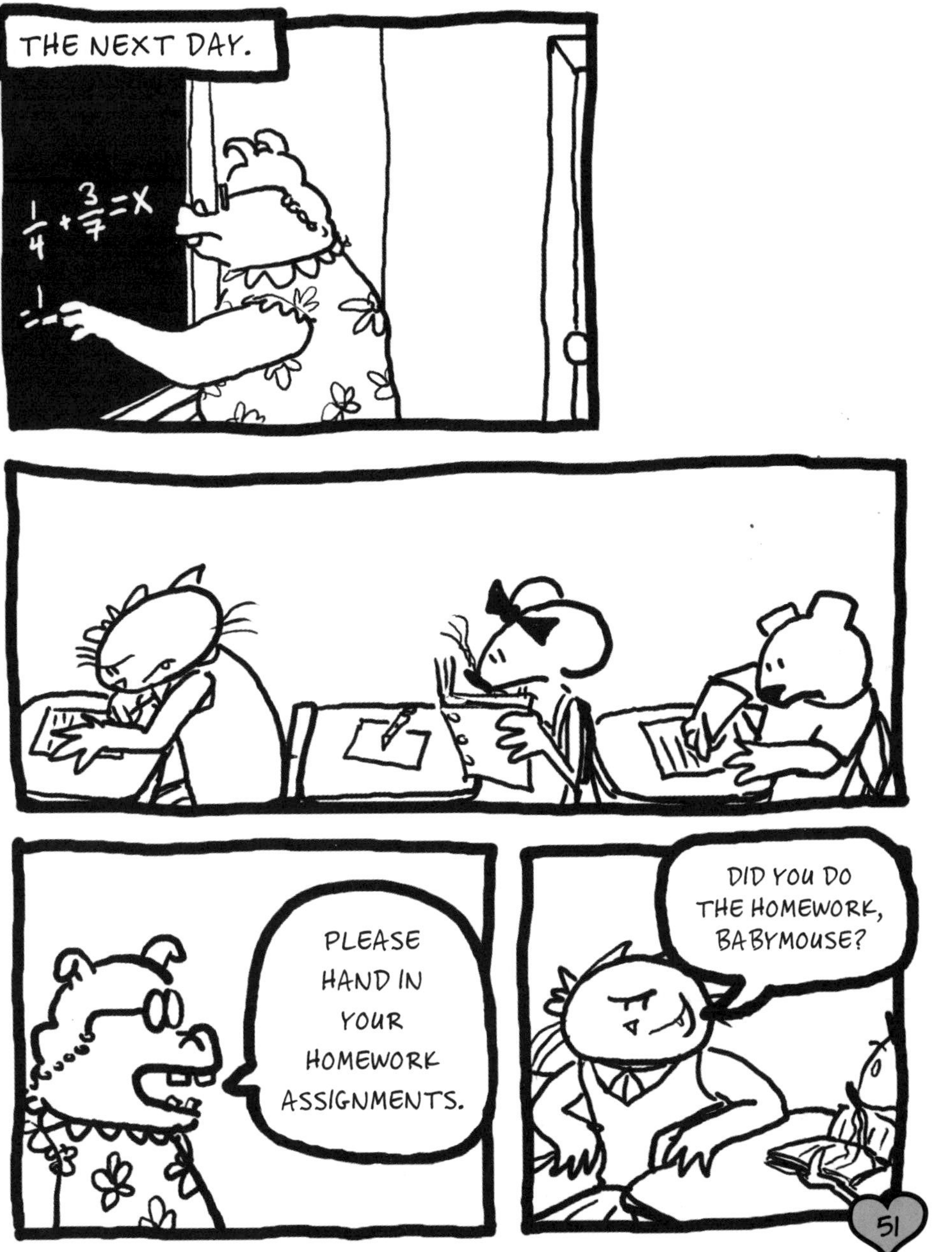
THE NEXT DAY.
1/4 + 3/7 = X
PLEASE HAND IN YOUR HOMEWORK ASSIGNMENTS.
DID YOU DO THE HOMEWORK, BABYMOUSE?

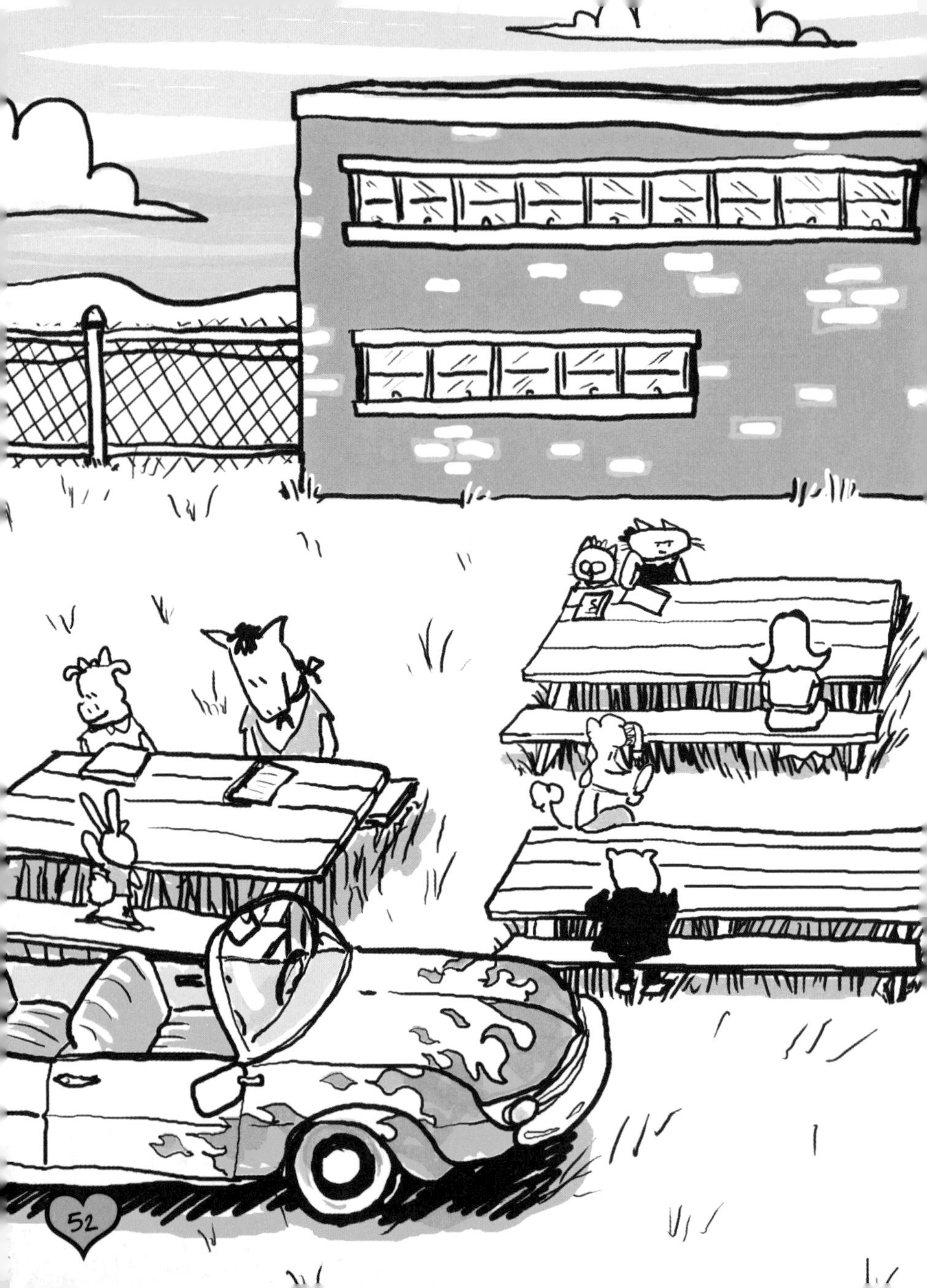

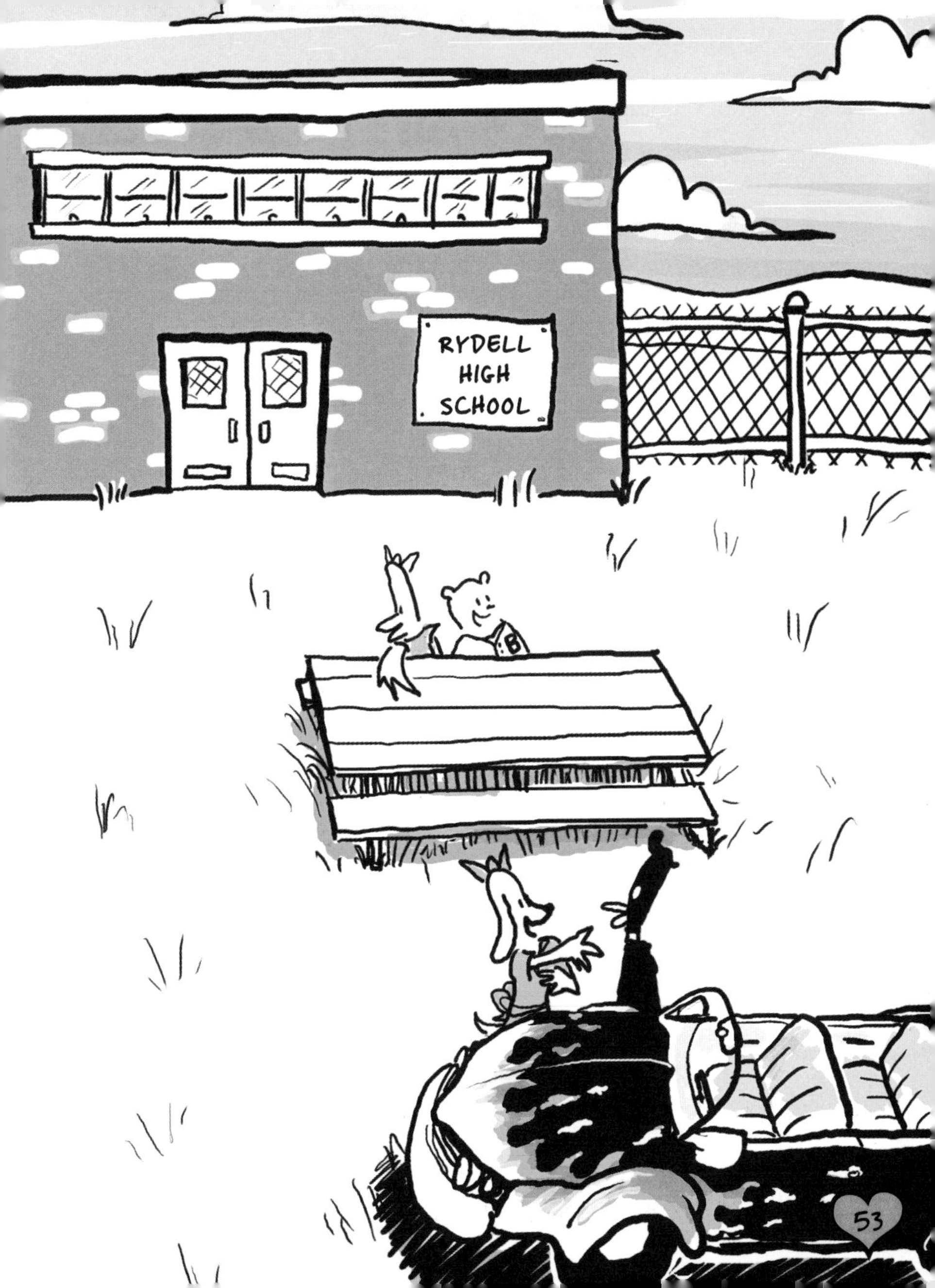
RYDELL
HIGH
SCHOOL

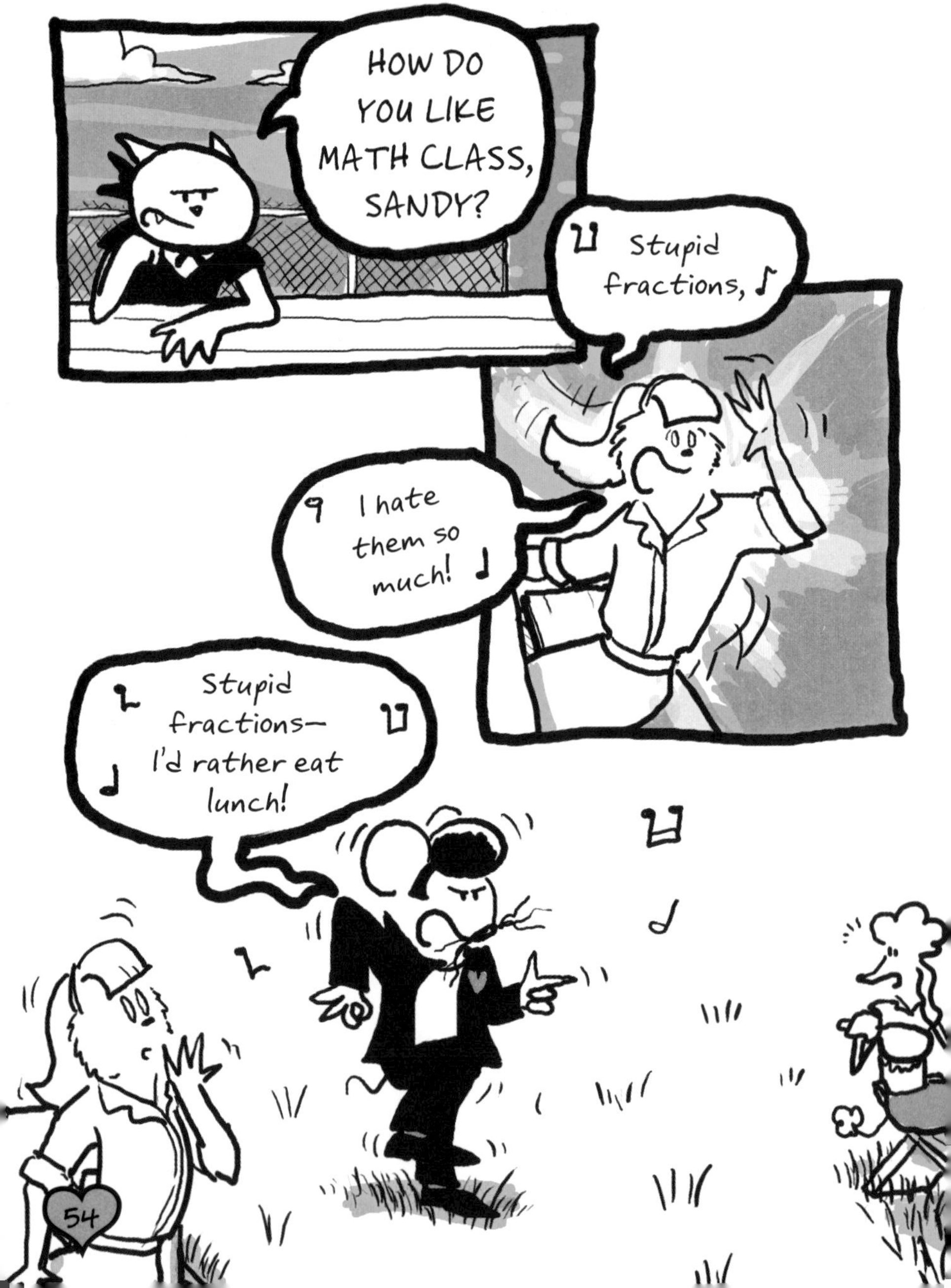
HOW DO YOU LIKE MATH CLASS, SANDY?
Stupid fractions,
I hate them so much!
Stupid fractions— I'd rather eat lunch!

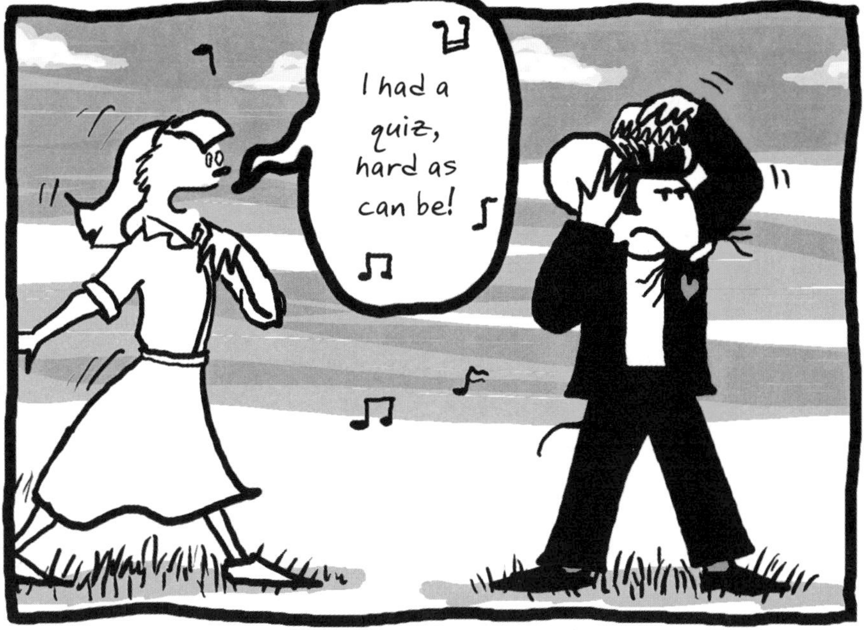
I had a quiz, hard as can be!

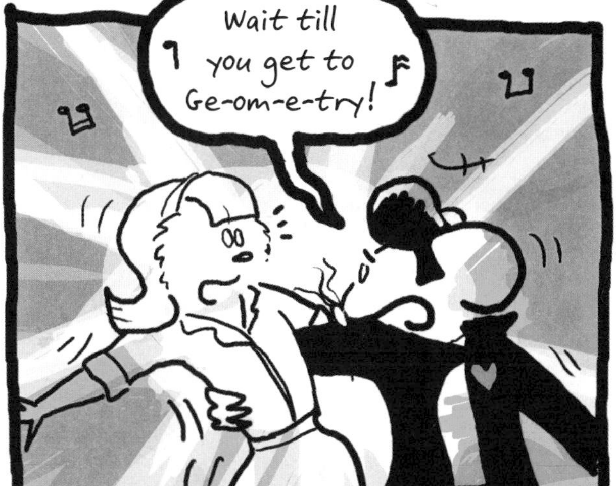
Wait till you get to Ge-om-e-try!

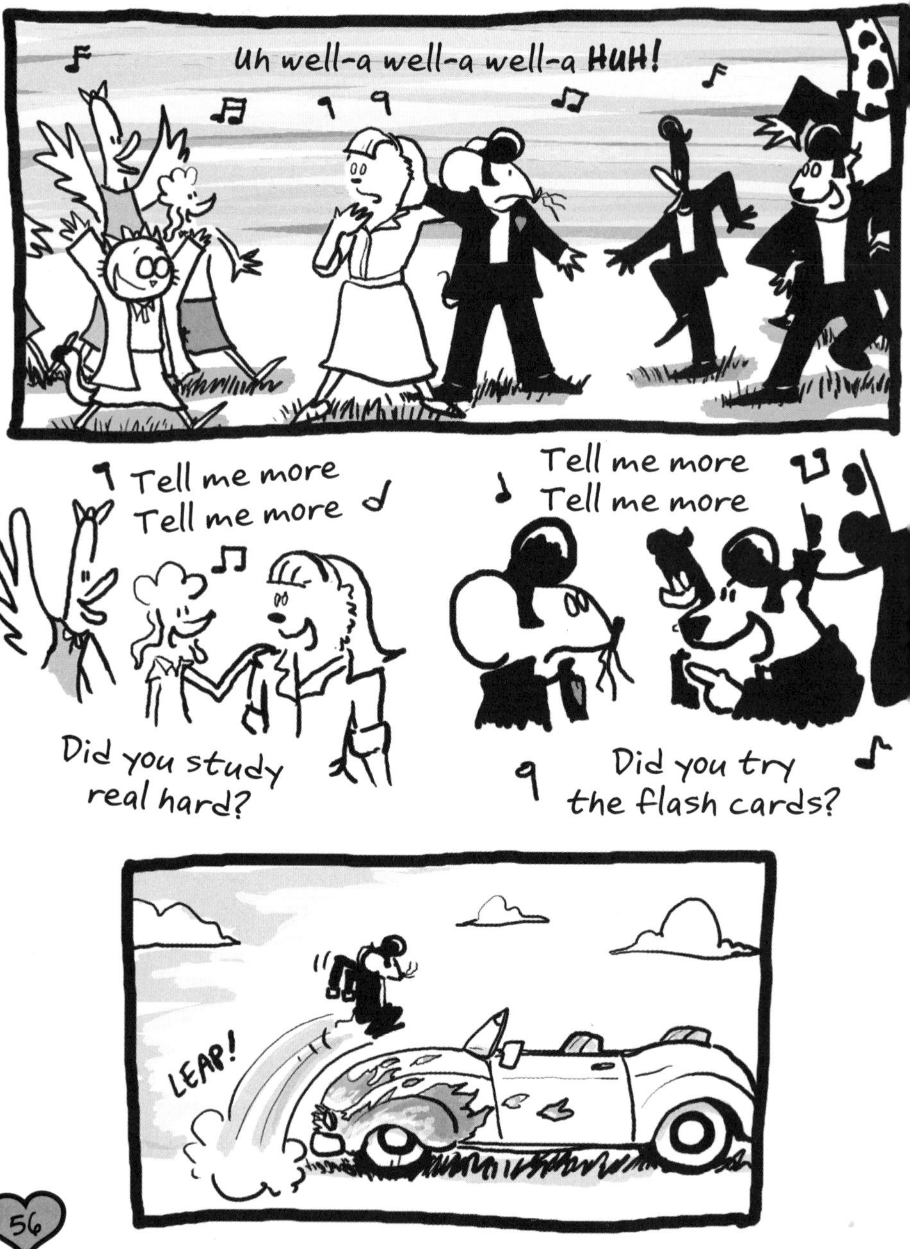
Uh well-a well-a well-a HUH!
Tell me more
Tell me more
Did you study
real hard?
Tell me more
Tell me more
Did you try
the flash cards?
LEAP!

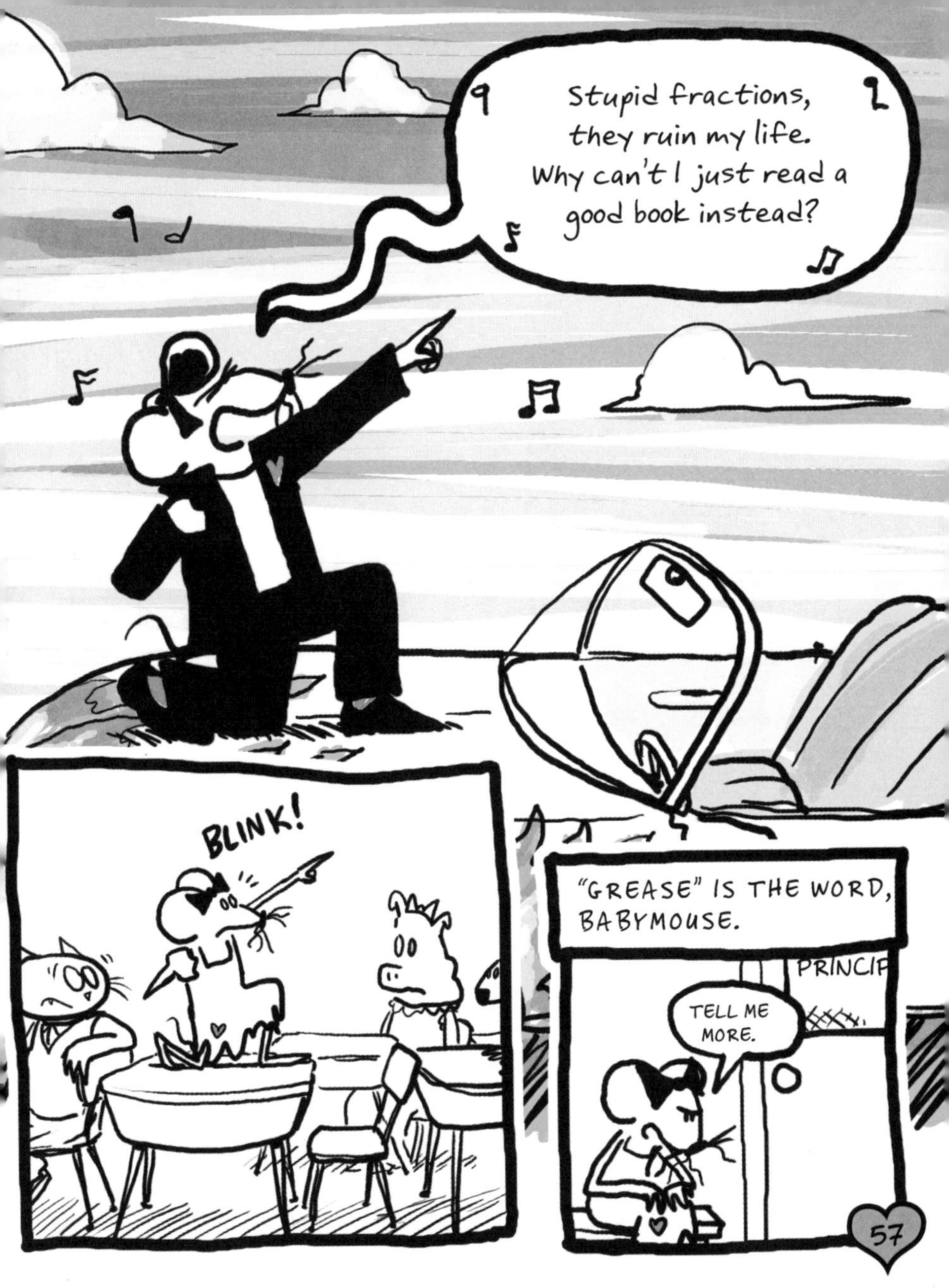
Stupid fractions, they ruin my life. Why can't I just read a good book instead?
BLINK!
"GREASE" IS THE WORD, BABYMOUSE.
PRINCIP
TELL ME MORE.

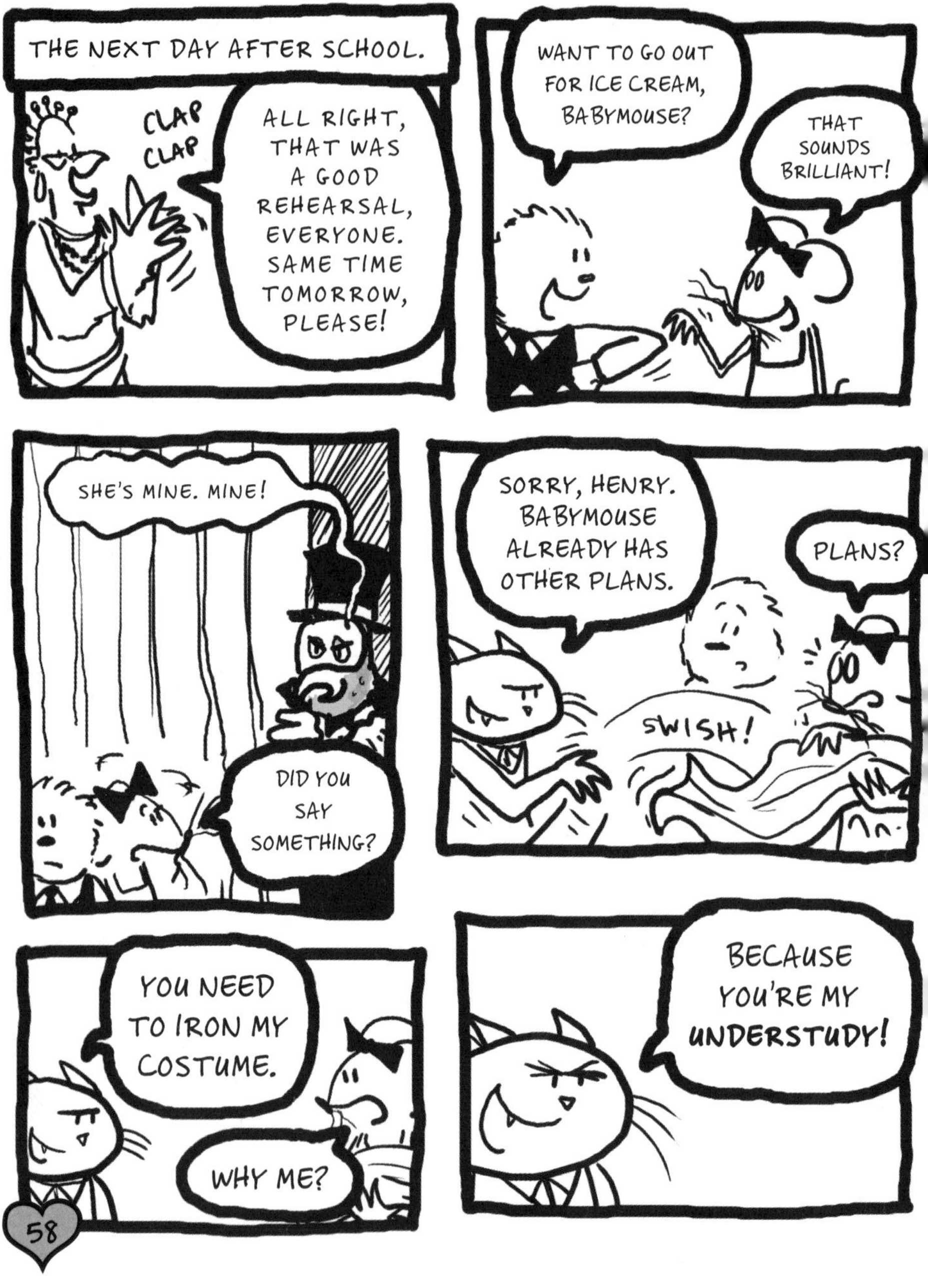
THE NEXT DAY AFTER SCHOOL.
CLAP CLAP
ALL RIGHT, THAT WAS A GOOD REHEARSAL, EVERYONE. SAME TIME TOMORROW, PLEASE!
WANT TO GO OUT FOR ICE CREAM, BABYMOUSE?
THAT SOUNDS BRILLIANT!
SHE'S MINE. MINE!
DID YOU SAY SOMETHING?
SORRY, HENRY. BABYMOUSE ALREADY HAS OTHER PLANS.
PLANS?
SWISH!
YOU NEED TO IRON MY COSTUME.
WHY ME?
BECAUSE YOU'RE MY **UNDERSTUDY**!

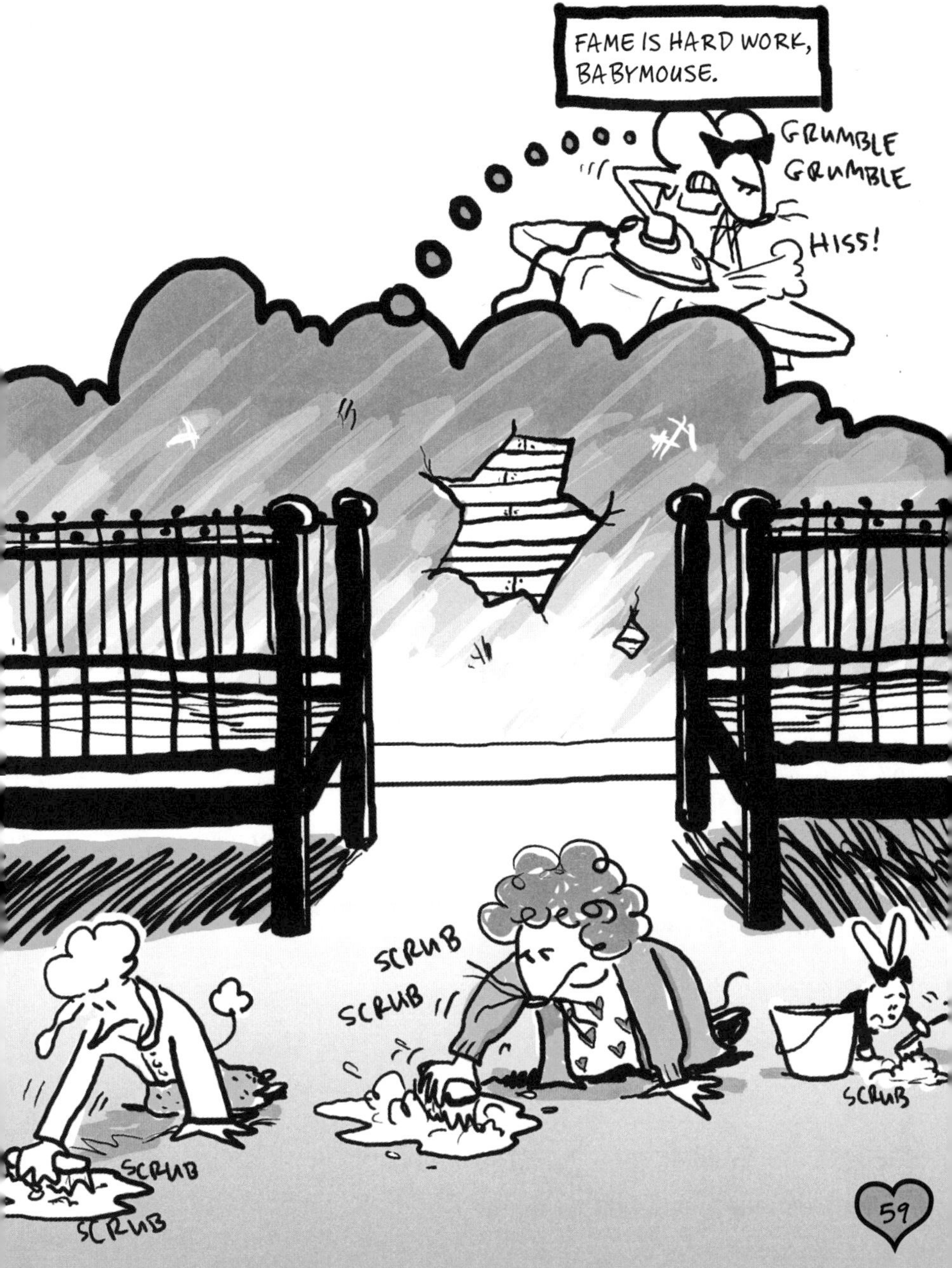

FAME IS HARD WORK, BABYMOUSE.
GRUMBLE GRUMBLE
HISS!
SCRUB
SCRUB
SCRUB
SCRUB
SCRUB

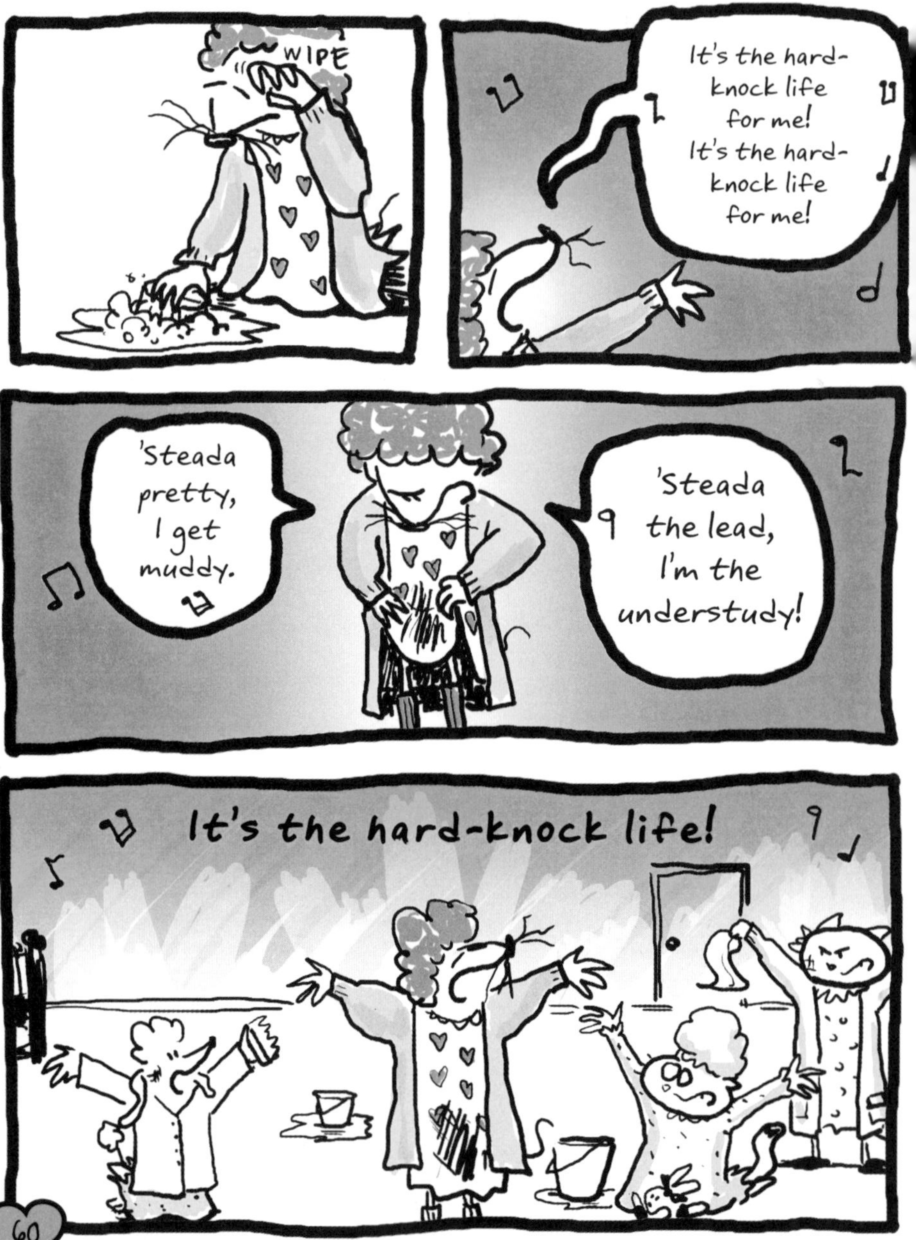
WIPE
It's the hard-knock life for me! It's the hard-knock life for me!
'Steada pretty, I get muddy.
'Steada the lead, I'm the understudy!
It's the hard-knock life!

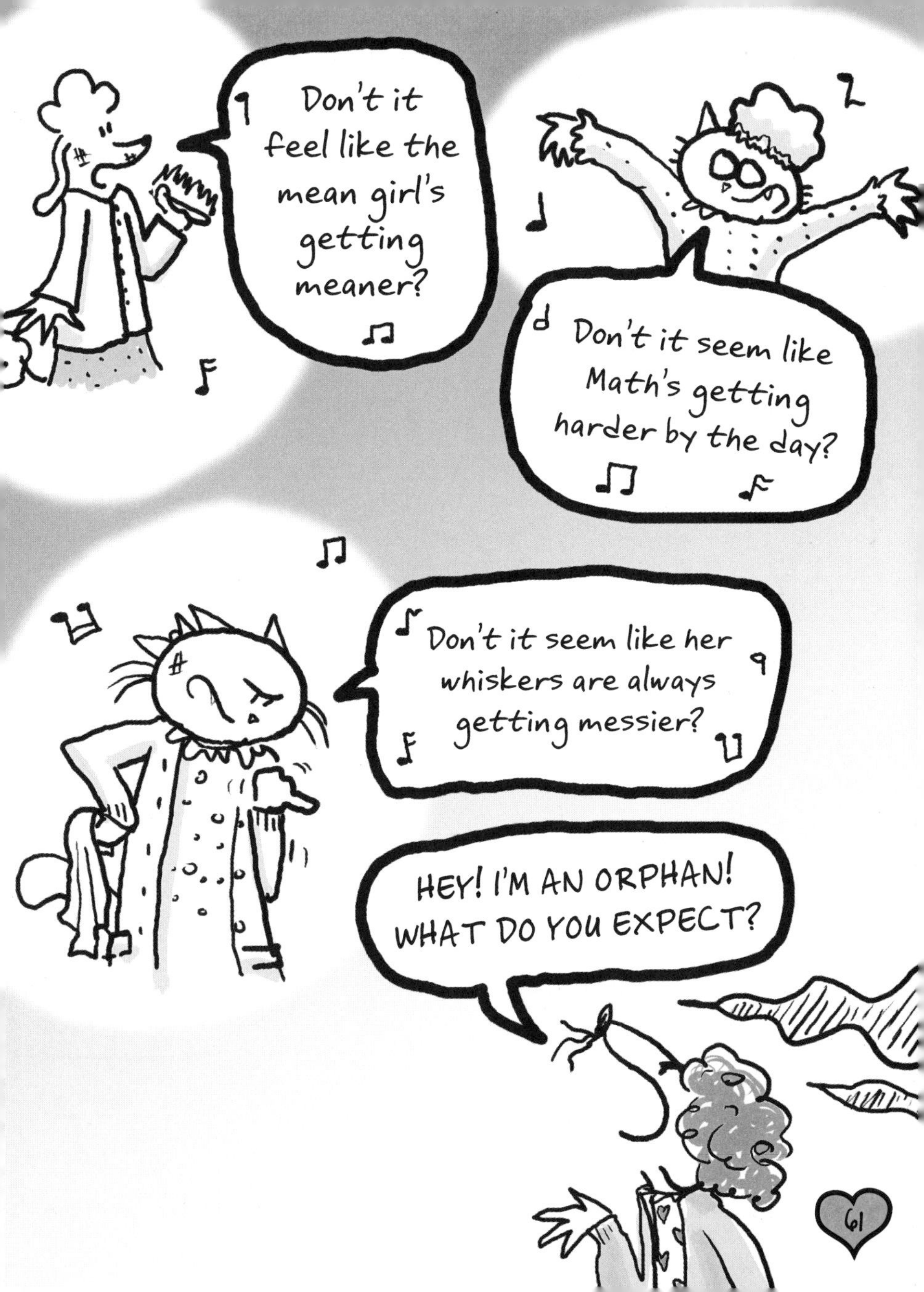
Don't it feel like the mean girl's getting meaner?
Don't it seem like Math's getting harder by the day?
Don't it seem like her whiskers are always getting messier?
HEY! I'M AN ORPHAN! WHAT DO YOU EXPECT?

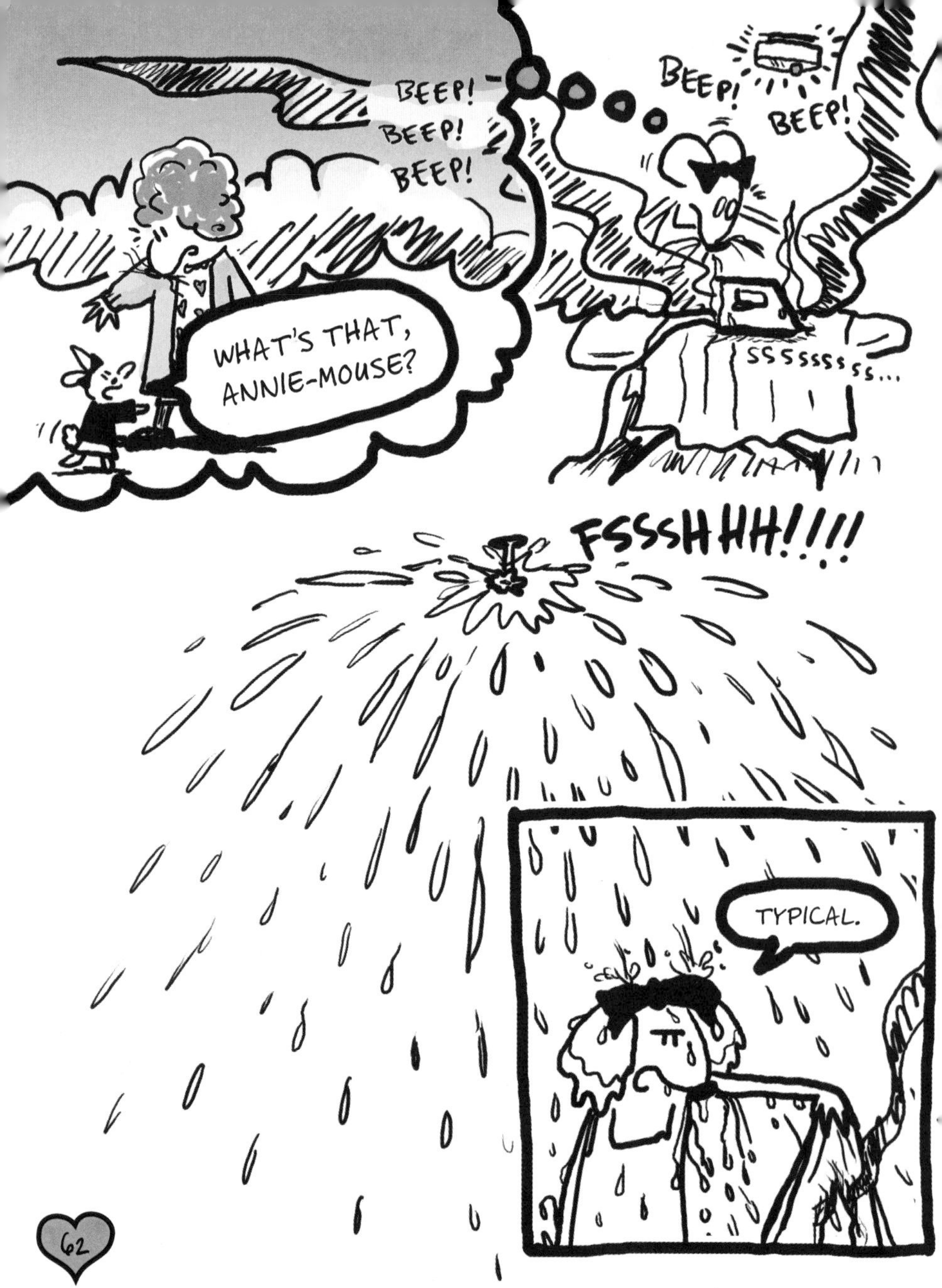
BEEP!
BEEP!
BEEP!
BEEP!
BEEP!
WHAT'S THAT, ANNIE-MOUSE?
SSSSSSSSSS...
FSSSHHH!!!!
TYPICAL.

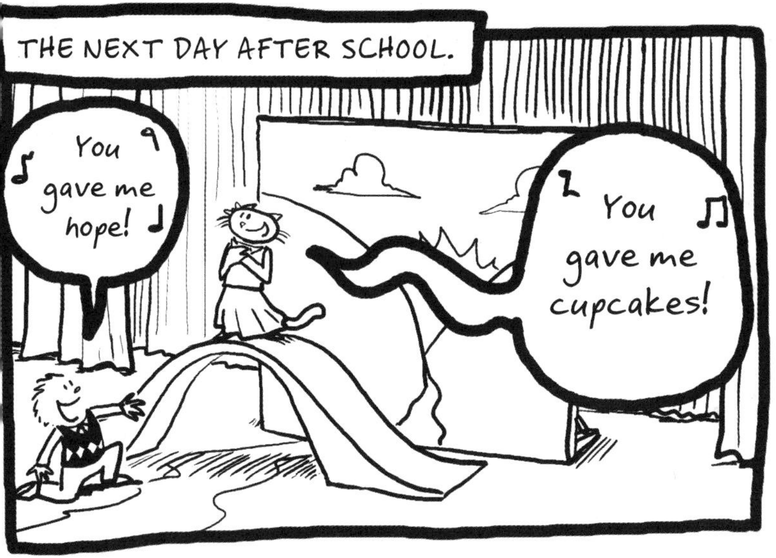
THE NEXT DAY AFTER SCHOOL.
You gave me hope!
You gave me cupcakes!

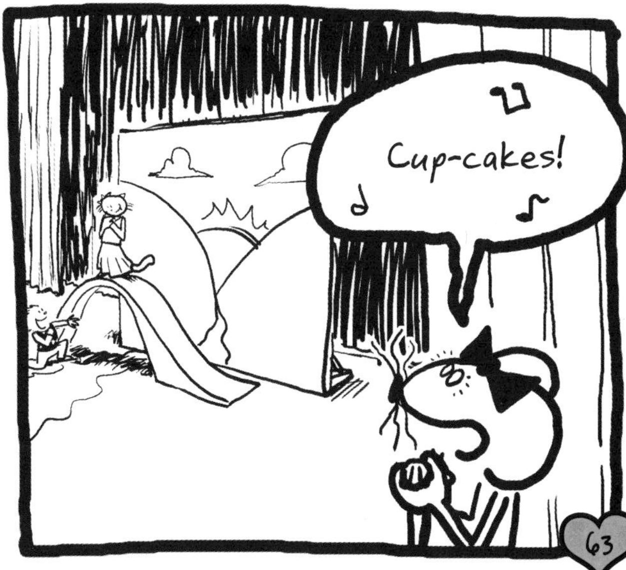
Cup-cakes!

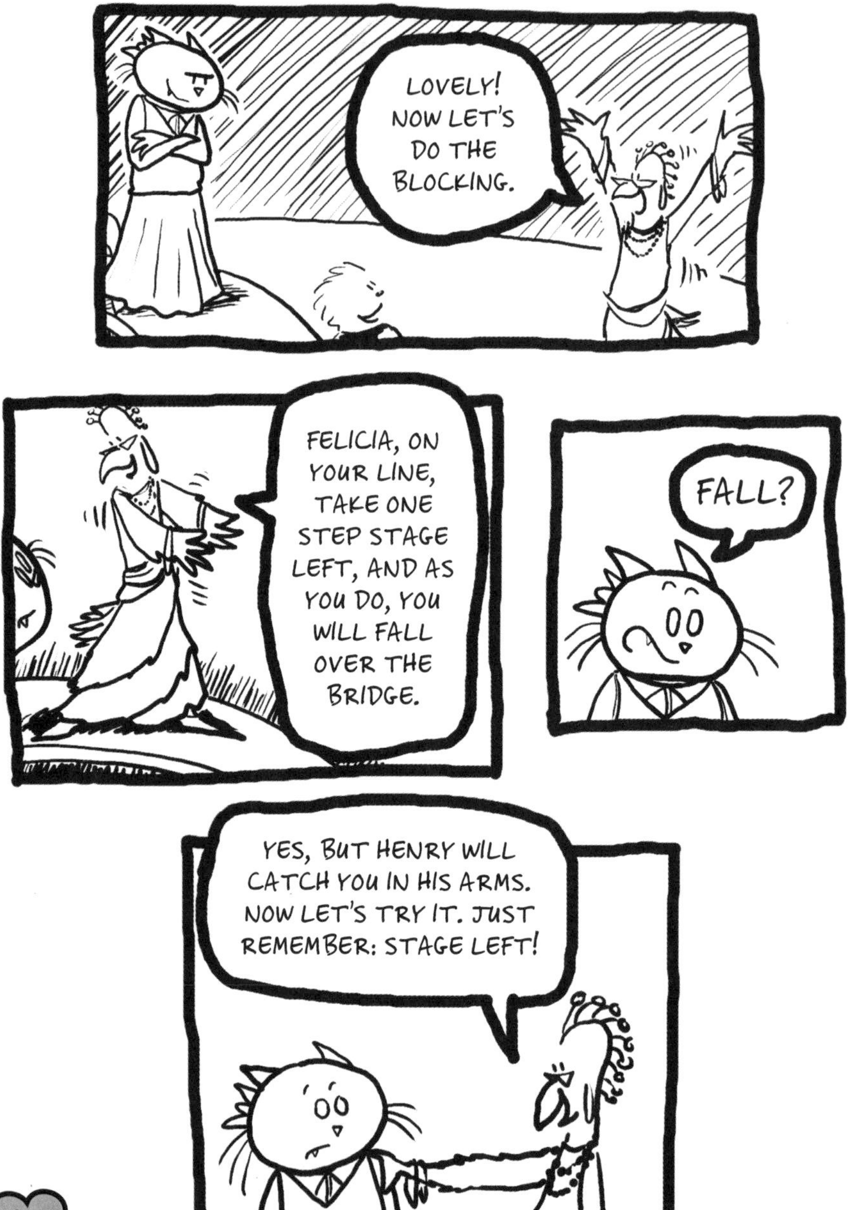
LOVELY! NOW LET'S DO THE BLOCKING.
FELICIA, ON YOUR LINE, TAKE ONE STEP STAGE LEFT, AND AS YOU DO, YOU WILL FALL OVER THE BRIDGE.
FALL?
YES, BUT HENRY WILL CATCH YOU IN HIS ARMS. NOW LET'S TRY IT. JUST REMEMBER: STAGE LEFT!

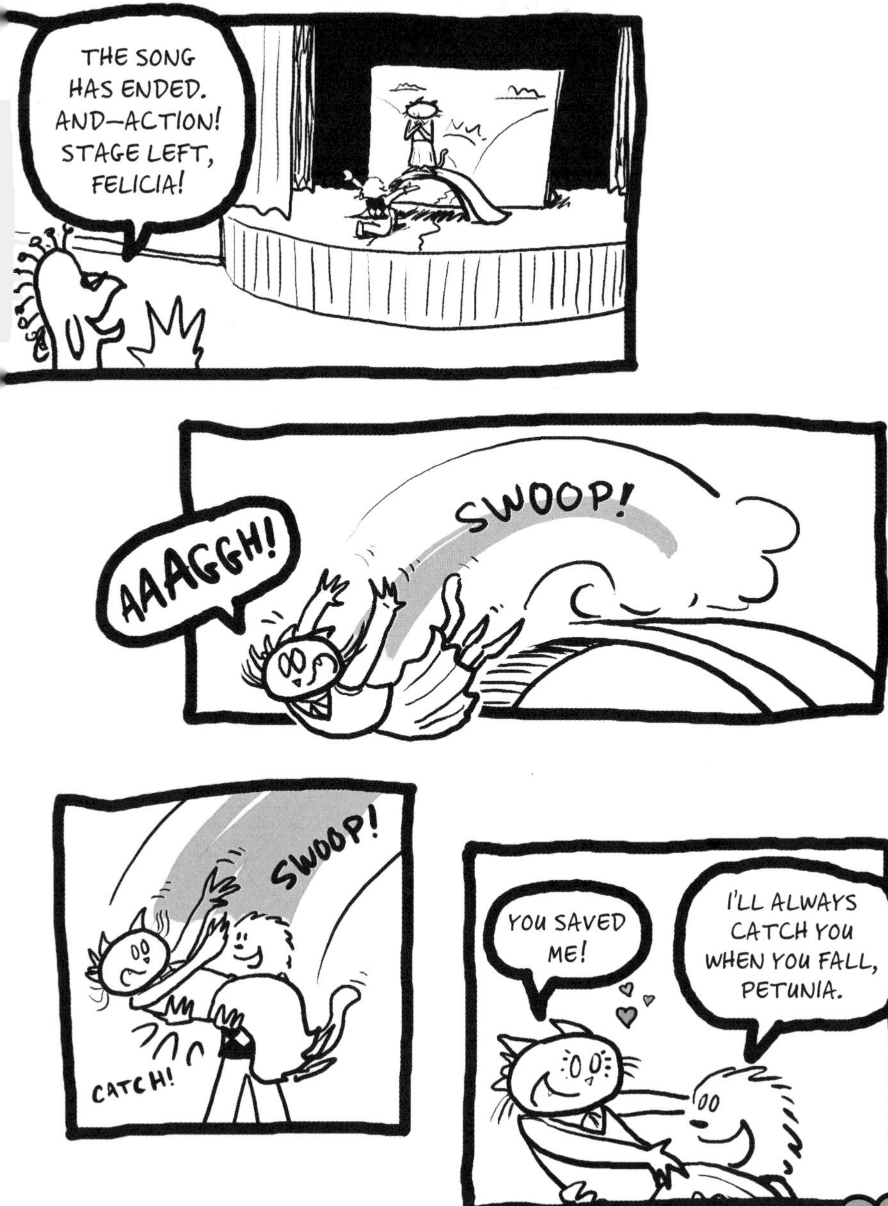
THE SONG HAS ENDED. AND—ACTION! STAGE LEFT, FELICIA!
AAAGGH!
SWOOP!
SWOOP!
CATCH!
YOU SAVED ME!
I'LL ALWAYS CATCH YOU WHEN YOU FALL, PETUNIA.

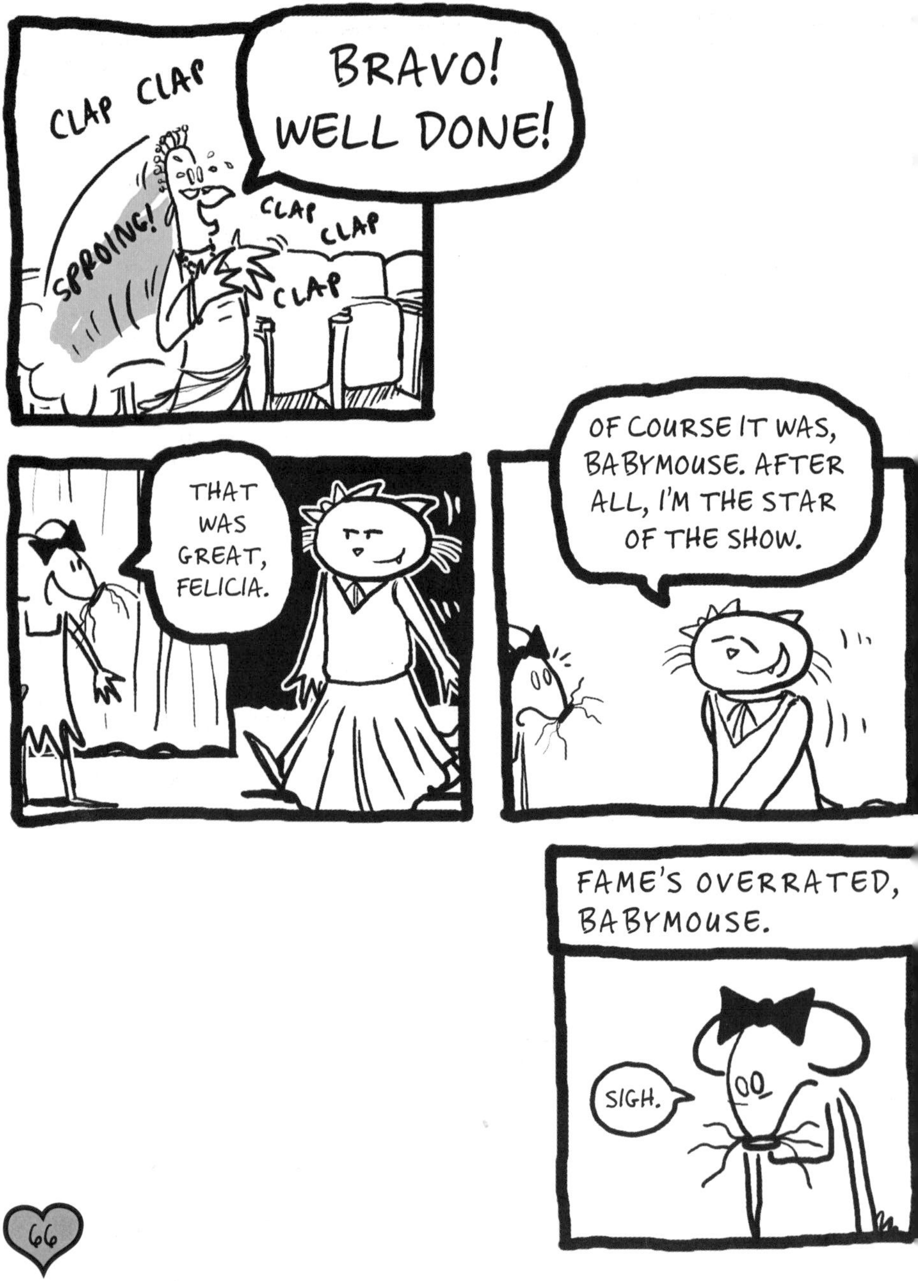
CLAP CLAP
BRAVO! WELL DONE!
SPROING!
CLAP
CLAP
CLAP
THAT WAS GREAT, FELICIA.
OF COURSE IT WAS, BABYMOUSE. AFTER ALL, I'M THE STAR OF THE SHOW.
FAME'S OVERRATED, BABYMOUSE.
SIGH.

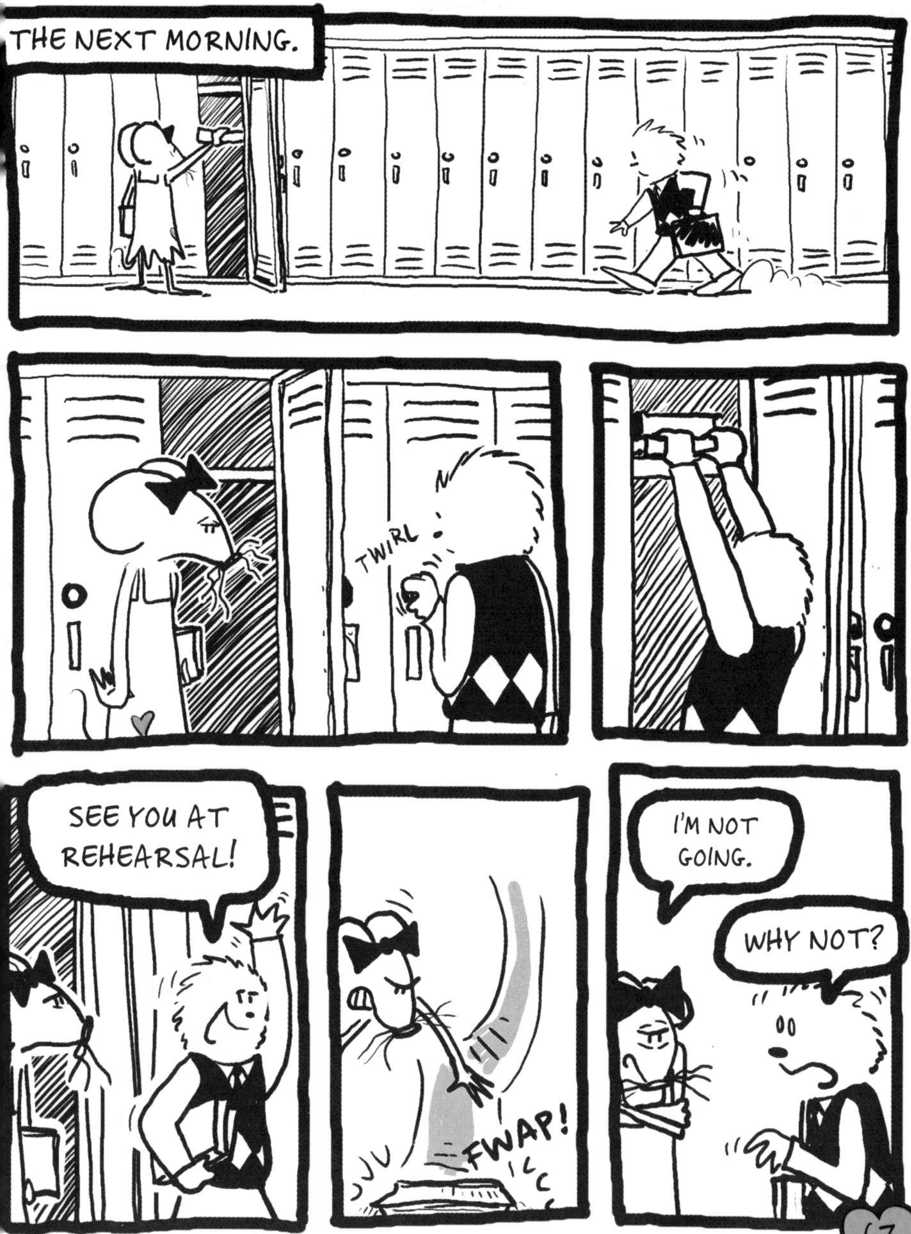
THE NEXT MORNING.
TWIRL
SEE YOU AT REHEARSAL!
FWAP!
I'M NOT GOING.
WHY NOT?

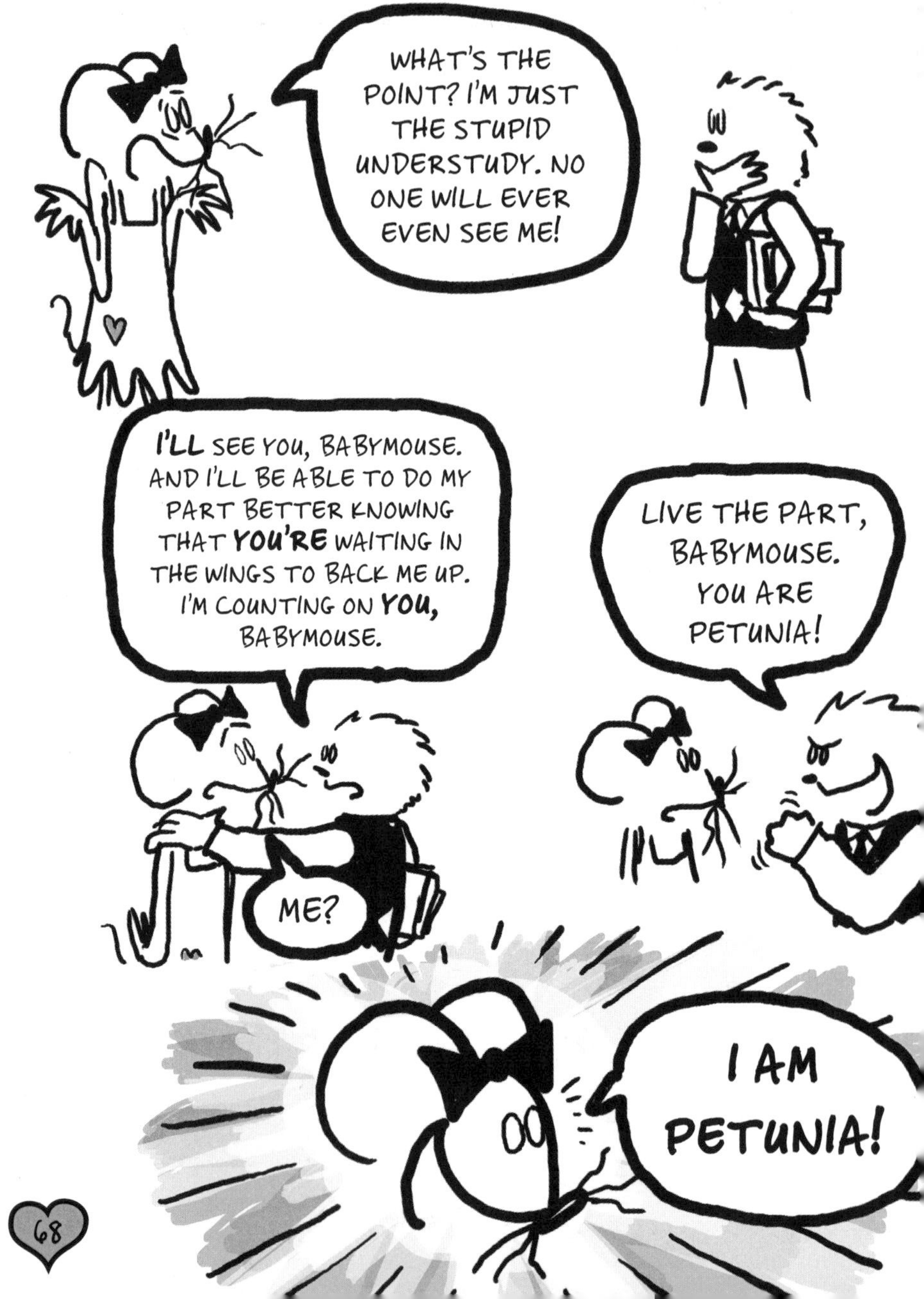

WHAT'S THE POINT? I'M JUST THE STUPID UNDERSTUDY. NO ONE WILL EVER EVEN SEE ME!
I'LL SEE YOU, BABYMOUSE. AND I'LL BE ABLE TO DO MY PART BETTER KNOWING THAT YOU'RE WAITING IN THE WINGS TO BACK ME UP. I'M COUNTING ON YOU, BABYMOUSE.
ME?
LIVE THE PART, BABYMOUSE. YOU ARE PETUNIA!
I AM PETUNIA!

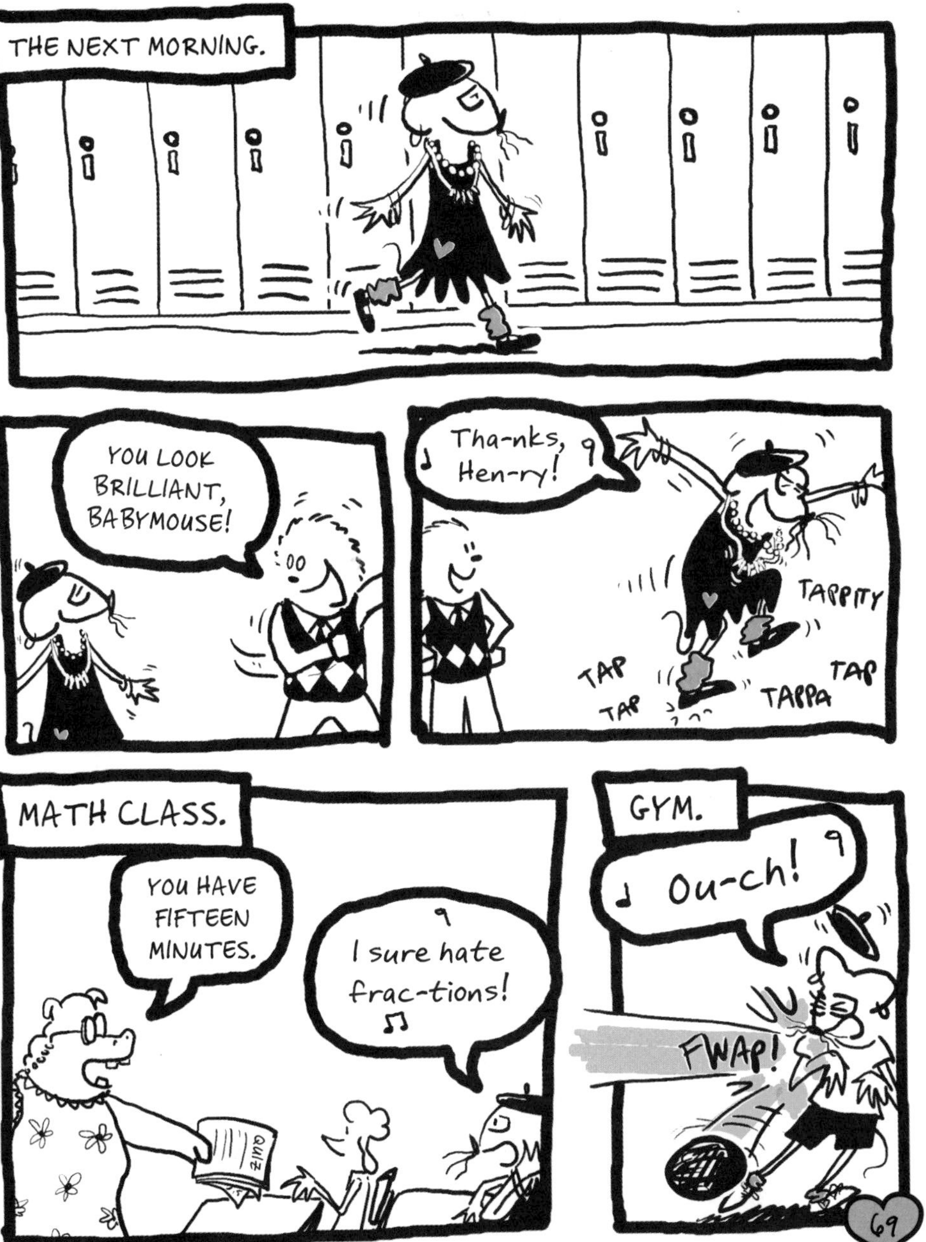
THE NEXT MORNING.
YOU LOOK BRILLIANT, BABYMOUSE!
Tha-nks, Hen-ry!
TAPPITY
TAP
TAP
TAP
TAPPA
MATH CLASS.
YOU HAVE FIFTEEN MINUTES.
QUIZ
I sure hate frac-tions!
GYM.
Ou-ch!
FWAP!

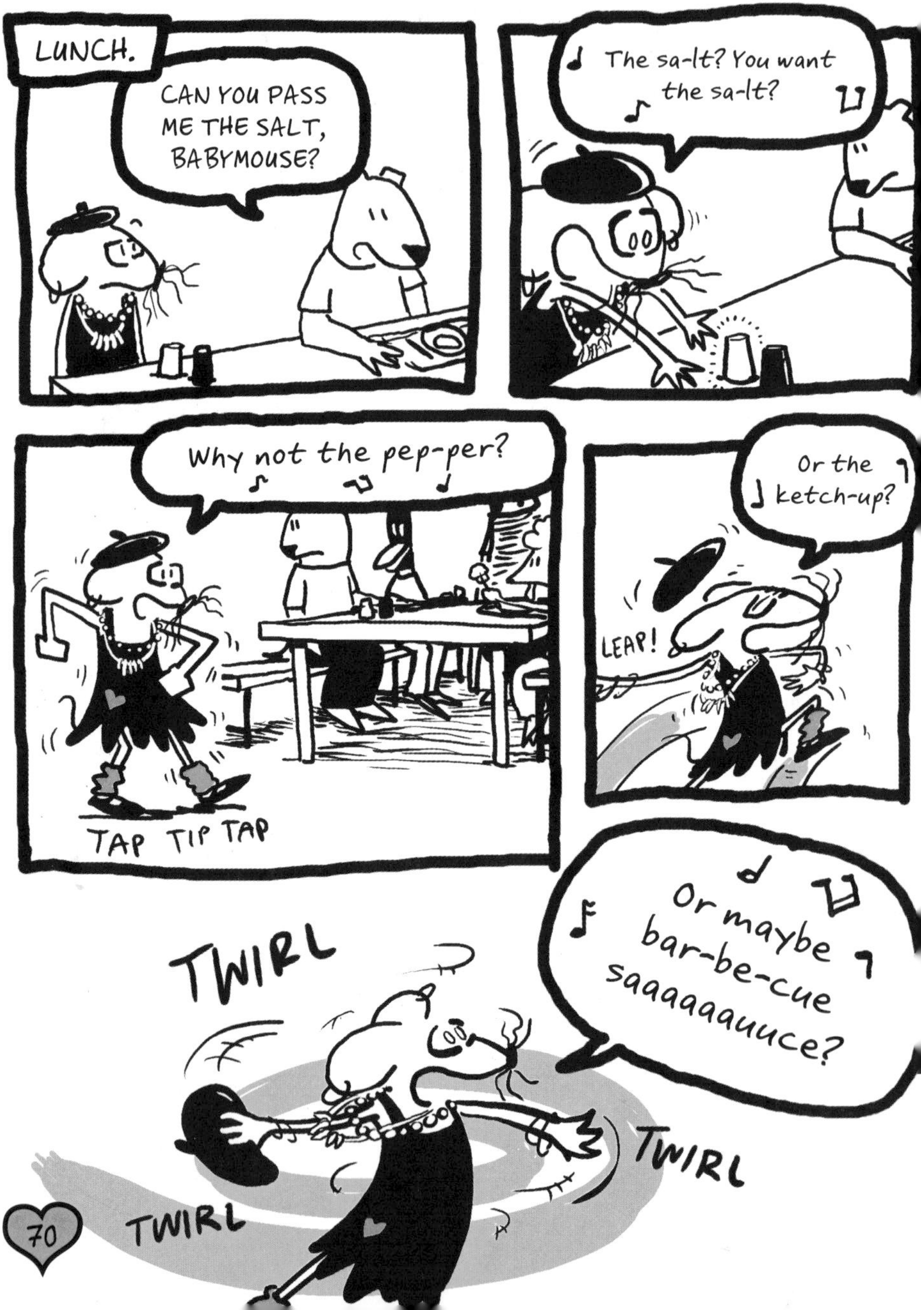
LUNCH.
CAN YOU PASS ME THE SALT, BABYMOUSE?
The sa-lt? You want the sa-lt?
Why not the pep-per?
TAP TIP TAP
Or the ketch-up?
LEAP!
Or maybe bar-be-cue saaaaaauuce?
TWIRL
TWIRL
TWIRL

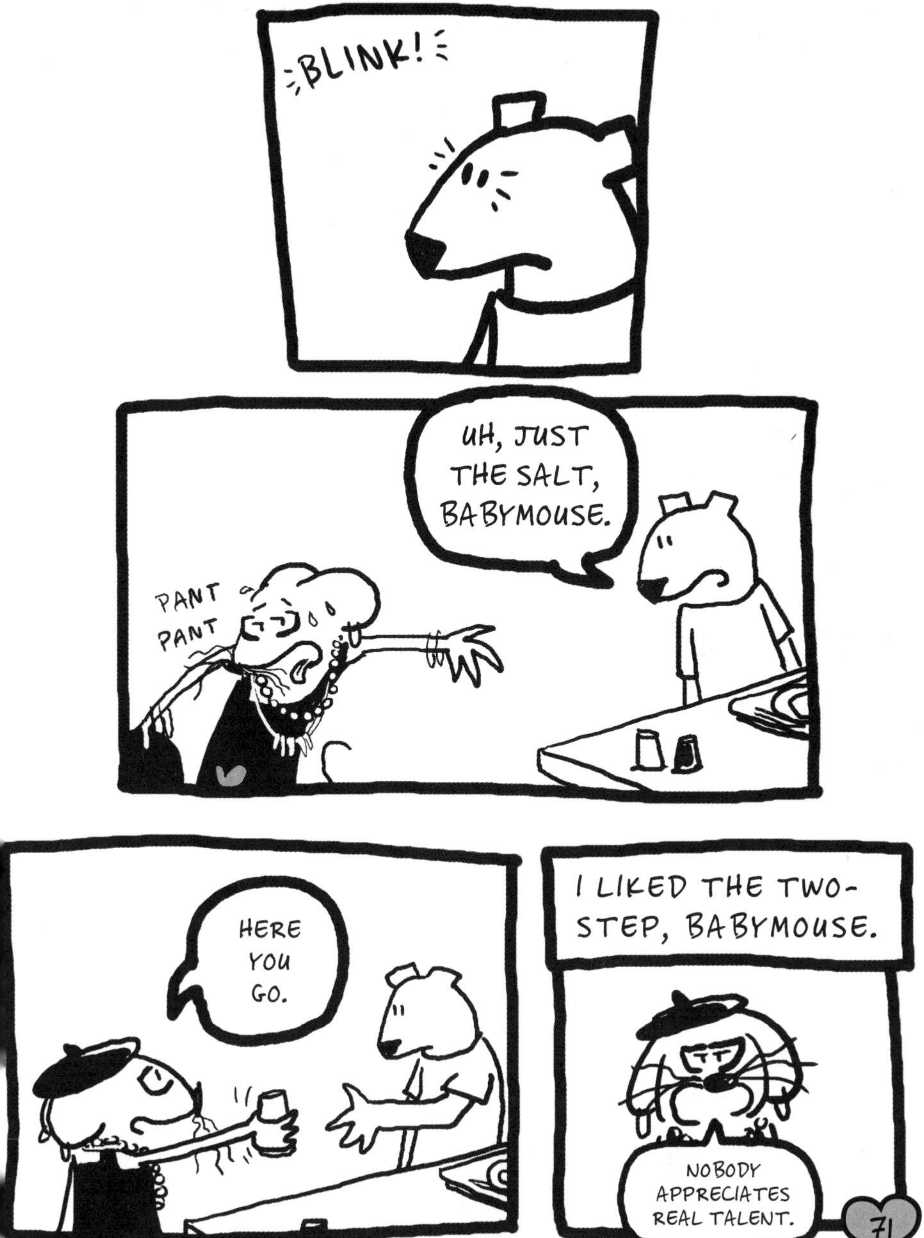
BLINK!
UH, JUST THE SALT, BABYMOUSE.
PANT PANT
HERE YOU GO.
I LIKED THE TWO-STEP, BABYMOUSE.
NOBODY APPRECIATES REAL TALENT.

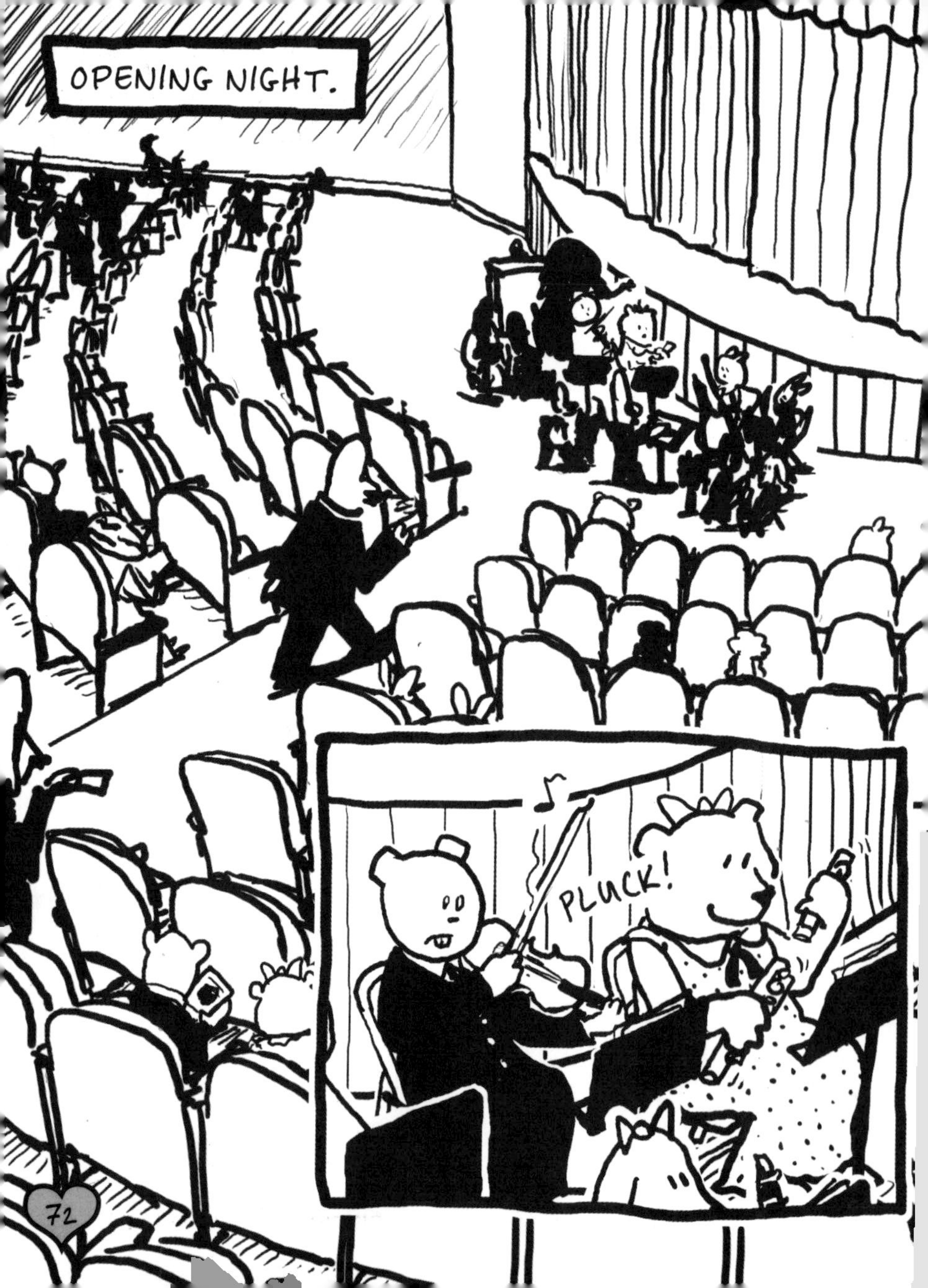
OPENING NIGHT.
PLUCK!

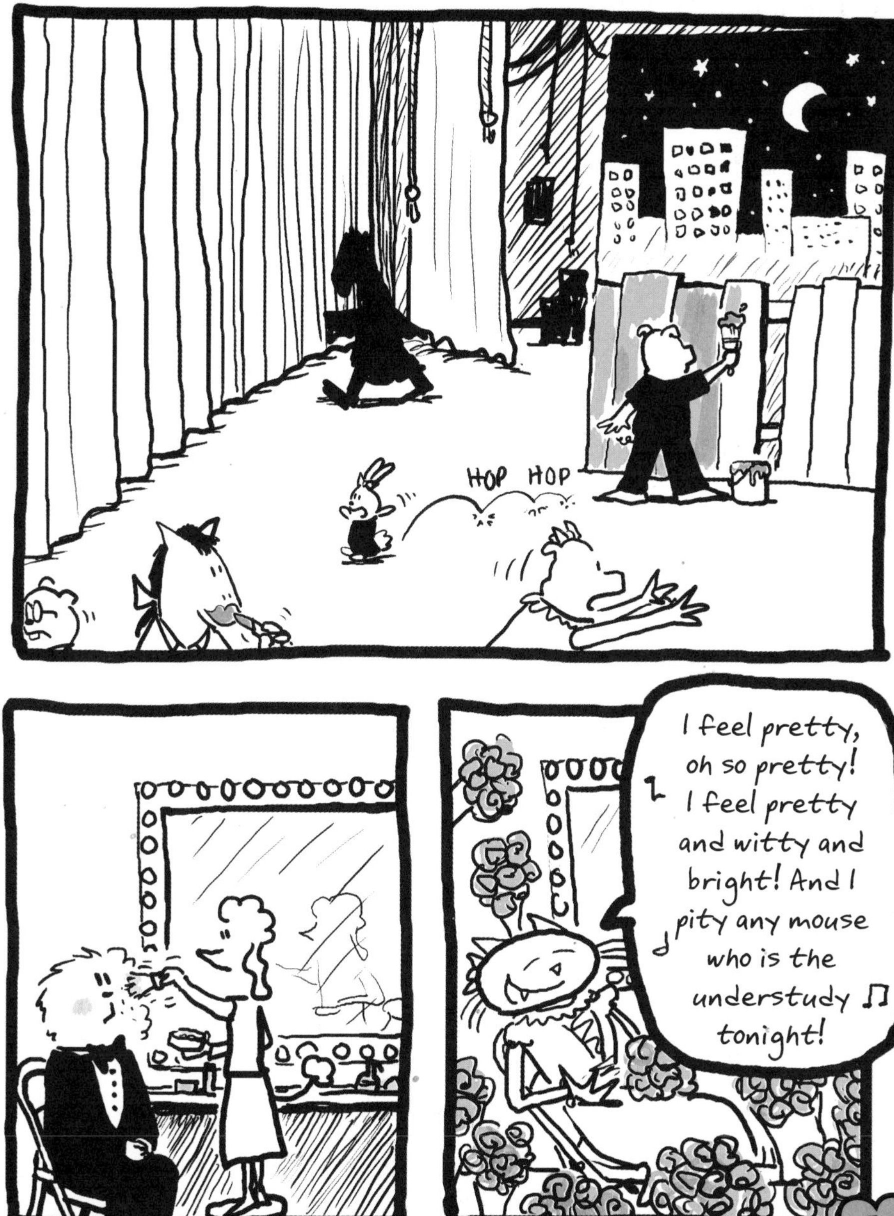
HOP HOP
I feel pretty, oh so pretty! I feel pretty and witty and bright! And I pity any mouse who is the understudy tonight!

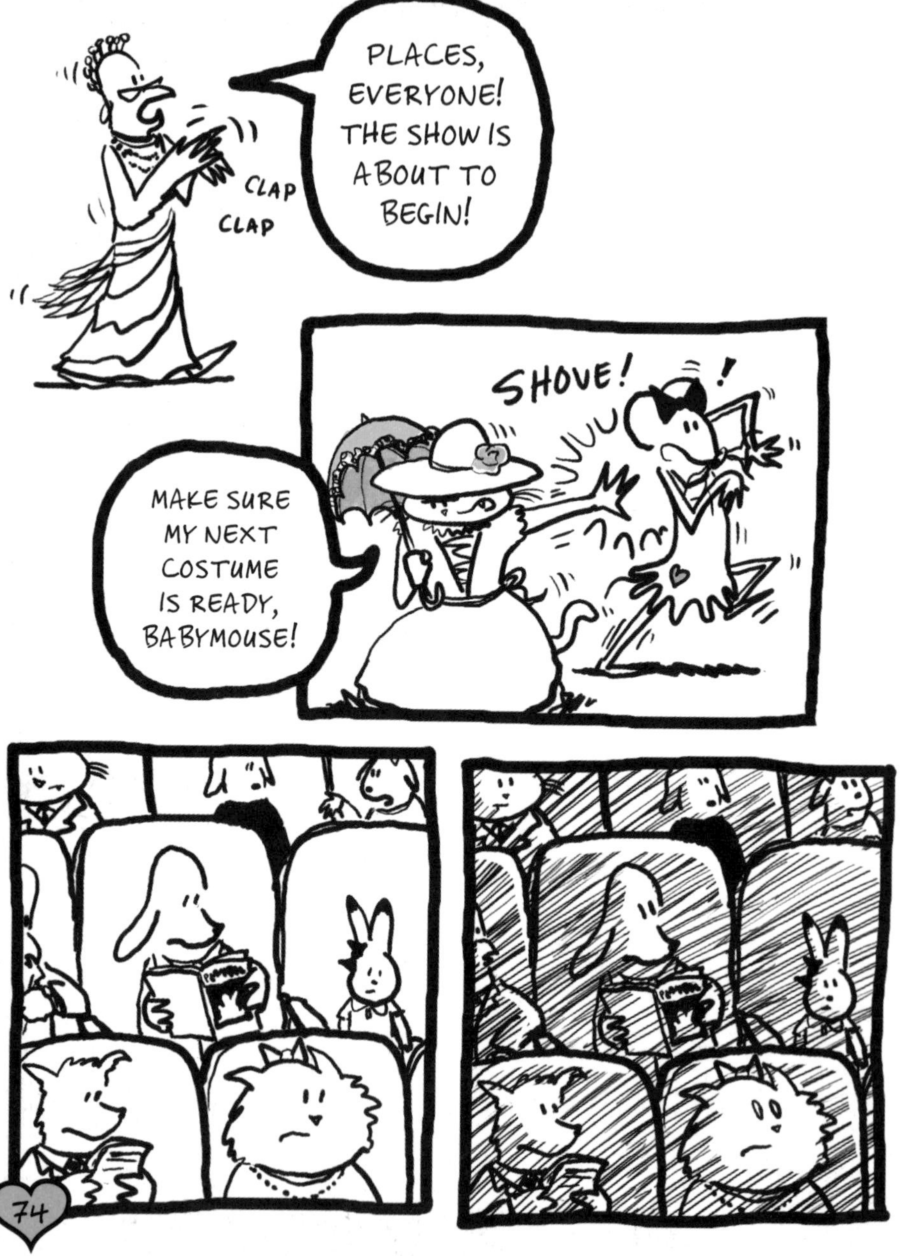
CLAP
CLAP
PLACES, EVERYONE! THE SHOW IS ABOUT TO BEGIN!
SHOVE!
MAKE SURE MY NEXT COSTUME IS READY, BABYMOUSE!

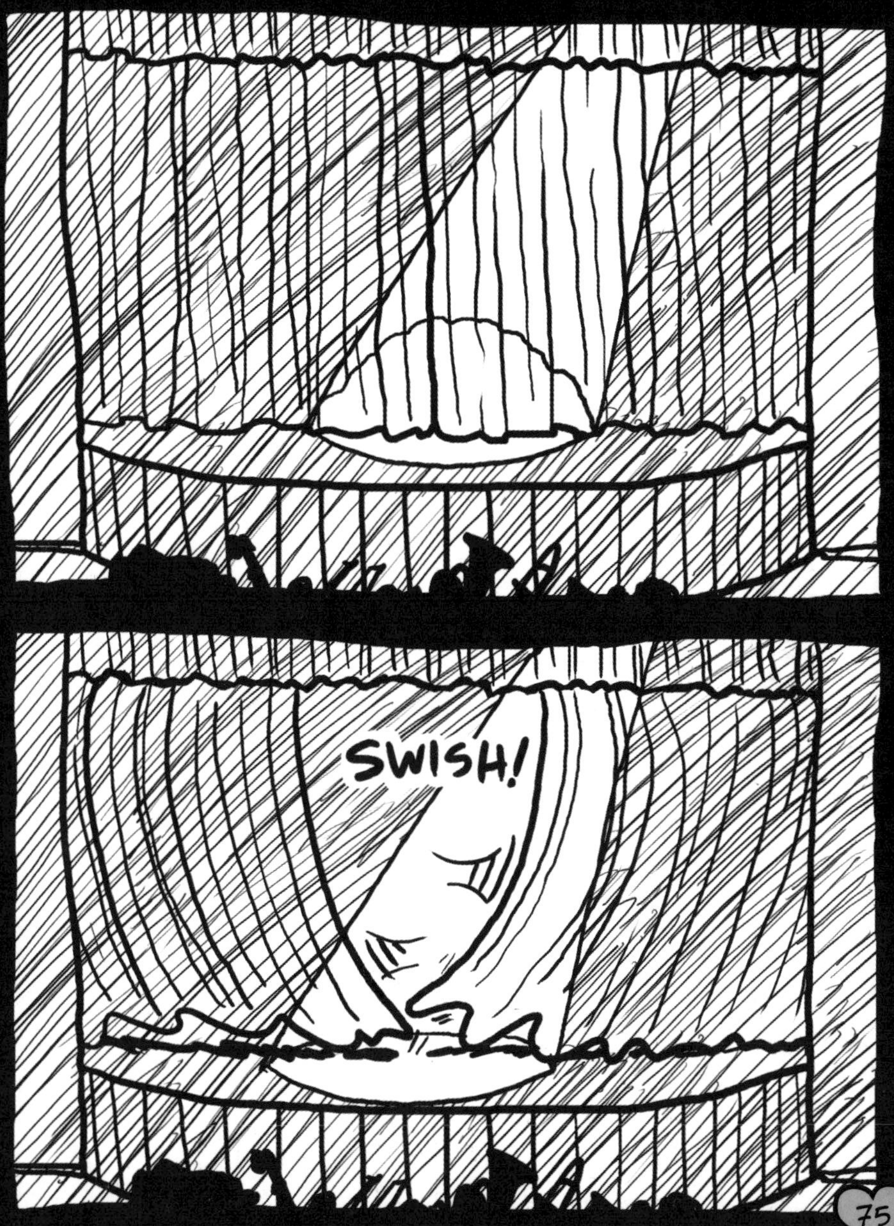
SWISH!

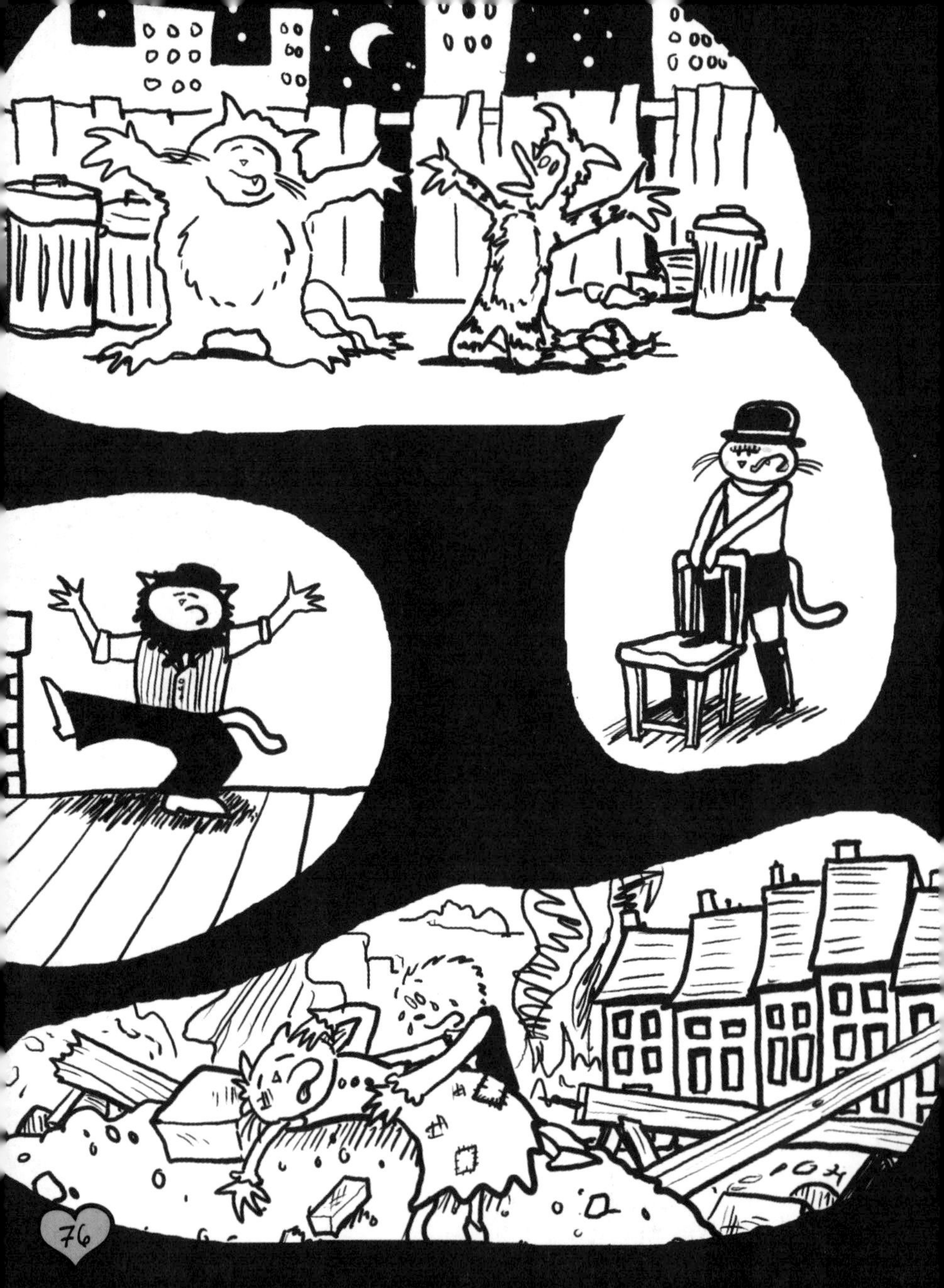

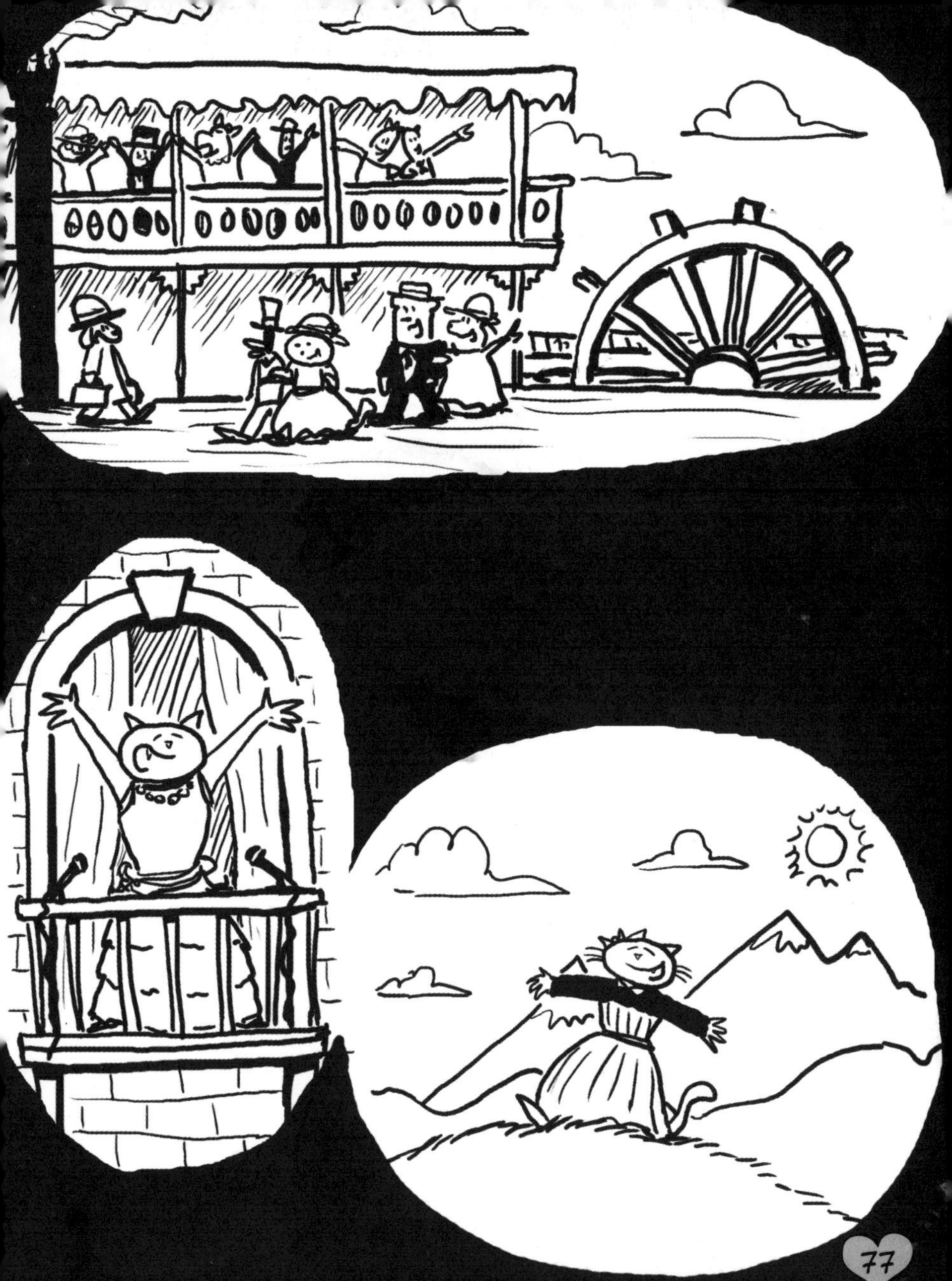

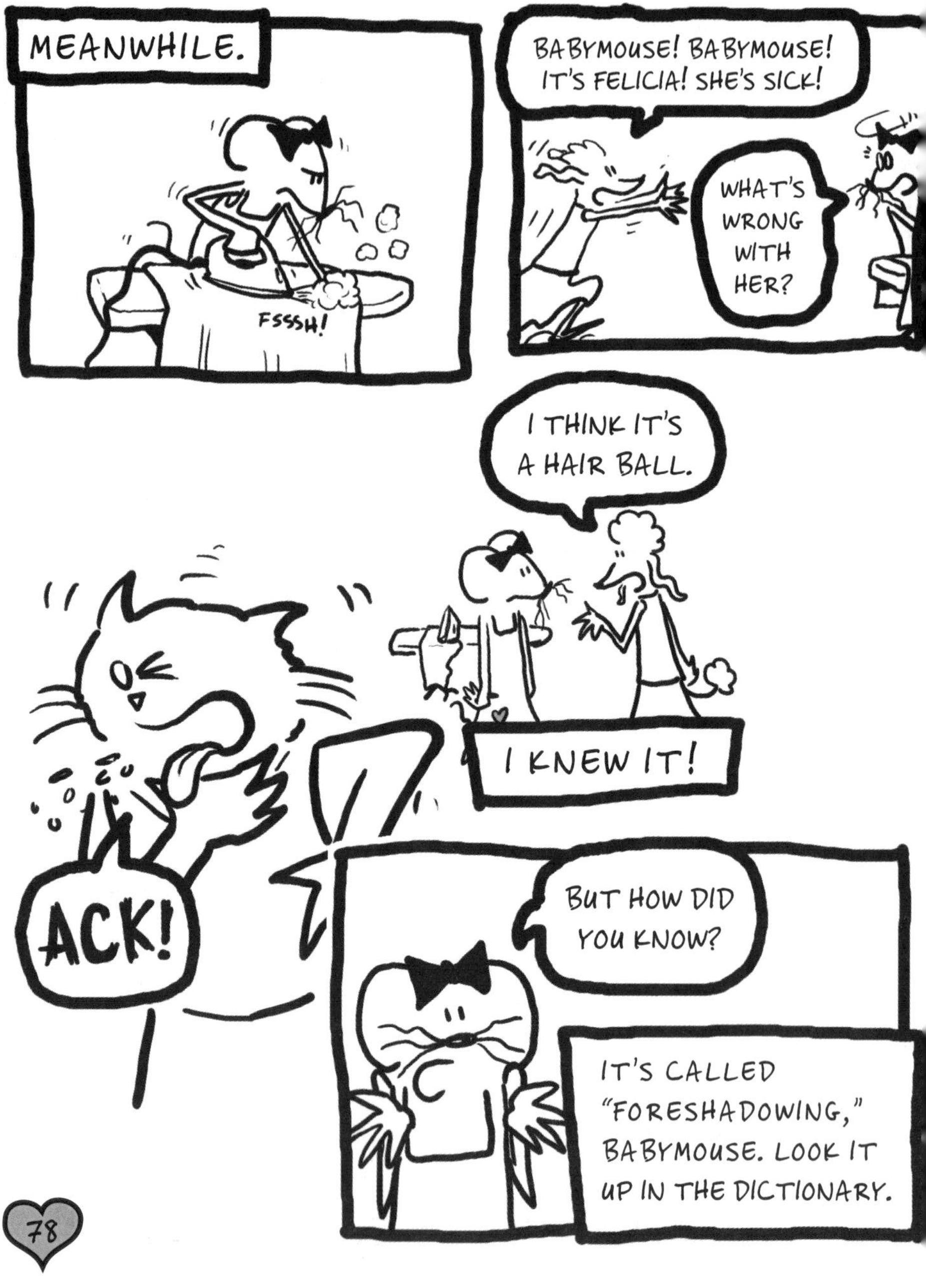
MEANWHILE.
FSSSH!
BABYMOUSE! BABYMOUSE! IT'S FELICIA! SHE'S SICK!
WHAT'S WRONG WITH HER?
I THINK IT'S A HAIR BALL.
ACK!
I KNEW IT!
BUT HOW DID YOU KNOW?
IT'S CALLED "FORESHADOWING," BABYMOUSE. LOOK IT UP IN THE DICTIONARY.

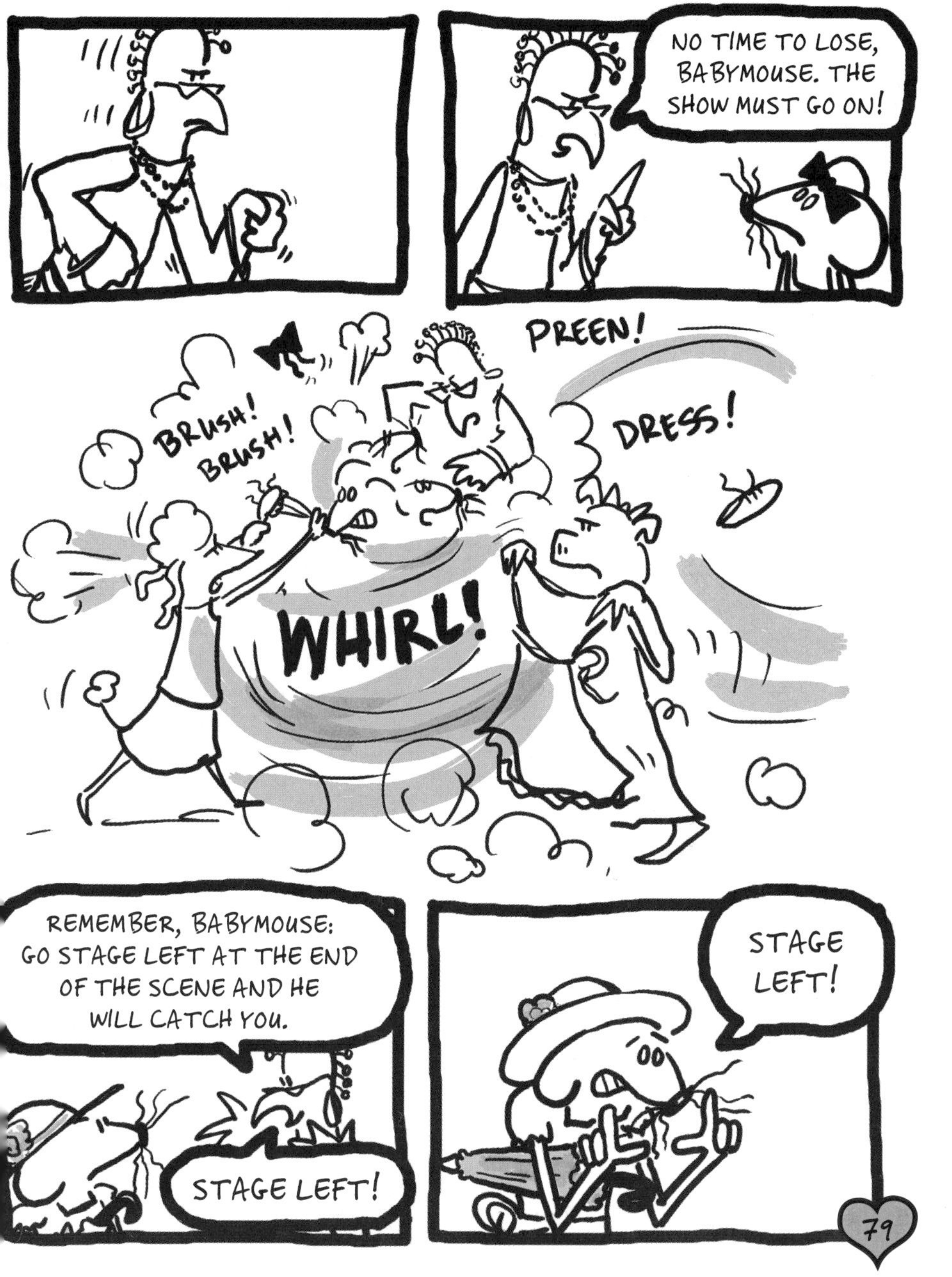
NO TIME TO LOSE, BABYMOUSE. THE SHOW MUST GO ON!
PREEN!
BRUSH! BRUSH!
DRESS!
WHIRL!
REMEMBER, BABYMOUSE: GO STAGE LEFT AT THE END OF THE SCENE AND HE WILL CATCH YOU.
STAGE LEFT!
STAGE LEFT!

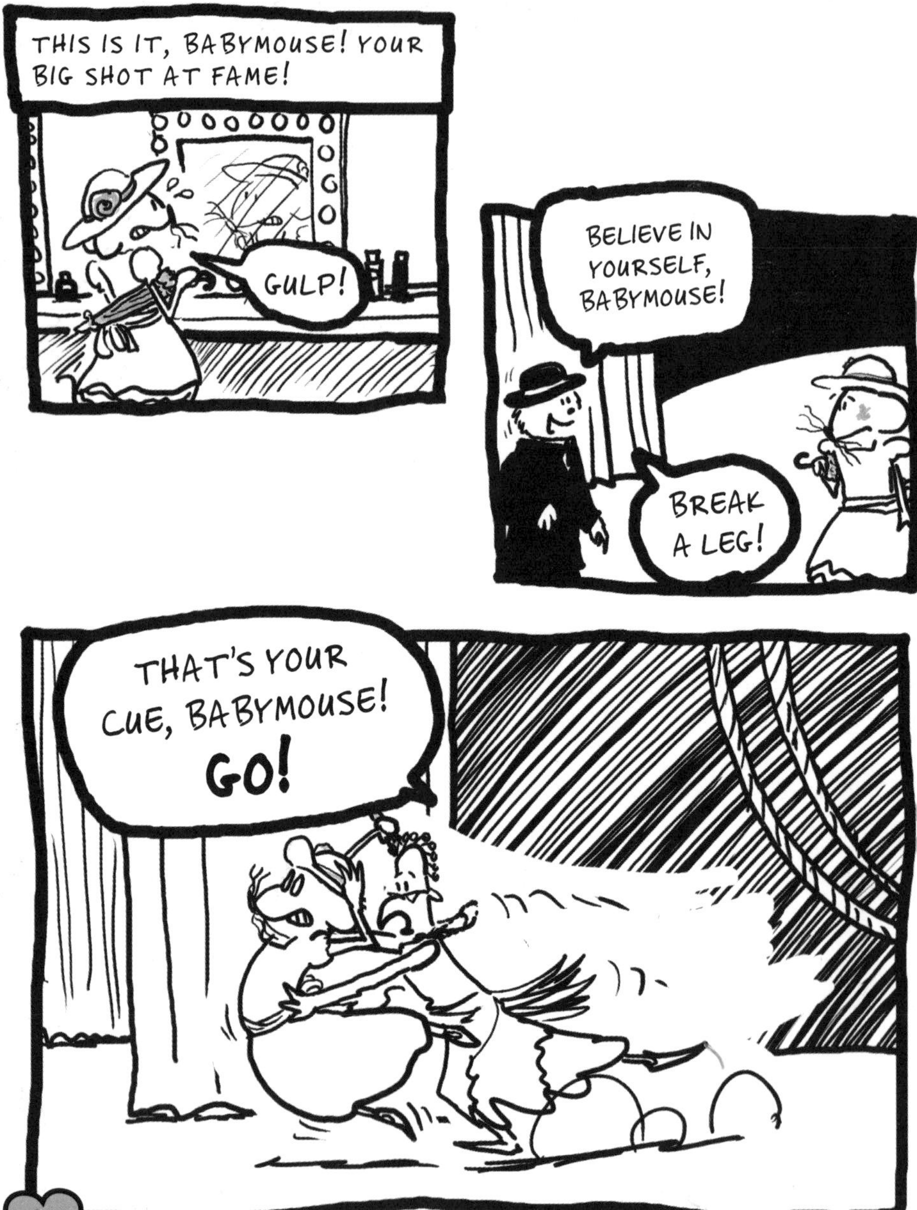
THIS IS IT, BABYMOUSE! YOUR BIG SHOT AT FAME!
GULP!
BELIEVE IN YOURSELF, BABYMOUSE!
BREAK A LEG!
THAT'S YOUR CUE, BABYMOUSE! GO!

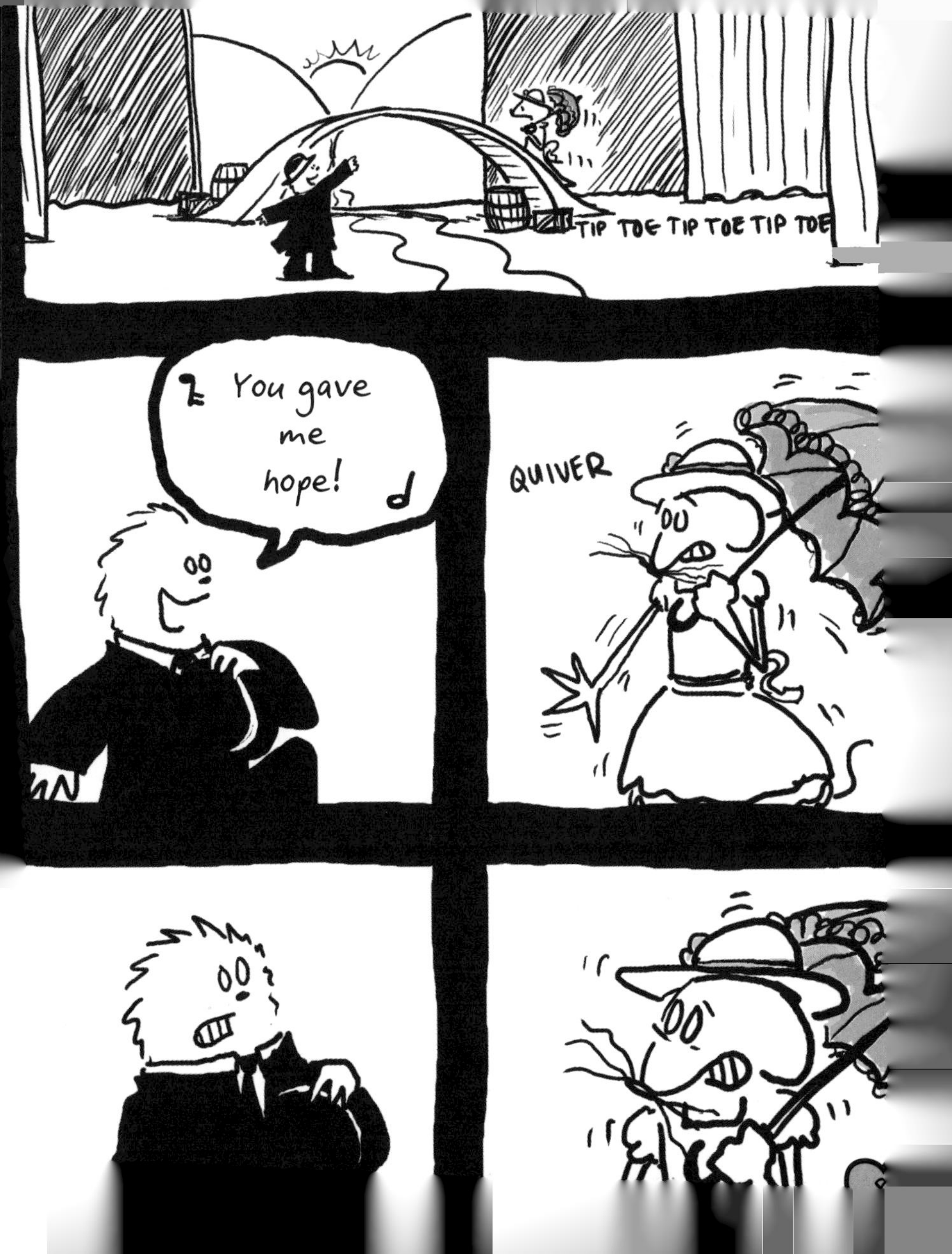
TIP TOE TIP TOE TIP TOE
You gave me hope!
QUIVER

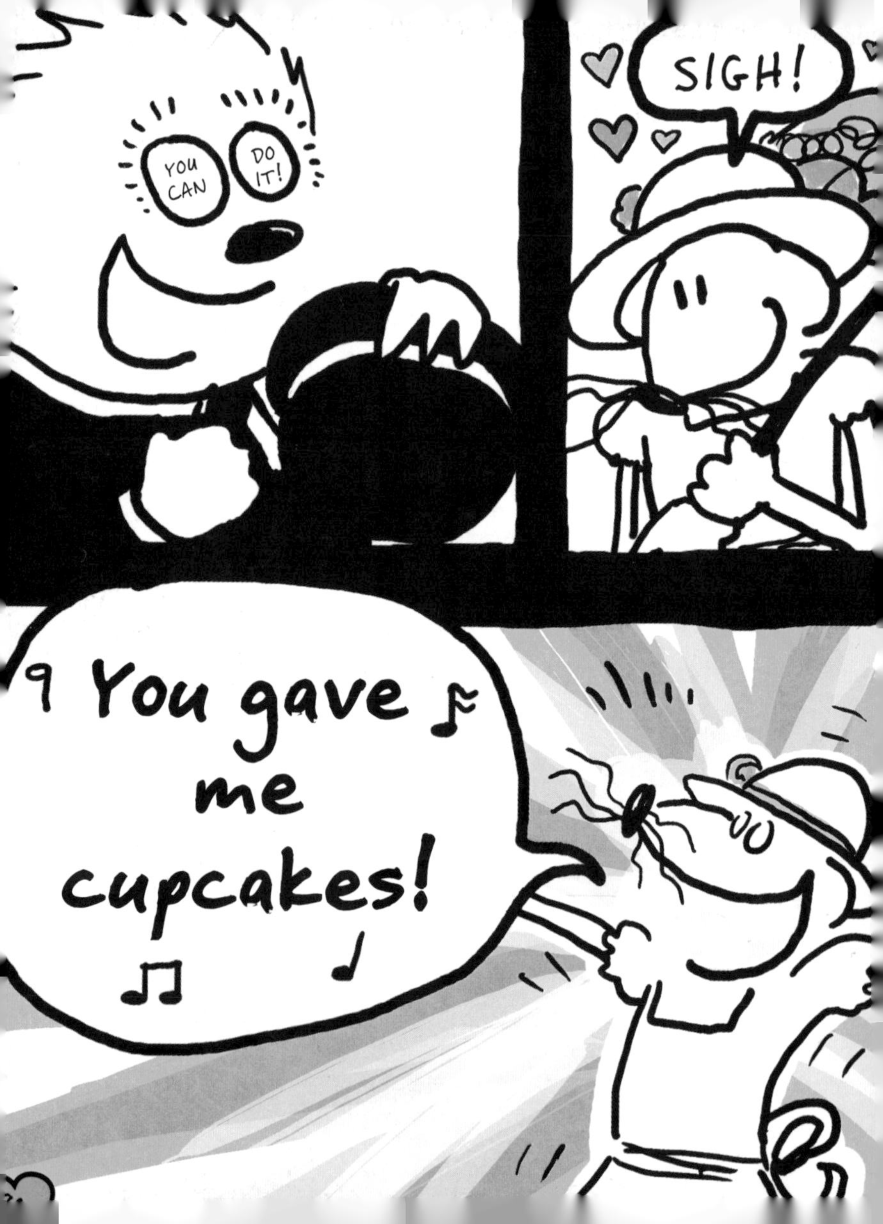
YOU CAN
DO IT!
SIGH!
You gave me cupcakes!

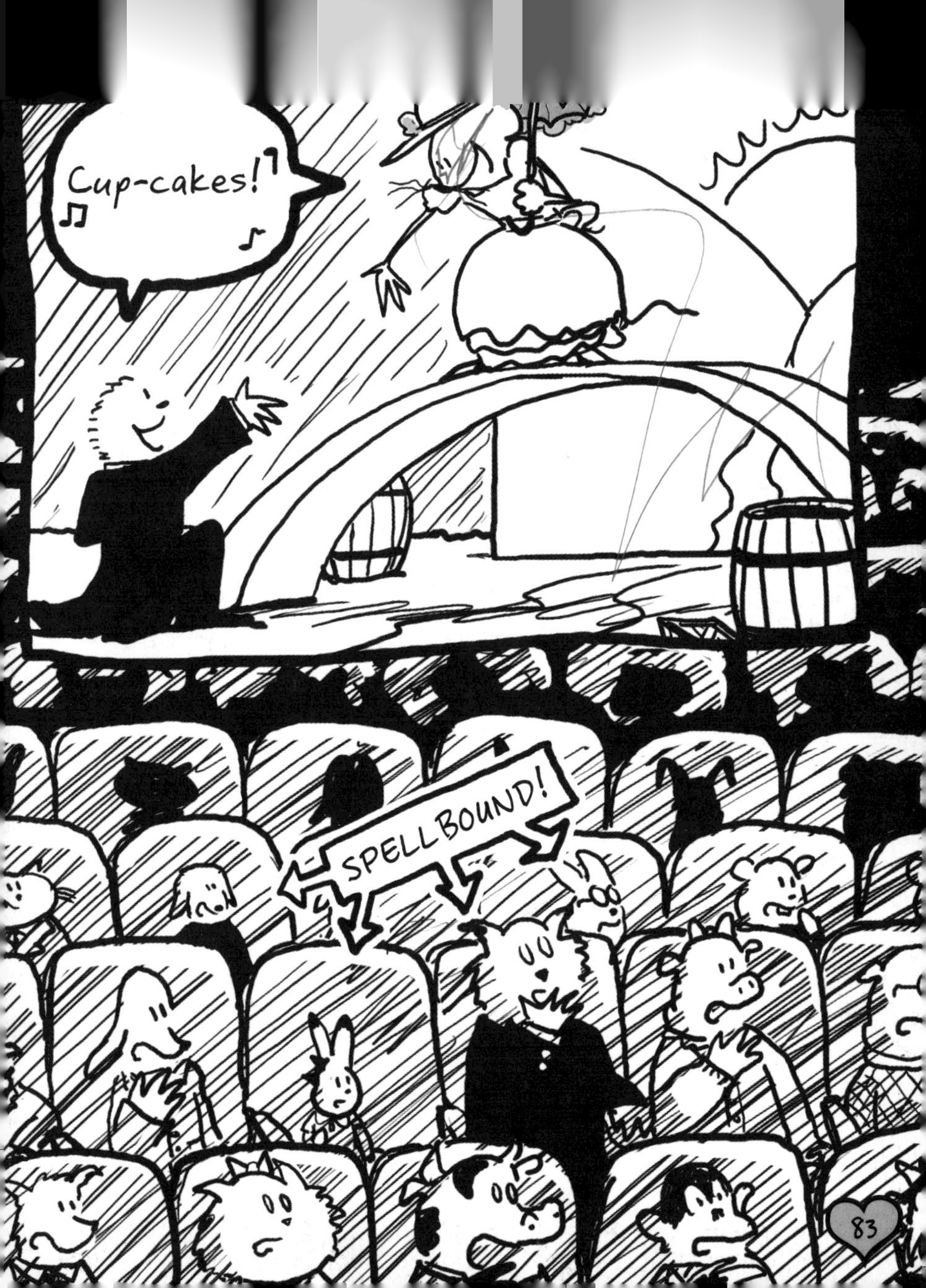
Cup-cakes!
SPELLBOUND!

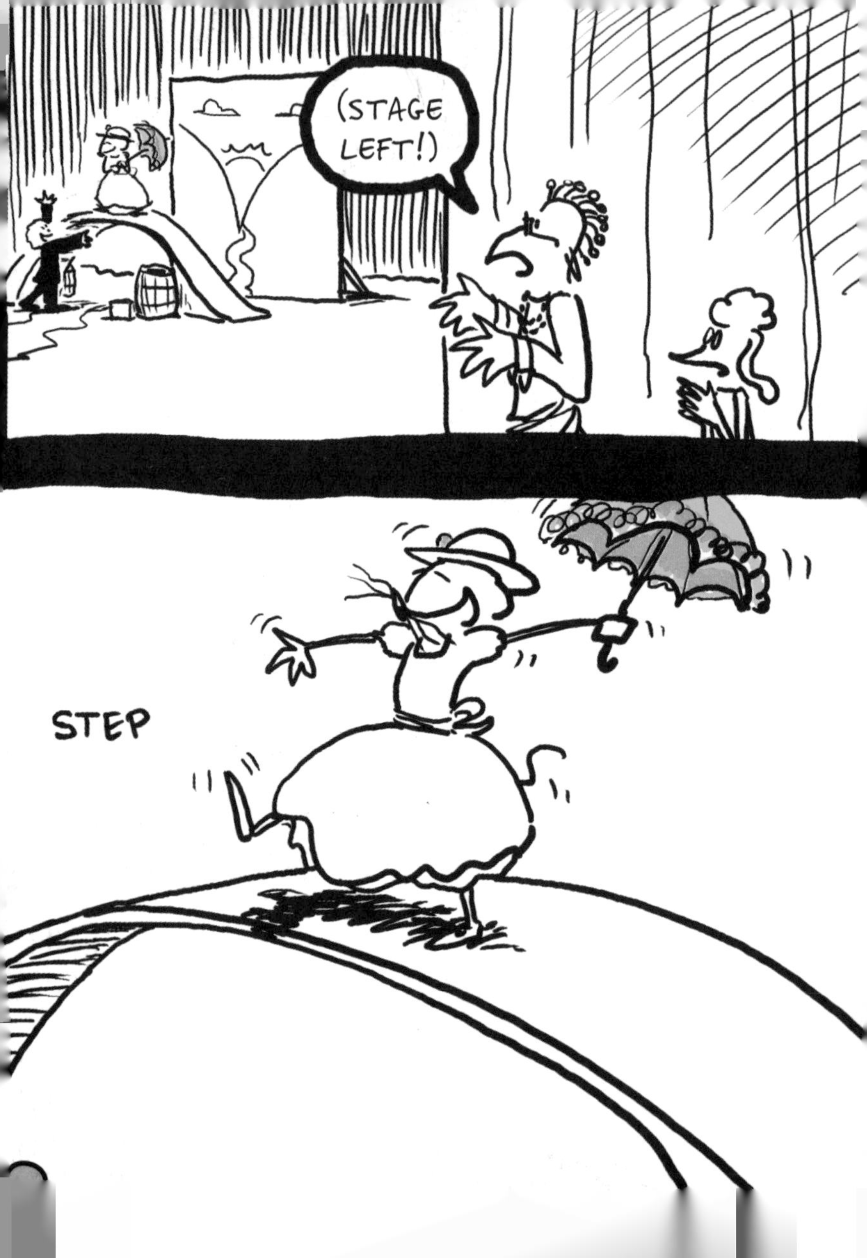
(STAGE LEFT!)
STEP

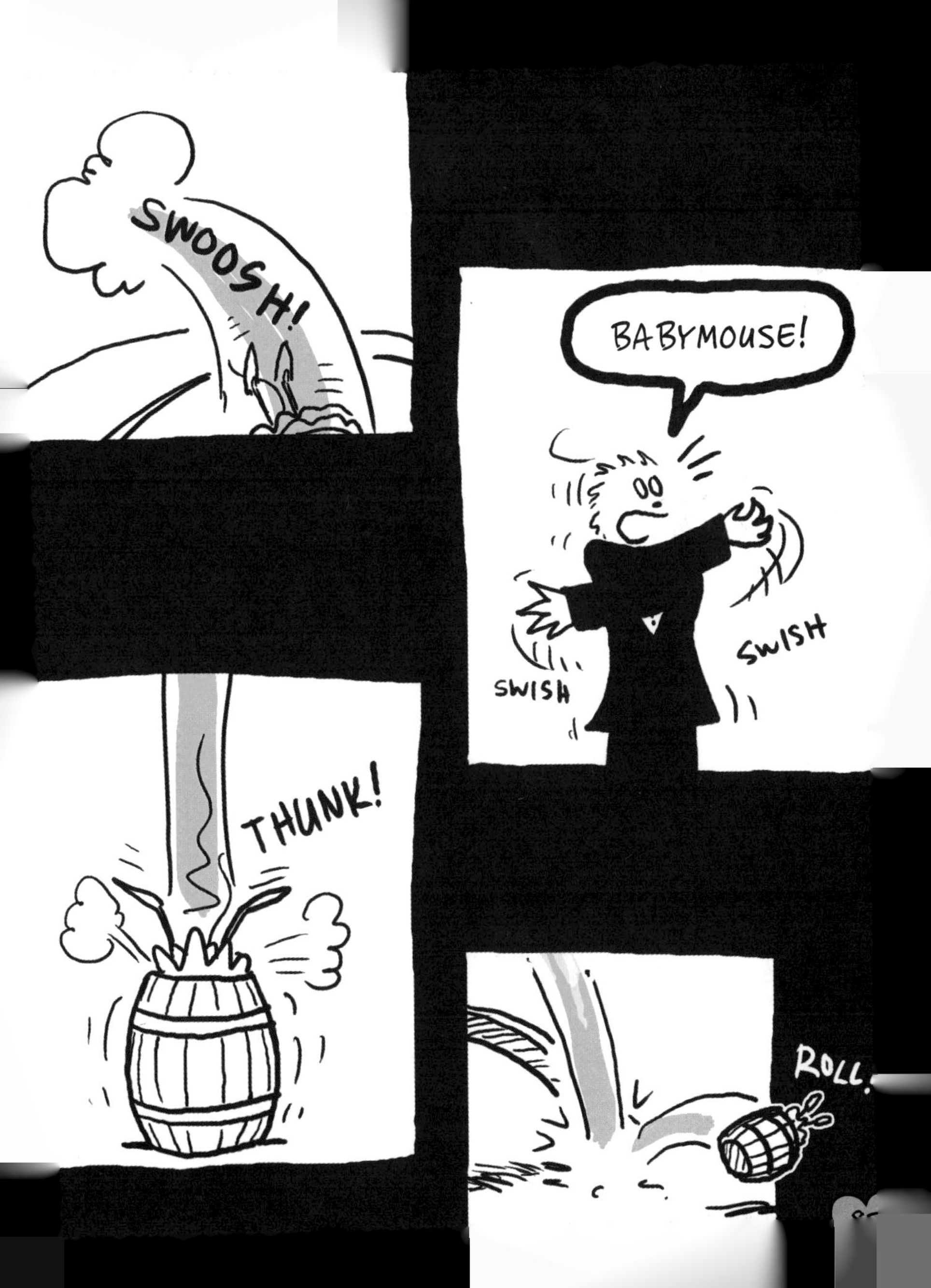
SWOOSH!
BABYMOUSE!
SWISH
SWISH
THUNK!
ROLL.

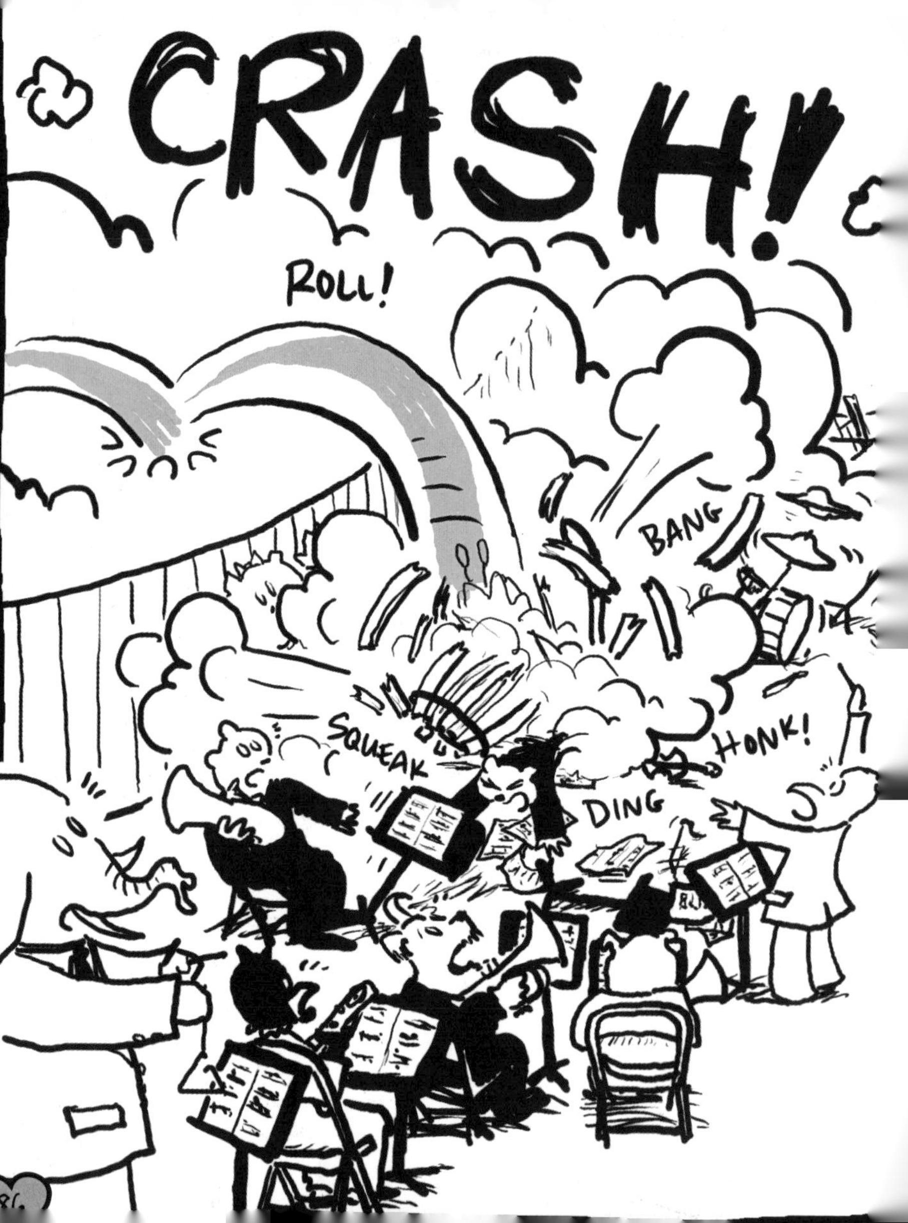
CRASH!
ROLL!
BANG
SQUEAK
HONK!
DING

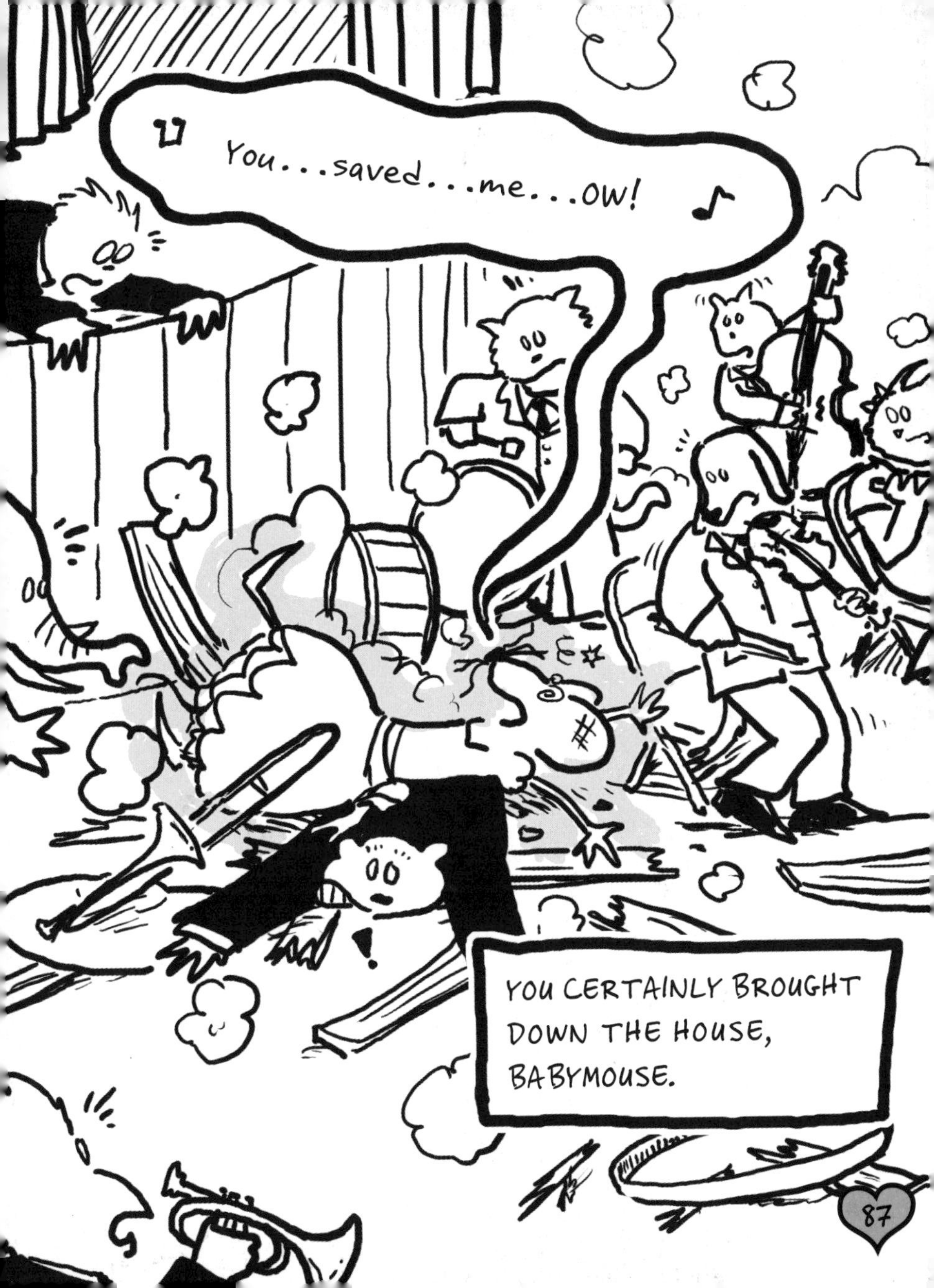
You...saved...me...OW!
YOU CERTAINLY BROUGHT DOWN THE HOUSE, BABYMOUSE.

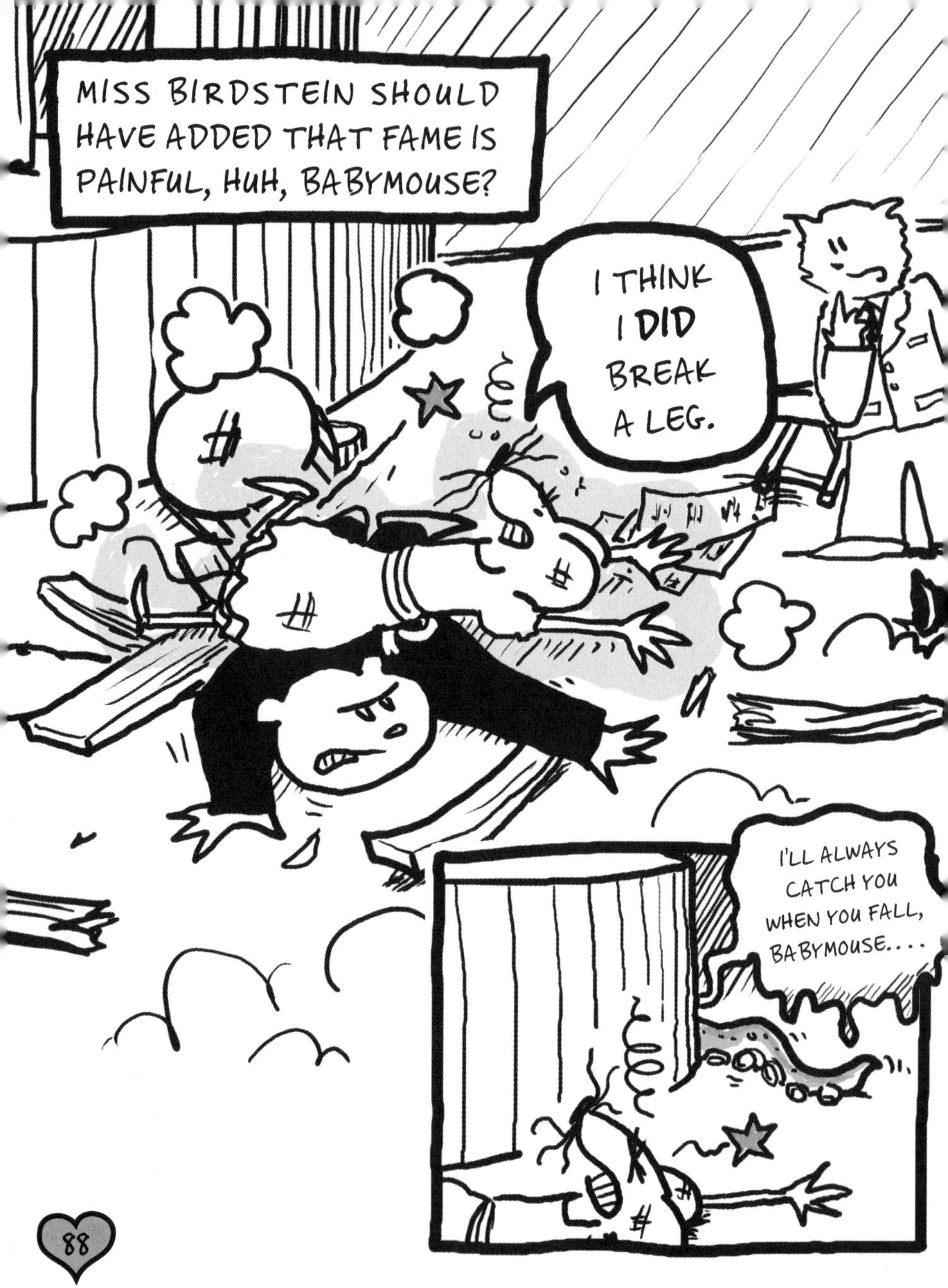
MISS BIRDSTEIN SHOULD HAVE ADDED THAT FAME IS PAINFUL, HUH, BABYMOUSE?
I THINK I **DID** BREAK A LEG.
I'LL ALWAYS CATCH YOU WHEN YOU FALL, BABYMOUSE. . . .

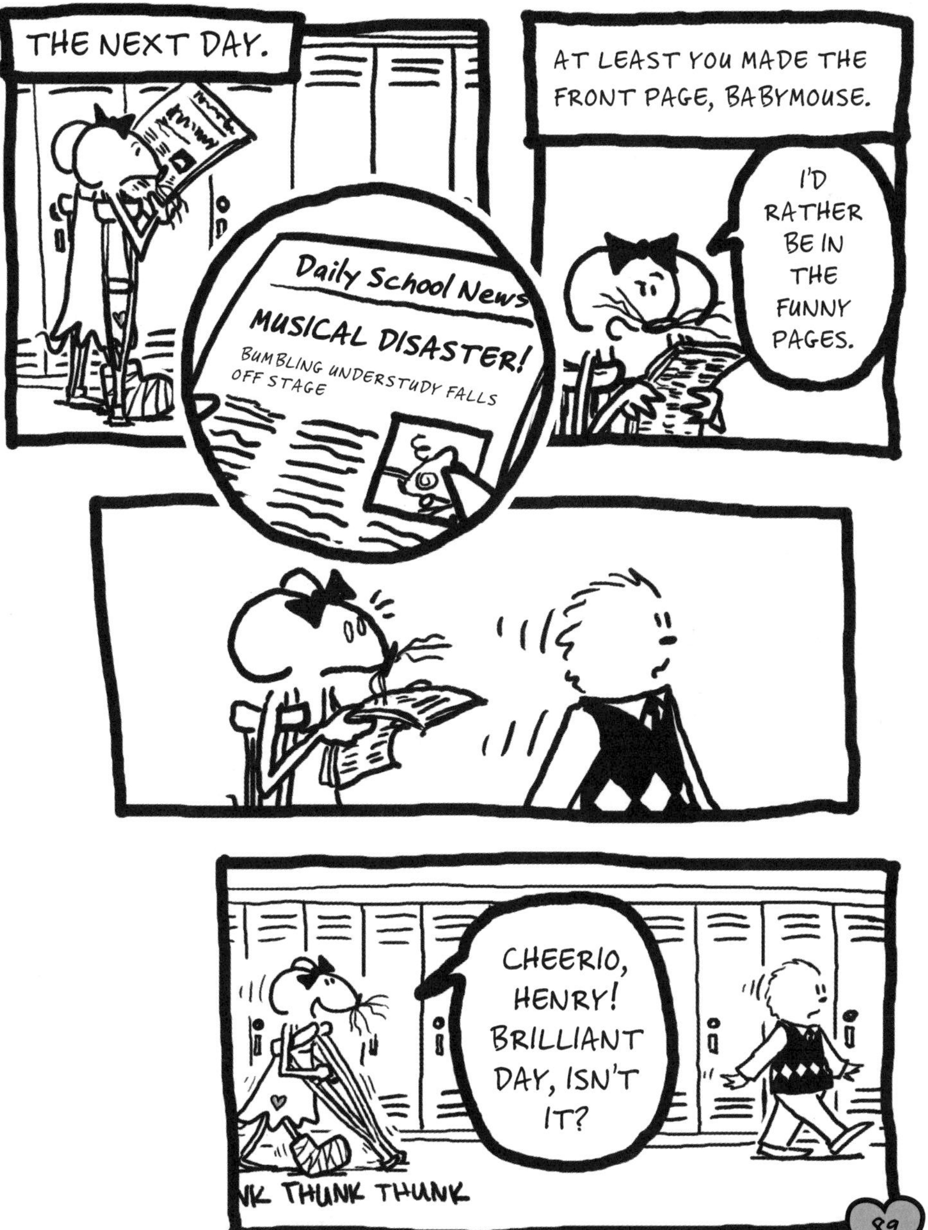
THE NEXT DAY.
Daily School News
MUSICAL DISASTER!
BUMBLING UNDERSTUDY FALLS OFF STAGE
AT LEAST YOU MADE THE FRONT PAGE, BABYMOUSE.
I'D RATHER BE IN THE FUNNY PAGES.
CHEERIO, HENRY! BRILLIANT DAY, ISN'T IT?
NK THUNK THUNK

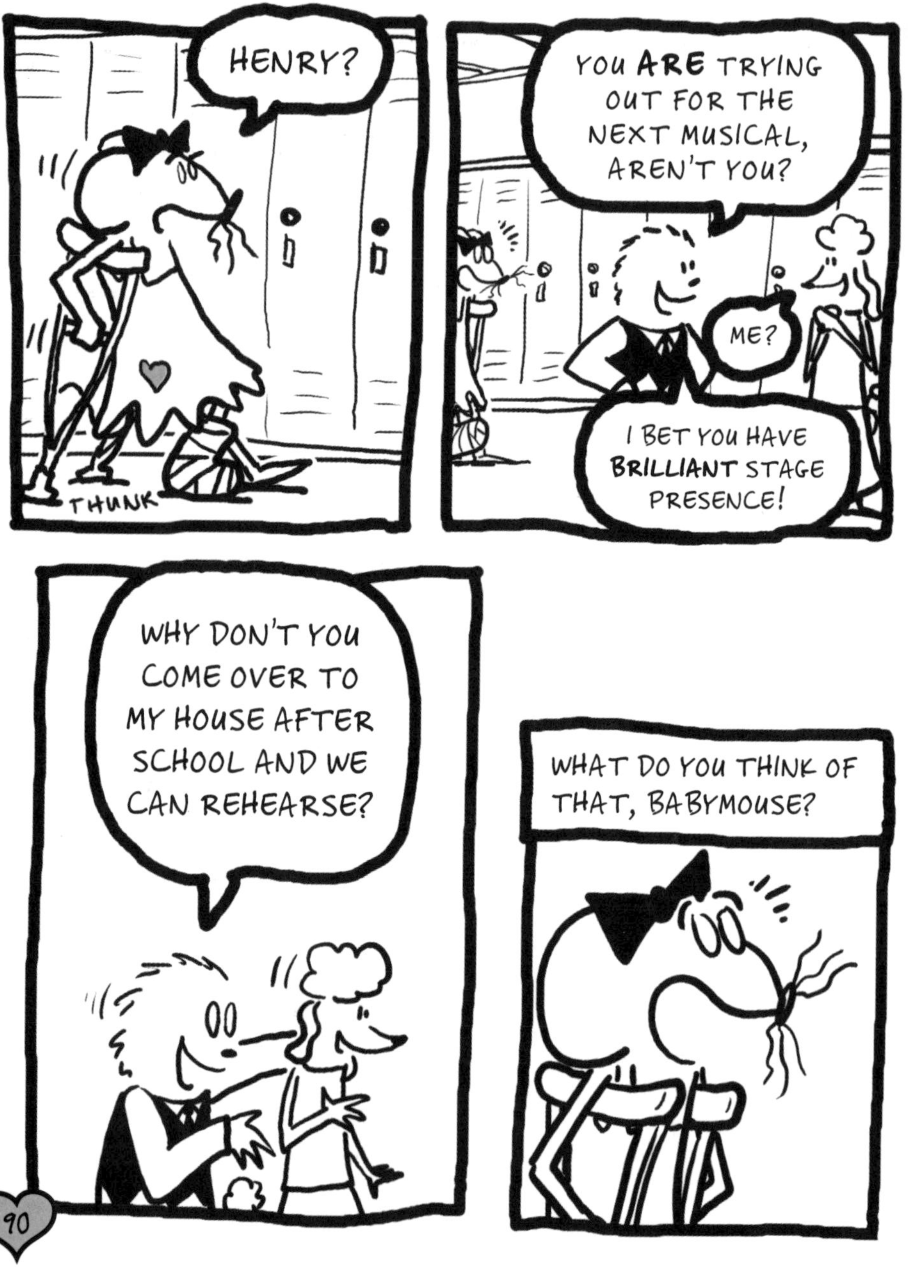
HENRY?
THUNK
YOU **ARE** TRYING OUT FOR THE NEXT MUSICAL, AREN'T YOU?
ME?
I BET YOU HAVE **BRILLIANT** STAGE PRESENCE!
WHY DON'T YOU COME OVER TO MY HOUSE AFTER SCHOOL AND WE CAN REHEARSE?
WHAT DO YOU THINK OF THAT, BABYMOUSE?

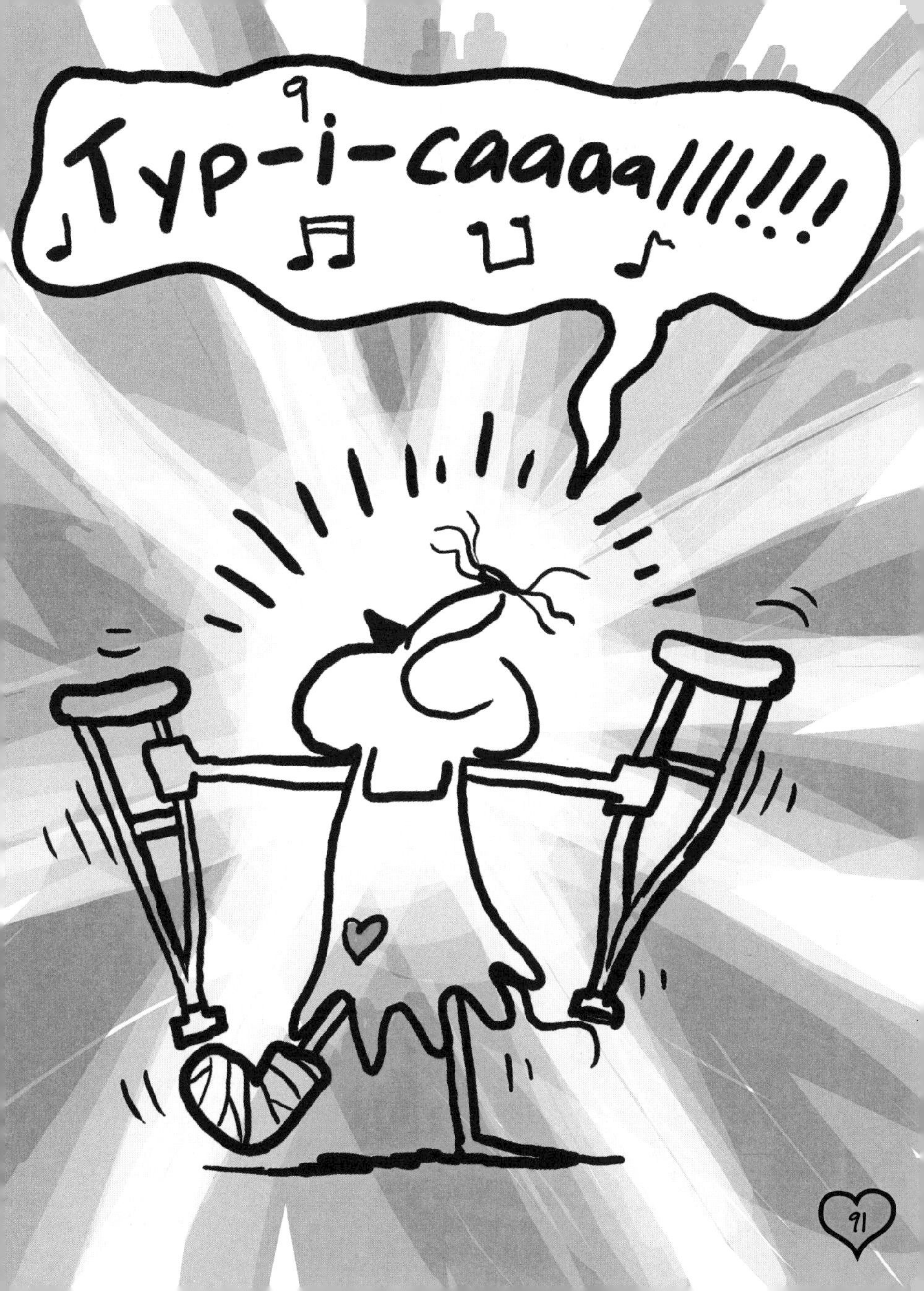
Typ-i-caaaalll!!!!

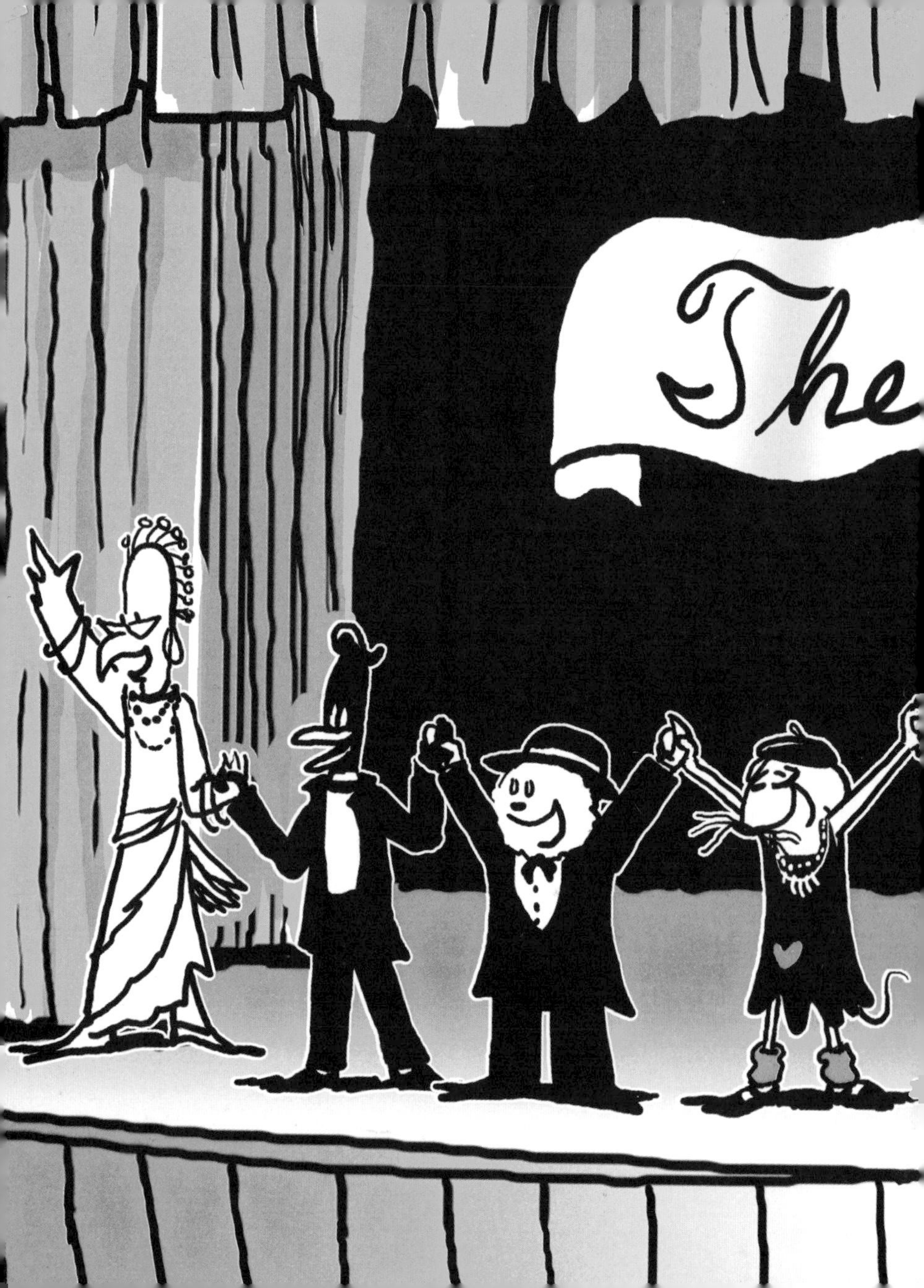
The

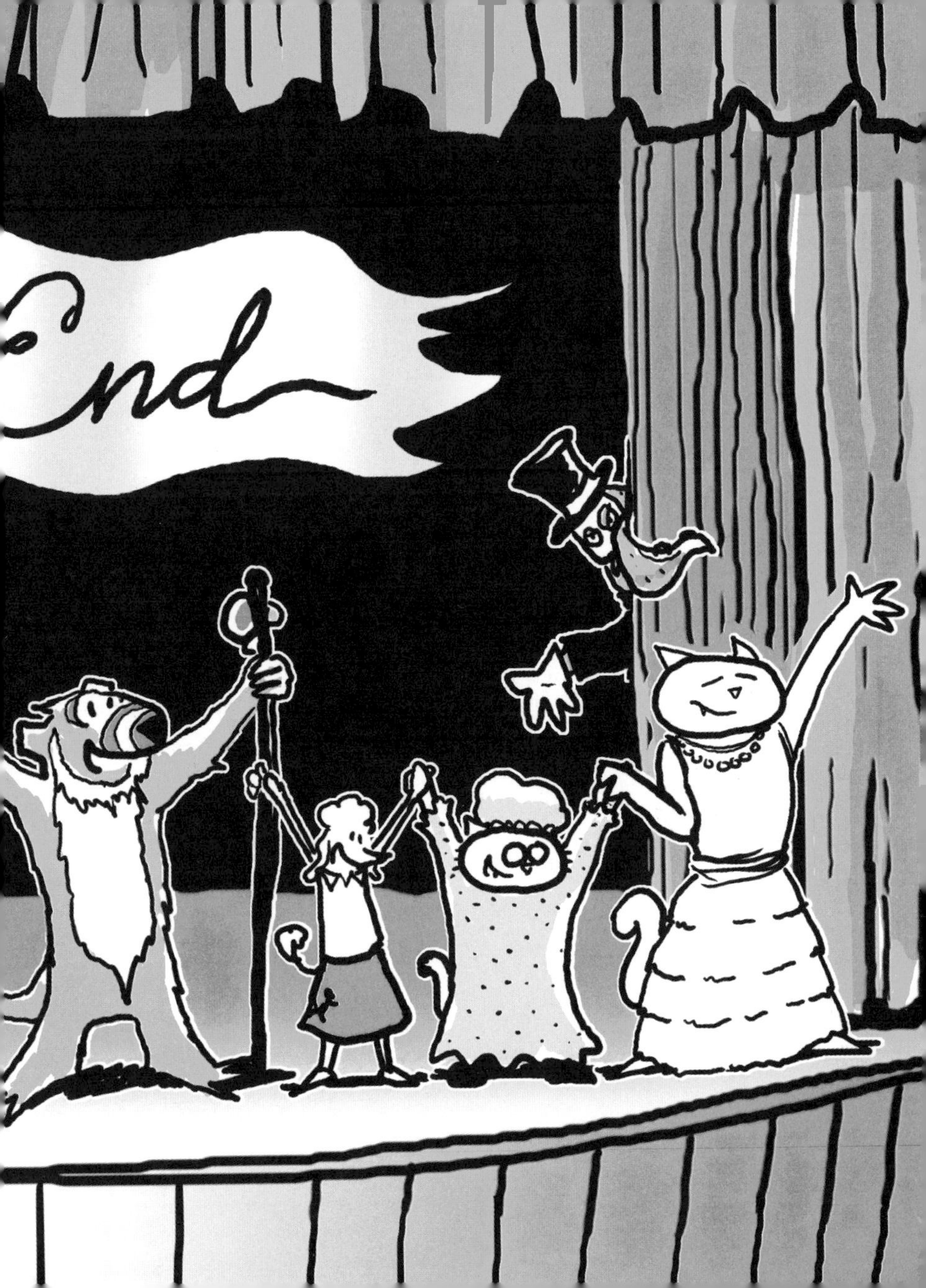
End

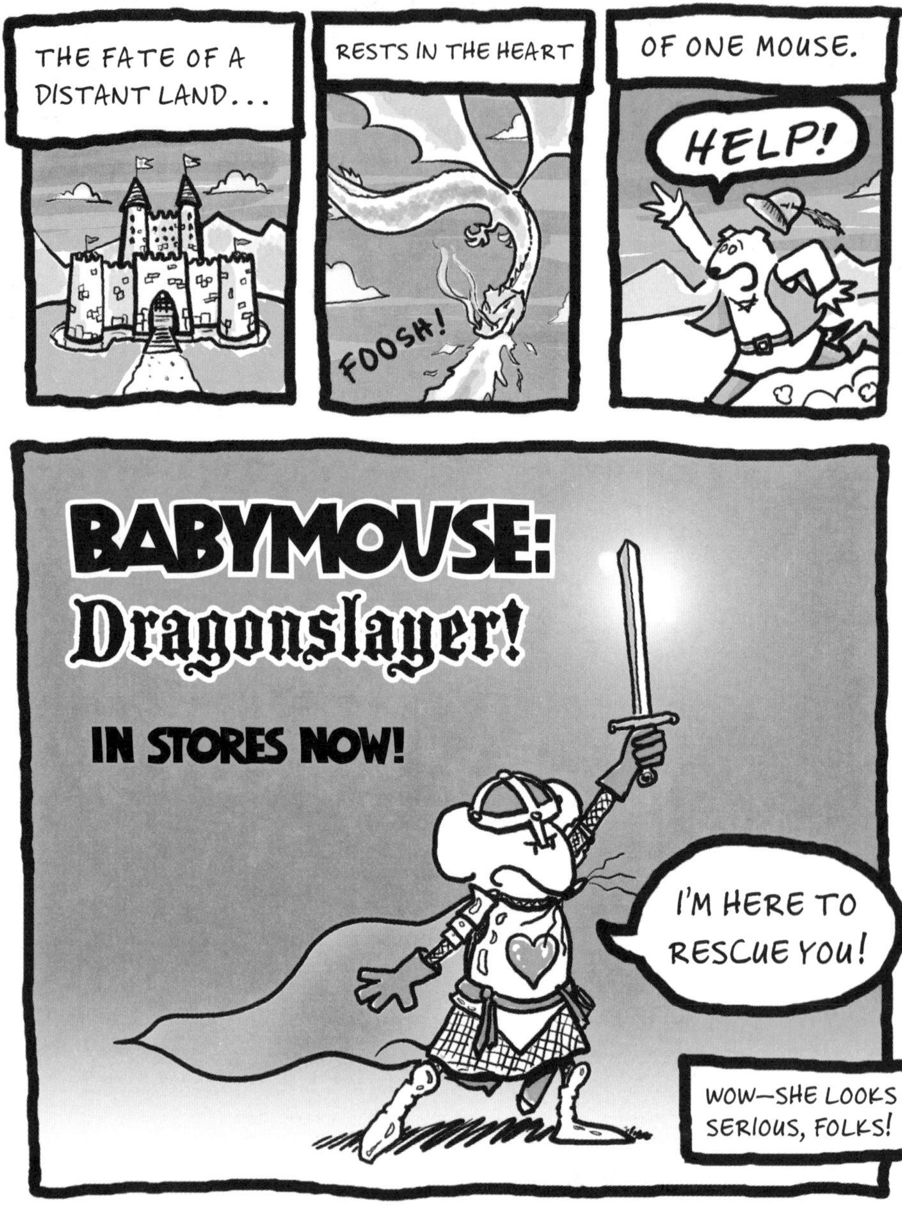
THE FATE OF A DISTANT LAND...
RESTS IN THE HEART
FOOSH!
OF ONE MOUSE.
HELP!
BABYMOUSE:
Dragonslayer!
IN STORES NOW!
I'M HERE TO RESCUE YOU!
WOW—SHE LOOKS SERIOUS, FOLKS!

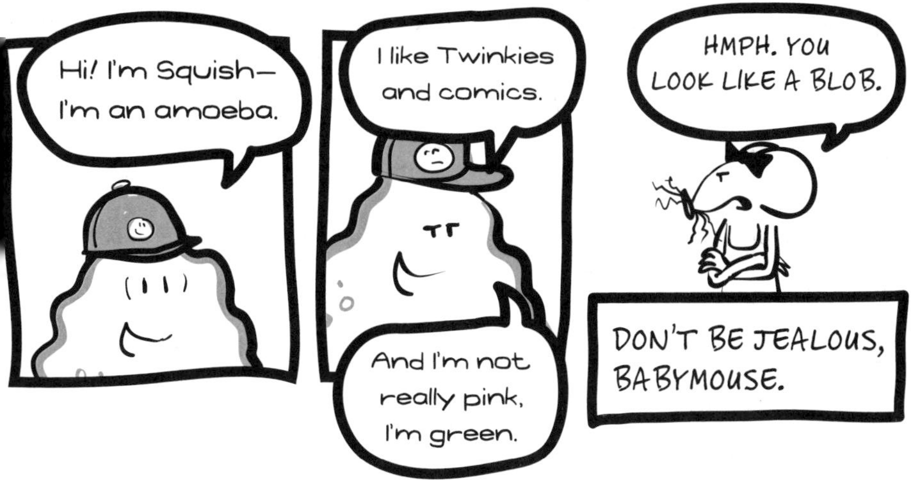
Hi! I'm Squish— I'm an amoeba.
I like Twinkies and comics.
And I'm not really pink, I'm green.
HMPH. YOU LOOK LIKE A BLOB.
DON'T BE JEALOUS, BABYMOUSE.

READ ABOUT SQUISH'S AMAZING ADVENTURES IN:

#1 SQUISH: Super Amoeba

#2 SQUISH: Brave New Pond

#3 SQUISH: The Power of the Parasite

#4 SQUISH: Captain Disaster

#5 SQUISH: Game On!

AND COMING SOON:

#6 SQUISH: Fear the Amoeba

★ "IF EVER A NEW SERIES DESERVED TO GO VIRAL, THIS ONE DOES."
—KIRKUS REVIEWS, STARRED

If you like Babymouse,
you'll love these other great books
by Jennifer L. Holm!

THE BOSTON JANE TRILOGY
EIGHTH GRADE IS MAKING ME SICK
MIDDLE SCHOOL IS WORSE THAN MEATLOAF
OUR ONLY MAY AMELIA
PENNY FROM HEAVEN
TURTLE IN PARADISE

THEY'RE
REALLY GOOD!
TRUST ME!